"I meant to ask about your neighbor, Sylvie. I hear he's really hot."

"Who said that, Kay?" Sylvie Shea stopped cold.

"You mean he's not?"

Sylvie shrugged. "I suppose, if looks are all you care about. He's a bit of a grouch. Which you'll discover if I don't get out there and save his daughter's cat. He'll yell at me through an upstairs window and order me to corral my dog."

"Joel Mercer has a daughter? Wow, I don't think the gals at the nail salon know he's married. A couple of them are drawing straws over him already."

Sylvie didn't mention that she hadn't seen a wife show up next door. Nor would she admit that Joel Mercer was better to look at than a chocolate fudge sundae. The last thing Sylvie needed was her mother or her sisters to get wind of the fact that she considered her neighbor worthy of a second glance. If Mercer was separated, as she'd begun to suspect, the last thing *he* needed was to get flattened by the Shea freight train—aka th

Dear Reader,

Ideas for stories come to writers in different ways. We don't have (as some people seem to think) warehouses brimming with plots and characters. Ideas pop into my head at odd times—like when I sleep, or travel, or I'm reading a funky weekly newspaper I found in an airport. I never know if a setting will grab me first or a character will. But I've learned to take whatever I get, in whatever form it arrives.

Sylvie Shea and Joel Mercer kicked around in my brain for months. She's a woman of eclectic talents who once left a small town nestled in the Smoky Mountain foothills and went to the big city, when she imagined fulfilling a lifelong dream. Her hopes dashed, she returns to Briarwood, North Carolina, a changed person.

He's a city guy who made his mark in his career, failed at marriage, but wants to raise his daughter in the warm, small-community environment he remembers fondly from boyhood summer visits. That place, too, is Briarwood, North Carolina.

I confess that it took me too long to see that Sylvie and Joel were meant to find each other. I always knew, however, that Joel's six-year-old daughter, Rianne, needed the unconditional love and acceptance of an extended family. A family just like Sylvie's.

I hope readers reach the same conclusion—that Joel and Sylvie belong together. Sylvie's sure that after being a bridesmaid thirteen times she'll never find a love of her own. And Joel, a confident man, a good father, a successful comic strip artist, is equally sure he's insulated against falling in love. I hope you'll enjoy discovering that they're both wrong!

I love to hear from readers. You can drop me a line at P.O. Box 17480-101, Tucson, AZ 85731. Or e-mail me at rdfox@worldnet.att.net.

Roz Denny Fox

ROZ
Denny
FOX

The Secret Wedding Dress

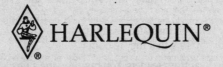

HARLEQUIN®

TORONTO • NEW YORK • LONDON
AMSTERDAM • PARIS • SYDNEY • HAMBURG
STOCKHOLM • ATHENS • TOKYO • MILAN • MADRID
PRAGUE • WARSAW • BUDAPEST • AUCKLAND

ISBN 0-373-75091-9

THE SECRET WEDDING DRESS

Copyright © 2005 by Rosaline Fox.

www.eHarlequin.com

Printed in U.S.A.

Books by Roz Denny Fox

HARLEQUIN AMERICAN ROMANCE
1036—TOO MANY BROTHERS

HARLEQUIN SUPERROMANCE

Chapter One

Through an open window in her sewing room, Sylvie Shea heard car doors slamming, followed by men's voices and, very briefly, a child's. Seated on the floor, Sylvie was busy stitching a final row of seed pearls around the hem of an ivory satin wedding dress. The commotion outside, unusual to say the least, enticed her to abandon her project. Her rustic log cabin, nestled into the base of the Great Smoky Mountains, didn't exactly sit on a highly trafficked street. Not that any street in her sleepy hamlet of Briarwood, North Carolina, could be called highly trafficked, she thought fondly. But because her family reminded her often enough that a woman living alone on the fringe of a forest couldn't be too careful, she'd better spare a moment to investigate.

Sylvie didn't expect anyone with a child for a fitting today. Nor was it garbage collection day. Russ Peabody's grandson sometimes rode with him in the truck.

Checking her watch, Sylvie saw she had at least an hour before Oscar, the Great Pyrenees belonging to Anita Moore, was scheduled to be dropped off for grooming. Her Mutt Mobile, as she'd named her mobile pet-grooming service, was Sylvie's second job; the first had always been making wedding gowns.

Pushing aside the dress form that held the cream-colored gown, she squeezed her way through eight other forms displaying finished bridesmaids' dresses for Kay Waller's wedding.

An eighth headless mannequin had been shoved into a corner. Sylvie automatically straightened the opaque sheet covering it, as she frequently did, making sure the dress remained hidden from prying eyes. Satisfied the cover was firmly in place, she finally reached the oversize picture window she'd had installed in what had once served as Bill and Mary Shea's sunporch. A year ago she'd converted the porch into a sunny sewing room.

The shouting outside hadn't abated. Sylvie parted the curtain she'd sewn from mantilla lace. Normally the filmy weave filtered the sun, which gave her enough light to sew, yet wouldn't fade any of the fine fabrics stored in bolts along a side wall. When she pulled aside the lace curtain, a bright shaft of August sun momentarily blinded her.

Blinking several times, she couldn't immediately see any reason for the racket. Then, as she pressed her nose flat to the warm glass, Sylvie noticed a large moving van had backed into the lane next door.

Iva Whitaker's home had been closed up for more than a year. Her overgrown driveway ended at a detached garage set apart from a rambling cedar shake home by a breezeway. Nearly ninety when she passed on, Iva had outlived Sylvie's grandparents. The Whitakers and the Sheas had always been best friends. Still, the house next door had been vacant for so long, Sylvie had practically forgotten there was a structure beyond her wild-rose-covered fence. At Iva's death, rumors abounded concerning her will. Who would inherit this house and property? Her land shared a border with Sylvie's. Iva's tract included a small lake fed by a stream running through Sylvie's wooded lot. She often wondered why, when each couple owned five acres, they'd built their homes within spitting distance of each other. Iva, though, had been a dear neighbor. If Sylvie was to have new ones, as the moving truck seemed to indicate, she hoped the same could be said of them.

Straining to see better, she watched a man with straight, honey-blond hair come out and unload a small pet carrier from a dusty white seven-passenger van parked to the right of the moving van. He was in his thirties, of medium height and a wiry build, with slashing eyebrows over a straight nose set in a hawkish face. He wore a pair of gold, wire-rimmed glasses. Good-looking, yes… Sylvie saw him as a sort of corporate version of country singer Keith Urban.

The man brought out several suitcases, slammed the hatch and disappeared behind a thicket of colorful sweet peas. Sylvie was left searching her memory for any details about Iva's will. If she'd heard anything about relatives, she'd forgotten the specifics.

Still, she might have missed the facts altogether, since Sylvie made a point of avoiding gossip. Gossip seemed to be the occupational pastime of too many people in Briarwood. Five years ago, she'd been the prime topic. Sylvie truly doubted a soul among the town's three thousand and ninety residents gave any thought at all to the pain caused by rampant rumors. Certainly, everyone in town was well aware that becoming a New York City wedding gown designer had been Sylvie's lifelong dream. Her best friends and their parents knew she'd imagined prospective brides coveting a Sylvie Shea gown with the same reverence the rich and famous whispered the name of Vera Wang.

So, yes, it'd shocked her that people whispered about her—when, at twenty-one, she'd abruptly left New York and returned home to live in the small house she'd inherited from her father's parents. They must have seen her distress over all the comments claiming she'd left Briarwood at eighteen with stars in her eyes and magic in her fingers, only to return at twenty-one with teary eyes and a heart in tatters. That was five years ago.

Broken by a man. Or so the gossips speculated—then *and* now. And rightfully so. Blessedly, the very few who knew the truth about how lying, cheating Desmond Emerson had stolen her dreams—and broken her heart in the process—said nothing. What really happened in New York should remain her humiliating secret. With a year under her belt, she'd almost worked through her crushing disappointment.

Almost.

Recently turned twenty-six, Sylvie was resigned to the fact that she'd never set the New York design world on fire. And she'd forged an okay existence here in Briarwood. Word-of-mouth sewing referrals paid the bills. Her pet-grooming service was growing steadily. In her spare time she managed Briarwood's children's theater, taught Sunday school and sang in the church choir. She occasionally hosted a gourmet cooking club that included her sisters and some old friends. She shouldn't complain.

If only certain busybodies would stop commenting that she'd sewn wedding gowns for all her friends at least once, and some twice, life in Briarwood might be enough. Oh, not to mention that she'd made gowns for her two sisters, both younger, while *she* remained single. It was too widely proclaimed that Sylvie Shea held the record for serving as bridesmaid more than anyone in the county. A total of twelve times to be exact, with unlucky thirteen coming up a week from next Saturday. She sighed, letting the lace curtain drift through her fingers.

The voices from next door had faded. Obviously, the movers and the man belonging to the white van had gone inside Iva's house.

If Sylvie's phone didn't ring soon, or if someone didn't otherwise clue her in as to what was going on next door, it was a cinch she'd hear all the details tonight at dinner. Today was her sister Dory's twenty-fourth birthday. The Shea family planned to gather at the home of their parents, as they did for every major life event.

Rob Shea, Sylvie's dad, a cabinetmaker by trade, also served as Briarwood's mayor. Her mother, Nan, volunteered—everywhere. Both were fourth-generation residents who had deep roots in the valley and love in their souls for Briarwood. The word *no* had never existed in the Shea vocabulary; they were considered the go-to family. Sylvie expected that her dad or her brothers-in-law would show up next door, offering to lend the stranger a hand unloading boxes. By morning, Nan and half the other women in town would have trekked to Iva's porch with casseroles, fresh canned goods, or baked goods piping hot from the oven.

Grinning to herself, Sylvie stowed her curiosity about her new neighbors, and returned to attaching seed pearls to Kay's dress. She'd barely finished sewing the last one in place when a vehicle crunched the gravel in her lane. The deep woofs that followed announced Oscar's arrival.

Sylvie was barely five foot two, and the Great Pyrenees weighed a hundred pounds and stood thirty-two inches at his shoulders. All the same, she loved every inch of Anita Moore's dog.

Taking care to latch the door to her sewing room, as she could well imagine what havoc Oscar might wreak, Sylvie stepped out onto her porch.

"Anita, hi." Sylvie raised a hand and waved. "You're still dressed for work. Let me get Oscar out of the Explorer for you." Anita's husband had the entire back half of the Ford renovated to accommodate the huge, shaggy white dog.

Bounding down her steps, Sylvie relieved Anita of a heavy-gauge leash, and quickly snapped it on Oscar's collar. He leaped out, barking joyfully. Just then Sylvie caught a glimpse of a cute blond-haired girl peering out through the sweet peas. Obviously this was the child she'd heard earlier. Sylvie flashed a smile, and the round face with the big blue eyes promptly withdrew.

"I'm sorry for what I'm about to ask, Sylvie. Can you possibly board Oscar? For a week or maybe two?" Anita said. "Not ten minutes ago, Ted got a call that his mom's in the hospital. He's on his way home to pack. I was already driving

Oscar here for grooming when he called me, or I'd have phoned to ask you first."

"I'd be delighted, Anita. We'll get along fine, won't we, guy?" Sylvie said, bending down to rub Oscar's floppy ears. "I hope Ted's mom doesn't have a serious problem." Straightening, she tightened her hold on the leash. Oscar had apparently heard noises next door and was ready to investigate.

"Sylvie, you're a lifesaver. Elsa had what her doctor thinks is a ministroke. Ted says we'll probably need to locate a nursing home, or at least some type of residential facility. Elsa's insisted on staying in her own home and she's always balked when we suggested she move in with us." Anita heard the bumping going on next door, and paused. "Has someone moved into Iva's house?"

"In the process of moving. See the van?" Sylvie squinted through the vines twined thickly in their joint fence. "You mean you haven't heard any scuttlebutt at work?" Anita was the loan manager for Briarwood's only bank.

"We wouldn't necessarily hear if there's no mortgage loan involved. Iva's great-nephew probably sold the property. I think he's employed by a newspaper in Atlanta. Iva used to brag on him. She said that, as a boy, he spent summers with her and Harvey. I can't remember, but I think he may have been Iva's only living relative."

"Wouldn't we have known if he'd listed the property for sale?" Sylvie ducked to see if she could ascertain what was going on next door.

"I suppose it's conceivable the nephew just retired."

"Then he's not the man I saw carrying stuff in from his car. And there's a little girl. She can't be more than six or seven."

"Huh. Iva talked about her nephew whenever he sent her a card or letter. She said he was super busy, and what a shame that was, since he loved to fish with your grandfather during the summers he spent in Briarwood."

that cat out of the tree, Oscar could never be allowed to go into her back yard.

The sun had dried most of the wet grass, Sylvie saw after stepping out a side door Oscar wasn't watching. Standing on her side of the fence, hands on hips, Sylvie studied the cat—and heard soft sniffling coming from the other yard. Concerned, Sylvie shinnied up the tree to its first fork. That placed her high enough to look into her neighbor's yard. "Hi," she said to a small girl who sat with both arms wrapped around her knees. "My name is Sylvie. Are you Rianne?"

The girl nodded, her face streaked with tears.

"I'm worried about my cat. Daddy's real busy, but Fluffy's only ever lived in a 'partment. I don't want to leave her, 'cause maybe she'll get lost."

"Ah." Sylvie considered the distance from her to the cat. It wasn't that the span was so great, but the limb seemed pretty frail. "Where was your apartment?"

"Atlanta. I'm six, almost. I loved my school and my teacher. Do you think they've got a nice school here?"

"I'm sure of it. I lived in Briarwood all my life, well, except for a few years I went off to work in New York City. There's a bunch of things that're way better here."

The girl stared at Sylvie with huge, watery eyes. "I'll like it okay. My daddy said it takes time to get used to somewhere new. What happened to your dog? My daddy said that dog's gonna be trouble."

Sylvie smiled at the girl who obviously planned to parrot everything her father said. No telling what she might discover about her new neighbors at this rate.

"Oscar isn't really my dog," she explained. "Normally he's friendly and loveable. I bathe pets and sometimes dog-sit, too. Look, honey, why don't I try to get Fluffy down?"

"I'd like that, thank you," the child said politely.

Sylvie inched out on the limb. "Is your last name Whitaker?"

"Uh-uh. Mercer. Rianne Mercer. My daddy's name is Joel, and my mommy's name is Lynn."

Creeping out several more inches, Sylvie absorbed those facts. It must mean that Iva's great nephew had sold his inheritance. She was about to ask, when she heard the limb crack. Her heart jackhammered wildly. The Mercers' back door flew open and the man with the gruff voice called, "Rianne? Where are you, sweetie? The movers need you to tell us where you want your bed."

The girl swung around. "Can I come in a minute, Daddy? Fluffy's still in the tree."

Sylvie heard dark muttering that mirrored the thoughts running through her head. Then she heard a sound like pebbles striking metal. Rianne's dad was pouring dry cat food into a bowl—but that only occurred to her when, big as you please, Fluffy leaped down from her perch. She landed safely below on all fours and dashed through her back door. Rianne shouted gleefully and raced after her pet.

Sylvie was glad her ignominious fall into her yard, limb and all, took place after her obnoxious, arrogant neighbor had closed his door. Luckily, her pride was all that suffered injury. Although, she mused, limping toward her cabin, who knew what aches and pains she'd have come morning?

JOEL MERCER had gotten a fair glimpse of his neighbor, wrapped tight around a sagging tree branch. His earlier impression had been of a scrawny dark-haired woman in her mid-to-late twenties, who behaved in a somewhat bizarre fashion. Hell, what was he thinking? She'd acted like a complete fruitcake.

Seeing her on to that branch was his second glimpse, and it did nothing to alter his first opinion. She'd changed clothes to climb trees, apparently. Her hair no longer hung straight to her chin as it had; she'd secured a twist atop her head with what resembled a large metal chip-bag clip. Spiky hair poked out every which way. Joel wondered if she'd been attempting to spy on him. Was that why she'd decided to swing through the trees like Jane of the jungle? God only knew, but Joel had run into of some pretty odd women hanging out in Atlanta's singles bars. Women he'd labeled predators. In spite of his weekly comic strip, which centered on a couple of zany cartoon girlfriends named Poppy and Rose and described their dating misadventures, Joel usually managed to keep his private life fairly tame. Making his life tamer still had been his one goal in moving to laid-back Briarwood, North Carolina, into the home he'd inherited from his great-aunt. That, and keeping Rianne from seeing her mother's face splashed all over half the billboards in town because it confused and upset her. Joel didn't begrudge Lynn her newly acquired high-powered TV anchor job. He did resent that she never made time to spend with their daughter.

"Rianne, let Fluffy eat in peace. I need you to come upstairs and pick the bedroom you'd like. Then we'll set up your bed."

The girl skipped up the curving staircase, landing hard on both feet at the top. "I never choosed my room in our 'partment."

"Choosed isn't a word, honey. It's *chose*. And you should say *a*partment."

"Why?" She slipped her hand in Joel's.

Answering his daughter's endless *whys* had been his second-biggest challenge as single dad to a precocious child. The first, he discovered, was figuring out how to safely shuffle Rianne in and out of women's public restrooms in restaurants, malls and parks. Now, *that* took charm and ingenuity. He always had to garner the aid of kind, elderly ladies; he'd learned to sense which faces to trust.

"The rules about using the proper words will fall into place when your new first-grade teacher gives you word lists. I'll help you study them."

"Daddy, the lady next door said I'll like school here. She

said she's lived here her whole life, 'cept for when she lived in New York City."

"She didn't live in that house, Rianne. I knew the couple who lived there. Mr. Shea taught me how to fish in the lake I showed you. His wife, Mary, baked the best oatmeal-raisin cookies I've ever tasted. I can almost smell them even now. Okay, snooks, this is the yellow room. Across the hall, the other room is painted…violet, I guess. One of its walls is covered in flower wallpaper. We can change the paint color and pick out new paper, if you'd like."

"I like this room, Daddy. Oh, look, there's a bench in the window. I can see Oscar playing in the lady's yard."

Joel knelt on the bench and gazed down on his neighbor's backyard. Given the amount of land attached to the Whitaker estate, he wondered why his great-uncle Harvey hadn't picked a more secluded spot to build. "Considering the size of the neighbor's dog and the way he scared poor Fluffy, I'd rather you stayed far away from that woman and her pet."

"Oscar's not hers. She baby-sits him. She gives doggies baths and sometimes dogs stay with her, like I did at my baby-sitter's the days when you worked late."

"Gr…eat!" Joel heaved out the word. "I see a dog run and kennels. Hmm. I wouldn't have thought that would be a legal business inside the city limits."

"Why?"

"Just because," Joel said, eyeing the neighbor's yard as the movers hauled in Rianne's bed. He turned from the window with a frown. He'd always sworn he wouldn't resort to answering his kids' questions with *just because.* As a boy he'd had an inquisitive mind. His parents, who fought constantly, never gave straight answers. Their bitterness had led to their eventual breakup and to his estrangement from them. Which was another reason this house and Briarwood held such fond memories for him. Iva and her good friends, Bill and Mary Shea, had nothing but time to lavish on a lonely, neglected boy. Joel's folks had finally split the year he'd turned fifteen. His dad, a career Army man, went on to a new duty station in Hawaii. He'd remarried ASAP, and his new wife had given birth to a son. Joel's dad seemed to forget he had an older son from his first marriage. He retired in Hilo, so Joel had never met his stepbrother. And his mom had continued with her job in Atlanta until she, too, met and married a new man. Seventeen by then, Joel elected to stay behind. His high school teachers and counselors secured him an art scholarship, for which he'd always be grateful. As a lonely child, he'd coped with moving from one army base to the next by drawing funny caricatures of the people around him. His drawing ability, combined with observational skills and a dry wit made him a good living from the time he'd hired on to create political cartoons a decade ago, to now. After a few years, the paper had offered him his own, more lucrative, weekly strip, which went into syndication a while ago.

"I'm going to have the movers bring in the posts for your bed, Rianne. How about if, after they go, you help me by handing over the bolts, nuts and wrenches I need? Then I'll assemble my bed. After I finish that, I'll fix us something to eat."

"What?"

"Whatever I find in the first food box I open. Tomorrow, early, we'll go grocery shopping."

Putting together beds soon became a chore that was next to impossible to complete. But by then, what to fix for supper was no longer an issue. Within minutes of the moving van's departure, a steady stream of Briarwood matrons started bringing in so much food Joel was astonished—and wary. Especially after the first talkative stranger, a woman named Millie McDaniel, informed Joel that she owned the only hair salon in town, and he realized that along with casseroles came questions. Briarwood's self-appointed welcoming committee was determined to find out the intimate details of his life. But ever since his very public divorce from a prominent news-chaser, Joel had learned how to smile politely and say nothing personal.

Seconds after he shut the door on a very persistent shopkeeper, Joel noticed his next-door neighbor striding down her lane. Where earlier she'd worn raggedy cutoffs, she now had on a floaty pink sundress. Joel hesitated just inside his door, juggling a layer cake in one hand and a macaroni-and-beef casserole in the other. Because she carried a covered metal pan, he assumed she was about to be his next inquisitor. Joel vacillated between meeting her head-on and pretending not to hear his doorbell.

Instead of escaping, he edged out onto the porch, admiring the change a dress made in her appearance. A full skirt swished appealingly around her slender ankles. On one ankle he identified a circle of gemstones winking in the setting sun. A minute or so passed while he enumerated her other attributes. Then two things dawned on Joel. One, she'd noticed him ogling her. Two, she wasn't going to his house. A car had pulled into her lane, and a spiffily dressed man emerged from the sleek black Mercedes coupe. He whipped open his passenger door and relieved the woman of her pan of goodies, then waited while she folded her full skirt inside the car. The man watched Joel, too.

Joel had barely darted inside before the driver handed the pan to his passenger and bent to say something that made her glance toward Joel's open door. He abruptly slammed it shut.

Big deal! So, the country mouse had a boyfriend with a few bucks. It was just as well. Joel hadn't come to Briarwood in search of dates. One mistake of the kind he'd made in marrying Lynn was all a man needed. Lynn had turned out to have a greater interest in skyrocketing to fame as a foreign correspondent, which had led to this new job as a high-profile TV anchor, than she'd ever had in staying in one place building a home with him.

"That cake is lopsided, Daddy," Rianne announced as Joel

carried the last gift into the big, country-style kitchen. "It sorta looks like the one you made for my last birthday, 'cept that one had my fav'rite chocolate frosting."

A stab of something like nostalgia had struck Joel as he'd watched the couple drive off in the hot car, but it faded instantly. Bending, he swung his daughter into his arms for a hug. If he hadn't met and married Lynn Severson, he wouldn't have Rianne. She was the best thing in his life.

"Can we eat the 'sketti the woman with the bright red hair brought?"

Joel grinned. "Bright red is accurate. I don't think I've ever seen that shade." As Rianne's blue eyes widened, Joel laughed and set her down. "If I let you, kid, you'd eat 'sketti every night. And it's *spaghetti*. Tell you what. I'll turn the oven on low and put this in to warm while we finish raising the canopy over your bed. I swear, we're not moving again until you're twenty-one. I'm not ever wrestling with that canopy again. I'd sure like to have a talk with the masochist who engineered *that*."

"What's a mas…maso—that word you said, Daddy? What is that?"

Joel nearly swallowed his tongue. "Never mind, honey. It's not a word you'll need to know in first grade—if ever," he muttered, taking the stairs two at a time to the first broad landing.

Chapter Two

Across town at her parents' home, Sylvie divided the time before dinner between sidestepping the issue of her new neighbor, and avoiding too much chumminess with the man her sister, Dory, had sent to collect her. *Where did her family dig up these guys?* Chet Bellamy's company had apparently sold Dory's insurance agency a new computer system, and he was in town for a week to see that it got up and running. Thank heaven the man had no desire to leave his thriving business in Asheville. And as he'd said he was on the road a lot, Sylvie couldn't really begrudge him this one evening in the company of her lively family.

Dory and Carline, twenty-five and twenty-four respectively, cornered their older sister in the rambling family kitchen.

Carline, eight and a half months pregnant and always focused on food lately, snitched several slices of cheese from a platter Sylvie was arranging. "I can't believe you sat and watched brand-new people move into the Whitaker place and don't have a thing to say about them."

Sylvie slapped her sister's hand as she polished off the two pieces of cheese she'd taken and reached for more. "Mom asked me to fix this to take out on the porch as an appetizer. If you keep grabbing everything I cut, Carline, the tray will look like a mouse got into it."

Dory cut a chunk of pepper jack for herself and nibbled

on it. "Jane Bateman passed the word at our insurance agency. She'd gone to the post office at noon and saw the moving truck, and knew they turned down Blackberry Road. She figured out they were headed to Iva's. I left work late, or I'd have gone by there with something from my freezer they can re-heat in a microwave. I wonder if the Mercers play bridge," she said, glancing at her sisters. "Peggy at the post office told Jane that's their name, Mercer. Peggy said their mail's being transferred from Atlanta. City people are more likely to play bridge, don't you think?" she asked hopefully.

Sylvie bumped against the refrigerator as she moved around the counter. The dull ache reminded her of her earlier fall from the tree. "They have at least one child, a little girl. And a cat," she added in afterthought.

"A girl? Great," Dory said, suddenly smiling. "How old? Kendra's age, I hope. They could play together when Kendra stays with you."

"This child, Rianne's her name, is probably a year or so older than Kendra. She asked me about the school here. I'd say she's in first or second grade." Sylvie looked out and saw her niece and nephew playing on the swing set outside. Kendra was an advanced four, and Roy a sturdy, delightful toddler.

"What did the girl have to say about her parents?" Carline asked, levering herself up on one of the stools that ringed the kitchen counter.

"Nothing much." Sylvie picked up the platter and prepared to go out to the porch where the men stood talking to her parents, Nan and Rob, as Sylvie's dad tossed steaks on a built-in barbecue. "She gave their names. You already know her dad's Joel. I believe she called her mother Lynn. I only saw him briefly, hauling luggage from his vehicle. I never caught sight of the wife."

"Maybe she stayed behind to tidy up the house they sold in Atlanta." Carline helped herself to a small cluster of grapes even as Sylvie tried to lift the plate out of her reach.

Stopping at the door, Sylvie turned. "That's something else the girl mentioned. She said her cat's only ever lived in an apartment." Sylvie was again reminded of her tumble from the neighbor's tree as she nudged open the screen with her hip.

"Gosh," Carline exclaimed, pausing with a grape raised to her mouth. "Maybe there is *no* Mrs. Mercer. I mean, if they lived in a city high-rise…"

Sylvie recognized the expression that passed between her sisters. Their dedication in matching her up with some—any—unattached male always shone like a thousand-watt lightbulb. "Stop right there! It's not too likely that a divorced guy with one kid would buy a home the size of the Whitakers'. Especially not in a backwater like Briarwood. Where's the future for him?"

Dory pounced immediately. "Who said Mercer's divorced? Did his daughter say that?"

Sylvie noticed the look again, and rolled her eyes. "Get this straight once and for all, you two. Capital N, capital O in foot-high letters. Whether he's divorced, widowed, never married or openly gay, you will *not* shove me in his direction, is that patently clear?"

"Openly gay?" the sisters chorused with laughter that was cut off when Sylvie banged the screen door.

Her neighbor's name didn't surface again during the meal, for which Sylvie was thankful. But as she and Chet prepared to leave, Nan Shea set a big plate of chocolate chip cookies on the pan Sylvie had brought a molded Jell-O salad in. "What are the cookies for?" Sylvie turned in surprise.

"Do you mind running them over to your new neighbors? I can't because tomorrow and the next are my days to volunteer at the library. Chocolate chip cookies are so much better eaten fresh."

A refusal rose to the tip of Sylvie's tongue. Knowing her mom, she'd rearrange her entire day to deliver the cookies herself if Sylvie didn't. Besides, Sylvie recalled Rianne Mercer's tear-streaked face. If anything would lift a homesick kid's spirits, it'd be chocolate chip cookies. "Okay, Mom…if Mercer's still up unpacking boxes when Chet drops me off, I'll bring the cookies over tonight."

Dory tried unsuccessfully to pull the plate from Sylvie's hands as she signaled her mom with an eyebrow. "I'll take them to Mr. Mercer in the morning, and add something from Grant and me. Mother, I'm sure Sylvie was planning to offer Chet a nightcap, weren't you, Sylvie?"

"Actually, no," she shot back, bestowing her most practiced smile on her escort. "I heard Chet tell Daddy he wanted to get an early start tomorrow for his drive back to Asheville. I wouldn't dream of keeping him up late. Maybe next time he's in town…" She let the suggestion linger, hoping against hope that she'd also heard Chet say he'd completed his company's project in Briarwood.

To the man's credit, he seemed to catch on to the fact that he hadn't elevated Sylvie's heart rate.

"Sylvie's right, Dory," Chet said quickly. "I intend to be on the road by 6:00 a.m."

"One drink, you two. How long would that take? Unless…" Dory pouted prettily, her meaning made plenty clear.

Sylvie opened the door and hurried out, but not before murmuring tightly, "Dory, honestly! Give me a break." Sylvie knew that few could pout like Dory. She had it down to a science. So much so, her husband, Grant, bless his heart, chuckled and playfully clapped a hand over her mouth.

Pausing at the gate, Sylvie thought of something she'd forgotten to mention. "Carline," she called, "Ted Moore's mom was taken to the hospital today. He and Anita went to Tennessee. They have no idea how long they'll be gone. I'm boarding Oscar. Did Anita get hold of you about sending their wedding gift directly to Kay and Dave?"

"She left a garbled message on my store phone. She must've been on her cell somewhere in the Smokies. Half the message was cut off. That's too bad about Mrs. Moore. I hope she recovers."

"A small stroke, Anita told me."

Nan Shea stepped off the porch. "No stroke is small when you're eighty, as Ted's mother is. If they left suddenly, they probably forgot details like watering the plants or having someone collect the mail. I'll call around tomorrow and see if anyone's doing it. If not, I'll get a volunteer from the community club."

"Mom, you're the best," Sylvie said from the car. "Your organizational ability puts us all to shame. I had Anita standing right in front of me and it never occurred to me to offer that kind of help."

Rob slid an arm around his wife's shoulders. "I recall Nan making a similar comment to her mom forty years ago. I'll tell you girls what your grandmother said, and I hope you remember, because it left an impression me. Lou said that what makes Briarwood so livable has to do with each resident practicing what she called 'good neighbor policies.'"

Sylvie and her sisters nodded, but Sylvie felt that her dad's eyes rested the longest on her. As Chet shut her into his coupe, she pondered her reluctance to extend any kind of neighborliness to Joel Mercer. Her father's admonition left her feeling guilty, and she hated the feeling.

"Do you get bombarded like that all the time?" Chet asked as he backed out of the drive.

Sylvie's still-guilty gaze flashed to her companion. "Pardon?" *Could this man read her mind?*

A sheepish expression crept over his face. "Dory simply would not let me wiggle out of coming to dinner tonight. She was even more persistent that I pick you up. I have to admit I expected you to be an ugly duckling." He flexed his fingers on the wheel. "You're so…not that…I can't imagine why she's selling you so hard. Are you the town's scarlet woman or something?"

Sylvie's jaw dropped, then laughter bubbled up. "To my knowledge, that's not a label anyone's attached to me. But if I thought it'd discourage my well-meaning family and friends from setting me up with any Tom, Dick or Harry who still happens to be breathing, I'd start the rumor myself. Oh, sorry." She covered her mouth. "I didn't mean to imply that you fell into the geriatric singles group. Some have, though."

"No offense taken. I have a mother and four sisters who can't abide the notion of anyone walking through life except as a couple. Change that to read a male and female couple. I heard your comment earlier. The one about a man being divorced, widowed or openly gay. I am. Gay, but not openly. My family would never accept that, so it's easier to sidestep their efforts to hook me up with some nice woman. I sort of wondered if you and I were in a similar boat."

Sylvie was awfully afraid she probably resembled the large-mouth bass often pulled from Whitaker Lake. "I, ah, no. I'm arrow-straight, really." She felt her ears burn and studied the pan and the plate of cookies resting unsteadily on her lap.

He winced. "Too bad from my perspective. I fancied I glimpsed a kindred spirit back there at your parents'. Forgive me for speaking out of turn," he said stiffly. "No disrespect meant, but I sort of hoped maybe we could do a long-distance appearance-of-romance thing. Maybe string my folks and yours along."

Thinking Chet had gone out on a narrow limb, baring his soul to a virtual stranger, Sylvie relented and gave him something in return. "I was badly hurt by a man in New York, whom I loved and trusted, Chet. My family doesn't understand why I can't embrace what they want for me, which is marriage. You and I probably do share a similar angst when we're placed in our families' crosshairs."

Chet swung down her lane. He left his seat to open her door, but didn't turn off the Mercedes's engine. Assisting Sylvie out, he brushed a limp kiss over her cheek.

"I wish you the best, Chet. For the record, if you come back to Briarwood, I will serve you that postponed nightcap."

"It's a deal. Shall I walk you to your door, or do you plan to deliver those cookies to your nosy neighbor?"

"Nosy?" Sylvie darted a quick glance at Mercer's well-lit window. Maybe a curtain had dropped, or maybe the window was open and the fabric had been stirred by a breeze. She couldn't tell.

Chet shrugged. "I know our comings and goings are being observed."

"I think I'll hold off delivering my mother's offering until after I put on sweats and change back into the real me. Have a safe trip to Asheville." She ran lightly up her drive. Sylvie didn't know what made her do something so uncharacteristic then, but she turned and blew Chet a kiss. If Joel Mercer *was* spying, why not give him an eyeful?

She set the cookies on top of her fridge and let Oscar out while she pulled on some comfortable sweats. Not five minutes after she'd tied her sneakers, all hell broke loose in her backyard. Tearing outside with flashlight in hand, she discovered her delinquent houseguest had once again treed Fluffy the cat. As if on cue, the back door across the fence banged open, and out charged a fire-breathing Joel Mercer.

"I understand that beast doesn't belong to you," he shouted.

"That's right." Sylvie was able, with difficulty, to hook Oscar's leash to his collar.

"How long will he be your guest? I can't run out here every few hours to rescue our cat. Out of curiosity, do you have a city license to operate a kennel?"

"Maybe that's how it works in Atlanta, but for your information this is the country."

A deep, clearly irritated masculine voice floated out of the darkness. "Who said anything about Atlanta?"

"Your daughter. Is there a reason you'd rather that didn't

get out? Oh, for Pete's sake, Oscar, you won't catch that cat, so quit barking."

The voice in the darkness drawled, "I suppose there's no noise curfew in Briarwood, either?"

"Next you'll demand I run up a red flag whenever I let Oscar into my yard. He has a perfect right to run around and bark if he wants. He's contained by my fence, after all." She could sound put-upon, too.

Her new neighbor might have bought into her self-righteous indignation had Oscar, the big lummox, not torn from her grasp, and in one plunge flattened a six-foot section of their joint wood fence. A fence that already sagged. For some time, Sylvie had meant to have her brother-in-law, the building contractor, check the posts. Since Oscar's leash remained wrapped around her wrist, Sylvie found herself once again sprawled on her face in the dirt. It was a very unflattering pose. She was sorry she'd gone out of her way to make a point.

Probably her worst humiliation came when she saw the cat leap from the tree into the dubious protection of her owner's arms.

Sylvie hadn't untangled herself from the leash enough to rise. In a blur, a shadowy man suddenly loomed over her.

"Are you hurt?"

"My vanity," she mumbled. Sylvie couldn't get a hand under her, because Oscar lunged so hard at his leash. Brushing hair out of her eyes, she saw, among other things, that the dog had switched allegiances and was licking the face of her nemesis.

"Sit," Joel roared, and Oscar sat with a surprised little yelp. Then he dropped to his belly and his coal-dark eyes blinked adoringly up from a muff of white fur.

"How did you manage that?" Sylvie asked as gentle hands assisted her to her feet. "He's the only dog I groom and board who ignores my commands. But really, in spite of it all, Oscar's a loveable oaf."

"He obviously knows you think so." Joel recovered the

flashlight that still shone across the fallen fence and thrust it into Sylvie's hand. "I can't see well enough to shore this up tonight. Can you corral Oscar in the house until daylight?"

"Uh, sure." She played the light over her broken fence. "It needed new posts. My fault. I'll pay," she said, and was surprised when her neighbor said they'd share the cost.

TOWARD THE END of the week, around 11:00 a.m., Sylvie pinned the bodice of her best friend's wedding gown. The lace curtains were half-open, and Oscar was safely outside in her yard with its newly repaired fence. Kay Waller, who was there for a fitting, began to fret about her approaching marriage. "Sylvie, I've never been this nervous about anything. Do you think it's wrong to marry David so soon after my ex-husband had the gall to walk his *pregnant* girlfriend down the same church aisle?"

"Mmfff." Sylvie had a mouth full of pins.

"I simply can't believe Reverend Paul agreed to perform their service when he already had my wedding date on his calendar. It's a slap in the face. I suggested postponing our service a month, but Dave says I'm being silly."

Sylvie carefully removed the pins and stuck each one in the wrist pincushion she wore. "Hold still, Kay."

"You're not being any help. What's a best friend for?"

"Honestly! Why are you worrying over what people will say? Is that what's caused you to lose so much weight? This dress is inches too big around the middle and I only put in the last stitch yesterday."

"I do care how people talk about me. I don't have your nerves of steel when it comes to pretending I don't hear their whispers."

Sylvie's fingers stilled on a new dart she'd pinched in the satin fabric. "Me?"

Kay nodded, her focus shifting to the draped dress form in the corner. She stabbed a finger at it, and the diamond ring circling her third finger glinted in a ray of sunlight. "Don't pretend I'm the only bride who's begged you to let her wear that special gown you keep under wraps. You and I have been best friends since the cradle, Sylvie. And if it fits you, I'm sure it'll fit me. *Please,* Sylvie. If word traveled about town that I got to wear a bona fide Sylvie Shea design—and not any design, but *the dress*—my wedding would be the end-of-summer highlight. Not a footnote to the way I've been upstaged by Eddy and his…floozy."

Sylvie sank back on her heels. She felt both palms go damp. "There are no more Sylvie Shea gowns, you know that, Kay. My ad clearly states that a prospective client must bring me a pattern of her choice. I'll sew any gown a bride wants. Friend or not, you accepted my terms, Kay. Your dress is gorgeous, and it's so you."

The other woman admired the two-carat solitaire on her slender finger. "It's the mystery surrounding *the dress.* There's not a woman in the valley—well, an engaged woman—who isn't dying to be the bride who'll wear your secret gown. Me, most of all."

Sylvie scrambled to stand, but was startled all the same by what Kay had said. "The only mystery to me is why people would covet a dress they've never seen. That's just silly, Kay. How often have you heard me preach about bridal gowns needing to fit a bride's unique personality?"

"Yeah, but it's not silly. Anyone who knows you is positive that dress has gotta be spectacular. Your sisters say you're always working on it, and we've all seen your previous designs. Mandi Watson claims you're keeping this one for your own wedding. Is that true, Sylvie?"

"Right!" Sylvie shook her head. "So when am I supposed to have time to work on anything for *me,* let alone find that mythical husband? If and when I ever get married, I'll probably end up with a dress off the rack. Don't you know it's the plumber's wife who has a clogged sink, and the shoemaker's kids who go barefoot?"

Sylvie impulsively gave her friend a hug. "Your wedding will be featured in our weekly society page, Kay. You'll be the most beautiful bride of this season. Who else will have eight bridesmaids, two candle-lighters and three flower girls? And your patterns came from France. Each one *is* an original. I've sewn all fourteen dresses with my own bleeding fingers over the past three months. I guarantee the guests will weep, you'll be such a vision," Sylvie said, laying it on a little thick. But she did have plenty of history with Kay, the drama queen. "If you'd relax, you and Dave will have lots of wonderful memories. People will say *Eddy who?* if that jerk's name ever surfaces."

Kay compared her soft fingers with Sylvie's callused fingertips, and had the grace to blush. "I'd have given you more notice, but David wanted that day. And you could've cut the dress count by one," she pouted, "If you'd let me buy *the dress*."

"I guarantee this gown suits you best," Sylvie said. "Come on, I have something to show you." Walking away, she looked quickly at the covered dress form in the corner. The unfinished gown beneath the sheet represented all that was left of her hopes and dreams, she thought, opening a cabinet and lifting out an old notebook. "Recognize this? It's the notebook I kept in high school home-ec." Her eyes misty, Sylvie flipped several pages, then handed the book to Kay. "This was your dream gown in tenth grade. See how closely it resembles this one? I knew your marriage to Eddy Hobart was doomed from the minute his whiny mother insisted you wear the dress she'd worn at her own wedding."

Kay snickered. "It was ghastly. And so is Flo Hobart."

Sylvie shut the book and returned it to the drawer. "Zero taste. Hold out your arms. I'm going to unbutton you. We need to get you out of this without losing my marker pins—and without sticking you."

They had the gown off, and on a padded hanger, when through the side window came the sound of furious barking.

"Oscar, Anita Moore's Great Pyrenees," Sylvie said nonchalantly. "I'm boarding him until Anita and Ted get back from Tennessee. Can you let yourself out, Kay? That's Oscar's 'I treed a cat' bark. I have to rescue my new neighbor's cat…again. Sounds like this time she's gone up my big dogwood."

Kay stayed with Sylvie. "I meant to ask about your neighbor, Syl. I hear he's a real hottie."

"Who said that?" Sylvie stopped abruptly.

"You mean he's not?"

She shrugged. "I suppose, if looks is all you're interested in. He's a bit of a grouch. Which you'll hear if I don't get out there and save his daughter's cat. He'll throw open an upstairs window and order me to corral my damned dog. And after Dory and Carline's husbands repaired our adjoining fence, too. For free," she added.

"Mercer has a daughter?" Kay ignored everything else. "Wow, I don't think the gals at the salon know he's married. A couple of them are drawing straws over him already." Kay worked at Nail It!, the local beauty parlor.

Sylvie didn't mention that she had yet to see a wife show up next door. Nor would she admit that Joel Mercer was better to look at than a chocolate fudge sundae. All Sylvie needed was for her mother or sisters to get wind of the fact that she considered her neighbor worthy of a second glance. Say Mercer *was* separated, as Sylvie had begun to suspect—the poor guy didn't deserve to find himself hustled into being her blind date before he could guard against being flattened by the Shea freight train.

Leaving Kay standing at the side gate, Sylvie raced into her yard. Sure enough, Oscar ran crazily around the tree, in which the long-haired cat huddled. "Oscar, stop. Bad dog."

Aware he was in trouble, the dog put down his head until his ears dragged the ground, and slunk toward Sylvie's back porch.

It took some coaxing, which she was getting proficient at, but she soon cradled the purring cat in her arms. As she'd predicted, the upper half of Mercer's body was leaning out his upper window. Darn, Sylvie couldn't see him as well as she'd like because she'd left the glasses she used for distance in her purse today. But even fuzzy, the man had a glorious physique. Not too skinny, yet not too muscle-bound.

"Hey," he called. "Rianne's on her way down. I've gotta say, for the record, a big reason I moved here is so she and her cat could quit being cooped up inside an apartment."

Sylvie nodded, pretty sure that would be a major factor for anyone moving from the city to the country.

"By the way, Rianne's supposed to thank you for the cookies you brought over the other night. They were a big hit. With me, too," he added.

Kay, who'd followed Sylvie into the side yard, hissed very near her friend's ear, "You took him cookies?"

Sylvie whirled. "I did, but—no, I didn't. Mom sent them home with me to drop off. Remember, I told you about Dory setting me up with that computer guy at our family barbecue? It was that night."

"Yeah? How did your date work out? According to Dory, Chet's cool, and he has his own business. I understand he drives a top-of-the-line Mercedes."

"He also lives in Asheville." Sylvie specifically didn't add that, from an unmarried woman's point of view, Chet had another major drawback, like being gay.

Joel Mercer's daughter exploded out their back door. The girl had clearly dressed herself today, as Sylvie noticed she often did. Sylvie was all in favor of comfort, but she felt colors ought to match. Today Rianne had on red shorts teamed with a pink-and-green knit top. Her shirt was stretched out of shape and had probably been in the wash with something black that had left behind a series of gray blobs.

"I'm sorry Fluffy keeps getting out, Sylvie. Oh, and Daddy said I should ask if I can call you by your first name or not."

Sylvie said yes, after which Rianne launched into a rehearsed-sounding thank-you for the cookies. Obviously ordered by her dad.

"I'll tell my mom you like her chocolate chip recipe. Rianne, this is my very dear friend, Kay Waller. She's getting married soon, so probably the next time you see her she'll have a new last name. Ramsey. She'll be Kay Ramsey."

The girl seemed shy all of a sudden.

"Rianne starts school in September, Kay. I told her she'll really like Briarwood Elementary."

"You will," Kay agreed. "Are you in second grade? If so, my cousin may be your teacher."

"I'm gonna be in first grade," Rianne supplied. "Daddy has to go there next week and take them records from my kindergarten."

"I suppose you've already done your school shopping," Kay said politely.

Rianne shook her head. "Daddy's been too busy unpacking boxes and working."

"Working?" Kay had no compunction about probing.

"Yep. He used to have his office in his bedroom. Now he has a bedroom where he sleeps, and he's got an office upstairs, too."

Sylvie wanted to ask what her neighbor did at his home-based job, and she could tell it hovered on the tip of Kay's tongue to ask, as well. They were interrupted, however, by the arrival of the rural mail carrier. Because Homer saw the women over Sylvie's side gate, he honked and beckoned her over.

"Bye, Rianne. I'll see you later." Sylvie noted that the girl's dad had long since withdrawn from the upper-floor window.

Kay lowered her gaze from the spot where Joel had been, and checked her watch. "I didn't realize it was so late. I'm meeting David at the church for our last couples class in fifteen minutes. Do you want to fit my gown again tomorrow? If you do, I'll have to rearrange some client appointments."

"I don't see any need. If you lose weight between now and Saturday, it won't be enough to change the drape of the ma-

terial. Tell David I said to take you out for a steak and lob-
ster lunch after class. Fatten you up some."

Homer, the arthritic mailman, had climbed out of his mail
truck by the time the friends parted with a laugh and a hug.

"I have some mail for the new owner of the Whitaker
place, Sylvie. Plus a package. Certified, so he's gotta sign for
it," the old man said, eyeing the overgrown driveway. "Do you
have any idee if he's home?"

"Yes. Kay and I spoke to his daughter. Mercer came to an
upstairs window a few minutes ago. Would you like me to deliver the package for you, Homer? It appears you're not too
spry today."

"That would be right kind, Sylvie-girl. My old bones tell
me the less walking and climbing I do today, the better. Just
have the Mercer fellow put his John Hancock on the line with
the big black X. When you come back, I have a box for you,
too. Peggy said it's the lace you've been waiting for."

"Fantastic. I'll find it in the truck when I get back."

Sylvie didn't *intend* to spy on her neighbor, but the return
address printed in bold lettering on a fat manila envelope was
that of a major Atlanta newspaper. She assumed it was a few
recent editions of the paper; he must want to keep up with
news from home.

She dashed up Mercer's porch steps and rang his doorbell.
Listening to the fading sound of the bell, she whistled a tune-
less melody, swaying from side to side as she waited for Rianne or Joel to answer.

He took his sweet time, but eventually Joel Mercer did yank
open the door. His hair stood askew as if he'd been running both
hands through it. Sylvie again admired small, gold-rimmed
glasses that left his slate-blue eyes looking slightly myopic.

"I brought your mail." She'd also picked up a thistle in one
bare foot, Sylvie discovered, idly brushing one foot over the
other. "I see you're still taking a newspaper from your hometown. Seems silly that they'd require you to sign for it. I'll

bet if you'd ask our librarian, she'd probably subscribe to this paper, if she doesn't already. It'd save you the cost of shipping. Freda Poulson likes having news from other cities. There's no one more interested in world events." Sylvie grinned engagingly and extended the bundle.

Joel grabbed the stack out of her hands and gave her a fierce scowl. "What are you doing snooping through my private mail? Tampering with someone's mail is against federal law."

The form that was supposed to be signed by Mercer floated to the boards at their feet.

Her smile turned to a frown, too. "Our mailman has rheumatoid arthritis. I couldn't care less who sends you stuff. I volunteered to run this up to you to save wear and tear on poor Homer's joints."

"If he can't do the job he should retire." Joel moved to shut his door.

"Wait!" Sylvie neatly blocked his move. "This needs your autograph." Bending to scoop it up, she and Joel struck heads. Sylvie rubbed her forehead, allowing him to come up with the signature card.

"Do you have a pen?" he asked curtly.

Dazed by their collision, Sylvie stared at him blankly.

"Never mind. This mail system is so haphazard I'll just make other arrangements," he muttered after digging through all his pockets and finally coming up with a pen. A moment later he shoved the signed card back into Sylvie's hands.

Joel slammed his front door almost before Sylvie had negotiated a step back. "You have a nice day, too, buddy," she snarled, stomping down his steps and out into his thistle-littered lane. She landed on the thorn buried in her foot and ended up yelping and limping to where Homer waited patiently.

"Got it? Thanks, Sylvie. What's Iva's great-nephew like now that he's grown up? I remember him as a quiet tyke over the four or five summers he spent with Iva and Harvey. Quiet but eager to please. Seems a long time ago."

"Are you saying Joel Mercer *is* related to Iva? Are you sure he's not some city dude who bought the place from her nephew?"

"Nope. That's him all right. I hear he's got a daughter about the age he was when he first used to visit the Whitakers. Mercy, how time flies. Say, don't forget your lace," Homer called as Sylvie turned to give the Whitaker house a longer evaluation.

She lugged the heavy carton of laces she'd ordered from New York into her house, mulling over the latest tidbit Homer had added to the little she knew about her neighbor. Darned little. The man had acted downright surly about her touching his mail. What was the big issue? Did Joel Mercer have something to hide?

JOEL STOOD IN HIS ENTRY and ripped open the envelope of tear sheets consisting of his last two months' worth of cartoon strips. Enclosed was a big fat check that would have to last him until his accountant decided if he could retire on his investments or if he needed to seek another job. Lester Egan, his former boss, had attached a scribbled note asking Joel not to be hasty in his decision to quit the strip he'd started right after Lynn had divorced him. At the time, no one, least of all Joel, had dreamed that his satirical exaggeration using the backdrop of upscale Atlanta singles, would garner so much interest. Or that it would result in syndication and a whole bunch of new readers. Neither had Joel supposed his ex would return to anchor Atlanta's nightly news.

But Joel didn't see how he could continue drawing comic scenes about city singles from Briarwood. To do what he did on a daily basis necessitated haunting popular nightspots, where the upwardly mobile twentysomethings hung out after work and on weekends. Anyway, he'd about run out of situations for Poppy and Rose, his cartoon characters. Material of that type didn't fall out of North Carolina dogwood trees.

Speaking of falling from trees—his dingbat neighbor had a penchant for crazy stunts. Tree-climbing at her age… Joel watched her retreat, barefoot, down his lane. Each time he saw her she looked different. Today she wore her dark hair in two fat pigtails tied with ribbons that matched her shorts. He couldn't fault the shorts. They showed off her legs to good advantage. She did have nice legs. Maybe her best feature. Outside of that, nothing was remarkable except for her eyes. A warm hazel that reflected every nuance of her mood.

Leaning into the etched oval window in the center of his front door to watch her progress, Joel was sharply reminded of how lethal even a casual meeting with Sylvie Shea could be. He had a lump forming in the center of his forehead. And no idea how Sylvie made a living, other than to barge through life at warp speed. Oh, and pet-sit with humongous, ill-mannered dogs.

She did seem to have an active social life, he mused. There'd been the guy in the Mercedes. Yesterday, two muscle-bound dudes, both on very friendly terms with her, appeared like magic to rebuild her fence. One or both had hugged and maybe kissed her before taking off. And today, a girlfriend had shown up to visit for an hour or so.

He watched Sylvie dig a package out of the mail truck and then scamper out of sight. Joel continued to stare out the window. His fertile imagination began fashioning caricatures of Sylvie Shea as a subject in his comic strip. A country cousin of Poppy or Rose. It started him thinking there might be a whole other side to the singles experience in Briarwood, North Carolina, than he'd believed. Having tired of political cartoons, he'd tripped over the idea of the singles strip after his divorce. After he'd been dumped into the singles scene himself.

Truthfully, after a number of years spent skulking around Atlanta's hot spots, studying unsuspecting females on the prowl for husbands, he'd learned how to observe without attracting attention.

And now, the longer Joel considered the idea, the more he

thought his neighbor's varied taste in male friends, combined with her zany capers, might just offer the perfect new opportunity for him to continue the strip.

Chapter Three

Sylvie dropped her stack of junk mail and bills on a sideboard that stood in her entry. She hunted down a pair of non-sewing scissors then with care cut open the box of imported lace. One roll of fine hand-stitched lace came from a specialty shop in Holland. The lace had been on back order for six months, and it was every bit as beautiful as she'd pictured. Every other piece in her order was nicer than anything she could purchase through online outlets, too. But the Dutch lace exceeded her expectations. Of course, it'd cost an arm and a leg. Eyeing it critically, Sylvie deemed it worth every penny.

As she pinched the lace edging into tiny pleats, her eyes kept straying to the covered antique dress form in the corner. Until Kay had referred to the dress as an object of envy, Sylvie had no idea the last gown from her private collection was of interest to anyone but her.

Human nature to speculate about something kept hidden, she supposed. She hadn't lied to Kay. The cover protected an unfinished project Sylvie rarely had the time or heart to work on—despite what Kay had heard to the contrary. The gown had been her intended wedding dress. She couldn't bear to part with it. But neither was there any likelihood of her ever wearing it. Moving it out of her client area seemed the best course of action.

This dress form was the first she'd owned. Fashioned of

brass and North Carolina hardwood, it weighed a ton. Sylvie's two dear grandmothers had run across it during one of their many antiquing forages into the Smoky Mountains.

As Sylvie wrestled the awkward thing into her bedroom, where the lighting was definitely poorer than in her sewing room, she fondly recalled the two women who'd nurtured her early dreams of becoming a wedding gown designer. Losing both of those dear souls had left holes in her heart. Yet she was thankful neither of her staunchest advocates were alive to see her slink home in defeat. Although, she mused, puffing as she dragged the form into a corner opposite her bed, many in the family said Mary Shea had possessed a sixth sense. And that might be why she'd willed Sylvie this land and cabin, when the logical recipient should have been Sylvie's dad.

Straightening, she dusted her hands. The form fit nicely below a shelf displaying old hat boxes. Those too had been Gram's. The grouping beckoned temptingly. Maybe it was an omen nudging her to—finally—assemble the lacy sleeves. After all, the arrival of the Dutch lace, coupled with the fact that autumn was coming and not as many weddings would be scheduled, meant there'd be time to do it.

Her bedside phone rang as Sylvie contemplated her workload. "Sylvie Seamstress, " she said cheerily into the receiver.

"It's Carline," came a muted response.

"Carline, what's wrong? Are you ill? Is it the baby?" Sylvie sank onto the crocheted bedspread, also an heirloom handed down in the Shea family. Carline's husband, Jeff, was twelve years older than his wife. Their baby, a boy, was probably Jeff's last chance to produce a Manchester heir, as doctors said his sperm count was low. They'd had a difficult time conceiving. The only other Manchester male, Jeff's twin, had died at sixteen in a parasailing accident. A tragic loss for any family, but especially for parents who needed their sons to take over the business—Manchester Sawmills. Not that they wouldn't have let any of their five daughters assume the helm; however, none of the girls or their spouses were so inclined. Feeling obligated, at twenty-two, Jeff had stepped into the role. The task had proved monumental and time-consuming, which resulted in zero opportunity to consider dating or marriage—until he walked into Carline's brand-new kitchen shop two years ago to buy a coffee grinder for his sister and fell instantly in love.

Sylvie always sighed over love stories that seemed to fall into place with such ease. Especially since she had a habit of falling for Mr. Wrong. Die-hard bachelors—guys who broke out in a rash at the word *marriage*. And that was even before Des had betrayed her.

Shoving aside those rambling thoughts, Sylvie gripped the phone nervously and strained to hear her sister's soft whisper.

"I'm fine. The baby's fine, Syl. I'm calling about Buddy Deaver."

"Who? Bucky Beaver?"

"Not Beaver. Deaver! And don't shout. He and his mother are in the next room picking out a gift for Kay. His real name is Jarvis. Jarvis the fourth, and they call him Buddy. He was in Dory's class, and went to university in Raleigh-Durham. An accounting major. Now he's a financial advisor or stock broker in Raleigh or something like that."

"Carline, this is all very interesting, but why do I need to know this?"

"Because I just suggested he escort you to Kay's wedding. His dad has a business associate flying into Asheville that day, so Mr. and Mrs. Deaver aren't going to make Kay and David's wedding. Which means Buddy has to go alone. He said he'd skip it altogether except that he hasn't seen his classmates in years."

"Carline, I can't conjure up a mental picture of this guy. But I'm Kay's maid of honor. That means I'm responsible for seeing that everything to do with the ceremony runs smoothly. What are you thinking?"

"That you're going stag to the reception and the dinner dance at the Elks club. Can you really think of anything more embarrassing?"

"Yes, being saddled with a financial guru named Buddy."

"Sylvie, why must you always be so sarcastic? I told him you'd probably have to take the flower girls or candle-lighters' dresses to the church. Mrs. Deaver said Buddy can drive his dad's Coupe DeVille. There'll be room."

"My Mutt Mobile has more. I've already scheduled time tomorrow afternoon to wash it and vacuum it out."

"Sylveeee!" Carline wailed, still in hushed undertones. "You can't humiliate me like this. Mrs. Deaver was thrilled to think Buddy won't have to stay home. She buys a lot from my shop. I can't go out there and say you won't go with her son."

"Make up an excuse. Say I have a prior date you didn't know about."

"*Lie?* Sylvie, what would Mother say? Or Reverend Paul?"

"Lord, deliver me from you and Mom when you invoke the name of our pastor. All right, Carline. I'll do this one favor. Don't commit me ever again or I swear I won't bail you out. Tell Buddy I'll take the dresses to the church early. That way he can drive his own car, whatever it is. I'm not going one mile if he shows up in his dad's Caddy."

"Thank you, thank you, thank you. You'll have fun, I promise."

Sylvie was saved saying she sincerely doubted it by her sister's banging down her phone. After hanging up, Sylvie went straight to the bookcase in the living room and pulled out the yearbook published in Dory's senior year. Sure enough, there he was, voted the school's best citizen and voted by his class as most scholastic. She groaned as she saw his perky bow tie and the absence of even a tiny smile.

She shut the book and slid it back in the shelf. One could

hope that working in the city had polished him up a bit. She really wished she hadn't suddenly remembered her father calling the fourth Jarvis Deaver a stuffed shirt. Oh well, it was only one night out of her life. She'd gotten through all the other blind dates scrounged up by her well-meaning family and friends by keeping that thought uppermost in mind.

Having stored the lace from her recent delivery, Sylvie had just finished checking the packing slip against the invoice when Oscar went berserk. Maybe this time he'd flushed a rabbit or a squirrel. Or else…the Mercer's cat was out again.

Sylvie knew that was the case the minute she stepped onto her back porch and heard Rianne Mercer calling for Fluffy. The girl's dad thundered from an upper window, "Rianne, what's the racket now? Tell me you didn't let Fluffy out!"

"It was 'nother accident, Daddy. Fluffy's on Sylvie's fence and I can't get her."

"All right. Give me a minute and I'll be down to help."

Sylvie was sure she heard his irritated sigh. Did that man do nothing downstairs? For crying out loud, did he live in that one room—a bedroom, if Sylvie recalled the layout of the Whitaker house. But then, Rianne had mentioned he worked at home and that he now had a bedroom and a separate office, instead of the two combined. Probably the sunnier corner room had become his office.

She wondered again what kind of career he had. Something to do with computers? Of course, her father had always worked at home, his cabinet shop was attached to the house. Until she'd gotten too involved with extracurricular activities at school, Sylvie had virtually been his shadow. She still loved the smell of fresh-cut wood and wood shavings. As well, she loved the way her father made gorgeous furniture from raw lumber and a pattern. Her love of crafting and designing clothing had probably come from spending hours in that woodworking shop.

She suspected that Rianne Mercer had no idea yet what a lucky girl she was to have her daddy working at home.

"Hi," Sylvie called over the fence to the child who was still trying to coax her cat down. "I'll put Oscar inside and come back and help you with Fluffy. Or maybe she'll jump down on her own like she did the last time."

"Okay, but Daddy's coming to help me, too."

"You can run in and tell him, so it doesn't interrupt his work." The girl glanced toward the house. "Yeah, that'd be good."

Sylvie dragged Oscar away from the fence, up her back steps and into the laundry room, where she checked to be sure he had food and fresh water. She dashed back outside and stood on tiptoes to grab the cat as Joel burst out of his house.

He met Sylvie at the gate to take the fat animal out of her arms. "I gave Rianne strict instructions to not let Fluffy out. I bought some litter and put her litter box in our laundry room."

"Yeah, but Daddy, it's so pretty in the yard. Fluffy likes to play dolls with me. I thought she'd stay there. I didn't see Oscar. I s'posed his owner took him home."

"There's a hopeful thought," Joel said. "It seems you and I are doomed to meet over the back fence to deal with our wayward pets, Ms. Shea."

"Having a pet next door is new for me. Iva didn't have any animals when I moved here, so my occasional boarders weren't an issue. After she passed on, I got used to the house being vacant. Uh—Homer, our mailman, said you're Iva's great-nephew."

"I am." He petted the cat, which snuggled happily in his arms.

"You're nothing like her, if you don't mind my saying. I was sure her relatives must've sold the land."

"I considered it. Her death took me by surprise. I had developers contacting me—and they all expressed interest in the land fronting the lake. At the time, my tax man said I'd be better off sitting on the property, that it would only increase in value." Joel raised one shoulder. "I didn't need the extra tax burden that selling would've added. One year ran into two, and two into three. Then…" He broke off speaking suddenly, and said, "It seemed like a good idea to move here."

Sylvie had seen the way his eyes shifted toward Rianne. She wondered if his abrupt departure from his rambling explanation had to do with his divorce. She assumed that was the case. Of course, she could be completely wrong. Maybe the Mercers had an open marriage. One of these days, his wife might show up.

"Well, I'm wasting time I ought to be using more productively," he said.

Sylvie airily waved a hand. "Yes, Rianne mentioned you work at home. Home-based jobs are certainly becoming more popular."

"They are. I feel fortunate that the arrangement works for me. Rianne, remember I said don't chatter and make a pest of yourself with Ms. Shea."

"Oh, she's not at all," Sylvie inserted quickly. "I don't mind a bit. I work at home, too, so I'm well aware of how people assume you have all the time in the world."

"You work at home? Oh, the kennels, you mean?"

"Actually," Sylvie explained, "I'm a seamstress. I board animals now and then. The kennels were my grandfather's. I assume you knew he was the only vet in town. After he retired, he bred and sold Red Bone hounds."

"Are you referring to Mr. Shea?"

"My grandfather, yes. Bill Shea."

"He didn't have dogs when I used to stay with Iva, which was shortly after my great-uncle Harvey died. I know he loved to fish. I came here four or five different summers and he always took me fishing. So, he was a veterinarian who later raised hounds? I probably should've known."

"It's odd to think you fished with Gramps, and yet I don't remember you."

"Nor I you."

"How old are you?"

"Thirty-three going on a hundred," Joel said, smiling.

"Ah, that makes me seven years younger. Depending on which years you stayed with Iva, I may not have spent much time here. My folks owned a beach house, and mom took us girls there most summers."

"So, are you studying to be a vet? Following in Bill's footsteps?"

"Not hardly. I operate a part-time mobile grooming service. Briarwood is a community where residents commute to the city for their jobs, or else they're retired. Both groups benefit by having someone—*moi*—groom pets in their homes. Because the kennels are out back, I occasional board someone's pet." She didn't mention that Oscar stayed in the house.

"So it's just my luck you're keeping a moose at the same time I move Rianne's poor defenseless kitty in next door."

Sylvie was intrigued by his uncharacteristic grin, which brought deep creases to his cheeks and fine laugh lines around his eyes. Or maybe it wasn't that uncharacteristic. She hardly knew the man.

Mercer seemed struck, uncomfortably so, by the fact that he'd stepped out of his tough-guy shell. Sobering, he said a quick goodbye and headed for his house.

"Hey, wait. I have to make spritz cookies for our Sunday school this week. If Rianne's at loose ends, maybe she'd like to come here and help."

"Daddy, can I? Please. Please?"

Joel turned slowly back, frowning.

"Sorry," Sylvie mumbled. "I shouldn't have asked in front of her. Uh, maybe your dad needs your help unpacking," Sylvie said in a rush. "If so, the offer remains open. I'll be making cookies another time."

"No. It'll be fine." Joel's grudging capitulation sounded anything but fine. "Just don't be talking Ms. Shea's ear off. And she has my permission to send you home if you ask *why, why, why* three or more times in a row."

Rianne ducked her head. "'Kay, Daddy. I'll try and re-member."

Sylvie laughed spontaneously. "I have a niece and neph-ew whose every other word is who, what, why, where or how. Rianne's very polite. I think we'll get on famously. Oh, and do call me Sylvie."

Joel rocked forward and back on his heels and narrowed his eyes, as if her request was an imposition.

What was the man's problem? One minute he seemed a nice, decent guy. The next, a grouch. Sylvie's concentration on the father was broken by a question from the daughter.

"I don't know what those cookies are, the ones you said you were making. Actually, I've never helped make cookies. Is it all right if I don't know how?"

Sylvie gazed down into the girl's anxious blue eyes. "Nev-er? Maybe your mom calls these sugar cookies. They're made from dough you refrigerate and squeeze out in different shapes from a cookie gun."

Rianne continued shaking her head. "I don't think my ma-ma makes cookies at all. She only talks on TV."

Sylvie felt herself nodding. "Oh, uh, then you're in for a treat, honey. I already have the dough made. You get to help with the good part, squishing it through the press and paint-ing the shapes with edible paints after they come out of the oven and set for a while."

The girl's dragging steps sped up and she gave a few lit-tle skips. "What's edible paint?"

"Just what it sounds like. Paint you can eat." Sylvie smiled over Rianne Mercer's obvious skepticism. "They didn't have such a thing when I learned to make cookies. My sister owns a kitchen shop in town. She first tried these paints last Christ-mas. Our Christmas plates did look fabulous."

"Daddy said the woman who used to live in your house made the yummiest oatmeal raisin cookies."

"Really? That would be my Grandmother Shea. Hers *were*

tasty. I have her recipe. If we have time, how would you like to mix up a batch to bake and take home to surprise your dad?"

"Yes, please." Rianne beamed.

"I'm fairly sure I have all the ingredients we need. Oh—" She paused. "Unless you and your dad have too many desserts on hand as it is." At Rianne's vigorous shake of the head, Sylvie led the way into her kitchen. "First we have to wash our hands," she announced.

"Why did all those ladies who don't know us bring us food, Sylvie?"

"It's called being neighborly," Sylvie said, sharing a towel. "People wanted to welcome you to town."

"Oh. Daddy thinks they just wanted to find out all about us."

"That, too." Sylvie laughed. "It's the drawback of living in a small town, kiddo. Everyone wants to know everyone else's business."

"Why?"

"That's a very good question." She got out the bowl of chilled dough and put the first batch into the press. Talk fell off as she showed the little girl how to push the plunger to create a slow, steady flow. As the dough softened, Rianne grew more adept, and her confidence soared.

"Are you sure you aren't teasing me about never making cookies before?"

"Nope. Daddy doesn't like to cook. And Mrs. Honeycutt, who watched me after kindergarten, has something wrong with her blood so she can't eat sweet stuff."

"Diabetes?"

"Yes. You're smart, Sylvie. You don't even know Mrs. Honeycutt."

"You're pretty smart yourself. I'll bet you'll be taking on some of the cooking soon." Sylvie was tempted to ask how long it'd been since the girl's father had assumed meal preparations in the Mercer household, but she didn't want Joel to accuse her of trying to pump information out of a kid.

The afternoon slipped by in a flurry of activity and laughter. Sylvie discovered the adorable little girl could converse intelligently at a level far above her age. And unlike the adults in Sylvie's life, Rianne didn't once question why Sylvie was still single. Why she'd never found some nice man to marry.

They'd painted all the designs on the sugar cookies and were sampling the ones that were broken as they waited for the last pan of oatmeal cookies to come out of the oven. Sylvie's phone rang. She checked the readout. "Hmm. It says unavailable. Probably somebody wanting to sell me something I don't need."

"Daddy doesn't answer those kinds of calls, either."

The caller didn't give up even after clicking into her answering machine. "Yeah?" she said to Rianne. "When you work at home, you learn that other people figure you aren't really working. Even friends and people who should know how busy you are take advantage."

Rianne wiped her hands on her shorts. "Yep. Daddy says if it's 'portant, the person wouldn't have any reason to hide his name."

Sylvie pulled on her oven mitt and bent to take the last cookie sheet out of the hot oven. Well, here, finally was an opinion she and Joel Mercer saw eye to eye on.

She had one row of cookies left to remove. In the back room, Oscar started barking furiously. The outburst was followed by someone banging loudly on her side door. "Can you ask whoever's there to wait a minute? Don't open the door, because I have no idea who it would be."

"It's my daddy!" Rianne announced.

"Oh, in that case, unlock the door and let him in."

He roared in like a whirlwind. "I was afraid something was wrong over here. Why the hell didn't you answer your phone?"

Sylvie calmly set the last cookie on the cooling rack before she turned to face him. "Was that you who just tried to call? It said unavailable, and Rianne told me you don't answer those calls, either. Is there a problem?"

Color streamed into his cheeks. "I…ah, Rianne's been over here for three hours. I thought I should see how you were doing."

"Good." Sylvie dumped the hot pan in the sink.

"Daddy, we had fun! Come see the cookies I squished out and painted all by myself." Grasping her dad's hand, she dragged him to the center island. He didn't make it all the way; instead, his piercing gaze stalled on the latest batch of cookies.

"Are those by chance oatmeal raisin?" He leaned down to peer at them more closely and sniffed the steam rising from the hot cookies.

His daughter flashed Sylvie an unhappy glance. "He spoiled my surprise."

"In that case, what can we do but give him a sample right now? Who better to tell us if these are as good as the ones he remembers?" Sylvie took a plate from the cupboard and piled it with cookies from the still-warm batch. Then she took three glasses, which she filled to the brim with milk. She motioned her guests to sit on the stools grouped at one end of her counter.

Joel bit into the first cookie gingerly, as if it might bite back. The grin that spread over his face spoke louder than any words of praise.

Sylvie nudged Rianne. "There's your answer. Your surprise is a big success. You and I should probably eat only one apiece. Especially since we shared the sugar cookies we broke."

"These are *fantastic!* I can't tell you how many times I'd buy some bakery cookies and remembered these. Nothing I've tasted has ever lived up to them. Still, I wondered if I'd blown them out of proportion." He grinned at Sylvie and then at Rianne. "I ask you, snooks, have you ever tasted anything quite this fantastic?"

Rianne nodded. "The chocolate chip ones Sylvie said her mother made. They're my very favorite, and I've never had any that tasted better."

Joel's face fell, but Sylvie burst out laughing. "There you have it. That's what I love most about kids. They're so honest."

"Meaning adults aren't?"

Sylvie lifted her glass of milk and touched the rim of his. "More power to you, Mr. Mercer, if in your thirty-some years of dealing with people, you still believe they are."

Considering that he twisted truths to make them humorous for his comic strip, Joel said nothing, but stole a second cookie.

"Ah, I see I made my point." Still, she was thankful when her phone rang again. Anyway, Rianne rushed to show her dad the edible paints and explain to him, as Sylvie had to her, that they were made out of vegetable dyes.

Sylvie, who tended to see her life as an open book, answered the phone on the second ring, knowing her sister Dory was the one calling.

"I hear voices," Dory said almost at once. "I won't interrupt, since you're with clients. Phone me back as soon as you're free."

"I'm free now, Dory. I'm in the kitchen with my neighbors. We're drinking milk and trying out Grandma Shea's oatmeal-raisin cookies. I haven't made that recipe in years, have you?" The phone crackled with static but was otherwise silent.

"Dory? Did you put me on hold?"

"You're serving milk and cookies in the middle of a work day?"

"I'm taking a break. Rianne Mercer has been over here helping me make the Sunday school snack."

"You're feeding Mercer's daughter, right? The kid from next door? For a minute there, I thought you meant you were entertaining Mr. Sexy himself."

Warning bells sounded in Sylvie's head, but she couldn't resist inquiring, "That description came from where, Dory?"

"From everybody who saw him in town this morning. Plus, I ran into Kay Waller at lunch. She agreed. Apparently she got a look at him while she was at your house for a fitting. She said you told her the guy has a wife. Hmm, funny, other people say Mercer only ever mentions his daughter. Kay and I think you should ask him outright about his marital status. If he's divorced, it gives you the perfect opening to invite him to Kay's wedding this Saturday."

"Why would I do that, Dory? He doesn't even know Dave or Kay."

"For one thing, it shows your intent to stake your claim. For another, you wouldn't be the only unattached female at the wedding dance. Kay and I feel—"

"*What?* I can't believe you two—"

"We're thinking of *you,* Sylvie. You need a life."

"Dory, I *have* a life. And I'll thank you to butt out of it." She'd spoken so sharply, Sylvie felt Joel Mercer's eyes boring into her back. Hunching her shoulders, she tried to step around the corner into the hall for some privacy. It was harder to ignore the tic of irritation that began to hammer insistently behind her eyes. "Look, Dory, I know you guys are sincere. But I guess you haven't talked with Carline since yesterday. I already have a date for the wedding."

"No kidding? You sly dog. Who?"

"Uh, Buddy Deaver." Sylvie almost dropped the phone because Dory screamed in her ear.

"Tell me this is a joke! I know his family has money and all, but Sylvie, he's a loser with a capital L."

The tic turned into a dull pounding at the base of Sylvie's skull.

"No one in the world is as boring as Buddy," her sister wailed. "Not only that, he's two full years younger than me, which makes him three years younger than you. People will think you're desperate, Syl."

"Carline said he graduated in your class."

"He did. He's a nerd who got bumped up two grades."

Sylvie's heart dived to her toes, but she wasn't about to give ground to her sister, especially after Dory had been the one to foist Chet off on her. "Look on the bright side, Dory. It's become the thing to date younger men." She ended the call before her sister could do more than sputter. Turning as she started to hang up the phone, Sylvie walked squarely into Joel Mercer. She felt a wave of heat emanating from his body and blindly aimed the receiver at the hook on the wall phone, but missed twice.

Eyeing her curiously, Joel plucked the receiver from her limp grip and dropped it into place. "That was my sister," she offered lamely.

"I gathered. Is everything all right?"

"Fine. Everything's fine." Sylvie shivered, stepped back and rubbed her bare upper arms.

"Okay, then. It's getting late, so Rianne and I will be on our way after she thanks you. We should hurry—she has to go to the bathroom." He grinned crookedly. "I'm embarrassed to admit I already polished off every cookie on the plate."

Releasing a hand she'd clamped around her arm for stability, Sylvie waved down the hall. "Don't make her walk all the way home for that. Rianne, honey, I have two bathrooms. The main one is down the hall, second door on your left. The other's between the two rooms on your right. That's for my guest bedrooms. And…uh…my sewing room."

"No need to trouble you." Joel might as well have saved his breath. His daughter sailed past him, headed down the hall at a dead run.

"Poor kid," Sylvie murmured. "She had a glass of water earlier, and that huge glass of milk with the cookies. I should've pointed out the location of the bathrooms earlier."

"She's not shy. She could've asked."

"At that age, ask a near stranger? Get outta here! Girls her age would burst rather than do that."

The look crossing Joel's face was one of pure horror. "Why are girls so difficult?" he muttered.

"You think she's difficult at…what—six, seven? Wait until she reaches the dreaded teens."

"She's almost six. And please don't mention *teenage*. I can't force myself to think that far ahead."

Though his tone was lighthearted, Sylvie sensed an underlying desperation to his remark. Just then she knew that, whatever the reason, her neighbor's wife was out of the picture. Joel Mercer was raising his daughter alone.

Sylvie couldn't offer him any help beyond the cookie-baking they'd done today.

Stepping around Joel, she knelt and pulled a disposable aluminum pan out of a bottom cupboard, where she kept a supply for taking dishes to church socials or family potlucks. Straightening, she began loading the pan with the oatmeal cookies.

Tension thickened the air until suddenly Rianne bounded back into the room. "Daddy, come see," she said excitedly. "Sylvie's got a whole room full of headless people, like at Dillard's 'partment store. They're all wearing beautiful dresses like I want for my Princess Barbie. There's even some dresses for kids."

The cover Sylvie started to snap over the cookie tin shot off and clattered to the counter. "Headless people!" She laughed. "Rianne, you had both of us going there for a minute. She's seen my dress forms," she explained to Joel. "I sewed gowns for an entire wedding party." Managing at last to get the lid on the container, she handed it to him.

"Rianne, honey," she murmured. "Something you'll learn about men—it's a rare one who can work up any enthusiasm for a dress. Unless," she added with a wink at Joel, "we're talking about the skimpy outfits worn by pro-football cheerleaders."

"You wouldn't be tarring all of us with the same brush, would you?" Joel drawled, refusing to be intimidated.

"Definitely." Sylvie's eyebrow spiked up.

"I suppose I'm guilty as charged," Joel said. "But I'm striving to become a more enlightened male," he said, grabbing his daughter's hand. "Let's go see those dresses, shall we, snooks?"

When he moved past Sylvie, she couldn't resist one last verbal jab. "Granted, it's not only cheerleader apparel that catches men's eyes. I forgot about the *Sports Illustrated* swimsuit edition, and Victoria's Secret catalogues."

Rianne tugged her father into the sewing room door, prattling nonstop. Joel stopped at the threshold.

Sylvie hung back, really not expecting him to comment. At first he remained silent, then she heard him utter a long, low whistle. "I may not know a damn thing about women's fashion," he said, "but I know a professional job when I see one. Mind if I ask why you bury your talent in a backwater like this? You could make a mint in Atlanta—or New York, for that matter."

He couldn't have hurt her more.

"If it's a matter of contacts," he said offhandedly, "I may have a few."

"It's not…I don't need contacts," Sylvie said quickly, trying to usher them out of room so she could shut the door. After all, she'd had a contact and the relationship had ended with her career in shambles.

"If working in Atlanta is so fabulous, why did you move to Briarwood?" she asked coolly.

"My reasons are personal." Joel stiffened, leaving a decided chill hanging between them.

"Exactly." Sylvie pursed her lips. "As you said a minute ago, it's getting late." She looked pointedly at her watch. "Don't let me keep you from more important things," she said, opening her front door.

"Bye, Sylvie," Rianne called over one shoulder as her father urged her gently down the hall and out the door. "Can I come back another day and watch you sew those pretty dresses?"

Sylvie didn't have it in her to crush any child's hopeful expression. Not even if that girl's father happened to have stumbled on to something she felt so sensitive about. "Sure, Rianne. You're welcome to come here whenever you want. Bring your Barbie doll. I'll make her a new dress. Or you can pick a pattern and we'll sew one for you."

"Really?" Rianne's thin voice rose.

"That's not necessary," Joel snapped. "Thanks all the same, but I can dress my daughter fine all by myself." The door slammed.

Sylvie detoured into the kitchen to pack the cookies for Sunday.

Later, she cried over a glass of white wine as she sat on her bed and stared at the covered wedding gown. She couldn't help it. She did envy the loving relationships her sisters had, envied Dory her kids, and Carline's burgeoning belly. Even Kay had David now, a really wonderful man.

It seemed now that she'd been terribly wrong when she'd assured herself last week that she'd gotten over double-crossing Desmond Emerson. He'd so carelessly and easily killed her dreams. What was worse, she sat alone weeping in her wine, was knowing that Des and his new wife, her own former assistant, suffered not one shred of remorse.

Chapter Four

Joel sat brooding over a cup of coffee in his kitchen. He doodled around the edges of a half-finished list of things he needed to do. His breakfast consisted of three oatmeal raisin cookies and black coffee. Fortunately for him, Rianne had slept in. He didn't want her developing his bad eating habits. Although Mary Shea used to say she put healthier ingredients in her cookies than most manufacturers used in their breakfast cereals. At times she used to alter her oatmeal recipe, adding in grated apple or cranberries and nuts. The newspaper's health columnist got after him one day over the disgusting meals he showed Poppy and Rose eating. The woman said a lot of young people read his strip, and that Joel should show a little responsibility. So he had Poppy going on a health-food kick for a time. Even used one of the columnist's lines, having Poppy tell Rose that there was more nutrition in the cardboard box than the sugar-coated cereal inside.

Remembering the furor that touched off in the paper's advertising department, Joel smiled. It was his first inkling of how powerful his work had become. He'd been summoned to a meeting with his editor, the editor in chief and ten suits from the ad division. The men shouted at each other and at him, all of them talking as if his characters were real people who'd committed a cardinal sin. Oh, it'd been sweet. He'd ended up getting a bonus, plus a fat raise. But he had to promise that Poppy and Rose wouldn't step on the toes of the paper's multi-million-dollar advertisers again.

"Daddy," a plaintive voice warbled down from upstairs. "Where are you?"

Jumping up, Joel quickly brushed cookie crumbs off the table into his hand, and dumped them in the garbage disposal on his way to the foot of the stairs. "I'm in the kitchen having coffee. What do you need, Rianne?"

"Nothing. I looked in your bedroom, and office, and I couldn't find you." She padded to the landing in her bunny slippers and long nightie, rubbing her eyes. A yawning cat twined about her legs. "The 'partment didn't have so many rooms."

Joel felt a stab of guilt for taking her away from all that was familiar. "Do you miss Atlanta so much, baby?" Rianne usually acted grown-up beyond her years. Except for early mornings or when she was ill. Running up the stairs to meet her, Joel held out his arms, and she stumbled forward and let him swing her aloft.

"I like it here 'kay. But I thought there'd be kids to play with." She pushed tangled blond hair out of her eyes. "Yesterday was fun. I loved making cookies with Sylvie. Daddy, why don't you like her? She makes me laugh. I *like* her."

"I don't dislike her…." he began, and realized he had no explanation for what had erupted between him and his neighbor yesterday.

"Come on, kid. Let's go fix you toast, juice and peaches."

"Are the peaches sour?"

"Nope. Sweet. I ate a whole one after you went to bed last night, and it was yummy."

"Sylvie had some in her fridge. She said they were good, too."

Joel set Rianne down to choose a seat. He rummaged until he found whole-wheat bread. As he shoved two slices in the toaster, his attention was again drawn to his neighbor. Joel thought he'd paid Sylvie's obvious sewing talent a compliment, but then he'd glanced at her, and her big, dark eyes were brimming with pain—as if he'd injured her with his comment. After that, she'd sounded shrewish. And her remark about sewing Rianne a pretty dress had hit him wrong, as if he let his daughter wear rags. It was too similar to a row he'd had with Lynn a few days before he decided to move to Briarwood.

His ex hadn't been back in Atlanta long, a month maybe, collecting her accolades and preening in the spotlight of her new TV job. Up to then, she hadn't contacted him or asked to see Rianne. Suddenly, out of left field, she phoned him at the paper and insisted he bring Rianne to a celebration of sorts—a party they were having for her at the station.

Rianne's toast popped up just as Joel finished slicing her peach. He buttered both slices, cut them corner to corner and turned the buttered sides together. He remembered with a start that it was how the woman who'd left him this house had served her toast. Iva followed rituals, and rituals created a sense of continuity. Yet she allowed Joel the freedom to be himself. A lack of that kind of tolerance lay behind the growing rift between him and his ex-wife.

Joel had notified the sitter that he'd collect Rianne early for the party. She'd worn clean jeans, sneakers and her favorite Dora Explorer T-shirt to kindergarten. Joel saw no reason to swing past their house for a change. On arriving at the sitter's, he'd taken a minute to wash chocolate milk off Rianne's face and comb her hair. He hadn't noticed the small chocolate stain that pretty much blended with a flower in Dora's hand. Probably no one else would have, either, if his so-perfect ex hadn't made a major production of it. Lynn claimed that Joel had purposely let Rianne come to the station looking like an urchin to humiliate her. She further announced, for all to hear, that he was unfit to raise their daughter. And ended by suggesting that her parents, who lived at a ritzy country club in Florida, might sue for custody. *Like they'd done such a bang-up job raising Lynn.*

Granted, when he'd met Lynn, Joel had been attracted by her perfection. Her face. Her figure. Her clothes. That had led to his buying a ring, and culminated in a huge wedding. It wasn't until the honeymoon began to fade in memory that Joel saw what it took to maintain twenty-four-hour-a-day perfection. Their first Christmas with Lynn's parents in their five-million-dollar mansion further revealed the source of his new wife's need to *have* the best, *look* the best, *be* the best. Lynn, her parents, a sister and an overachieving brother all spent an entire week trying to remake Joel in their image. It had been a rude awakening to discover that the woman he thought he loved, and hoped to live with for fifty years or more, hadn't married him for what he was but for his potential. As it turned out, he didn't have enough potential to suit Lynn, after all.

That day at her la-di-dah party, she made it plain that Rianne didn't measure up, either. Joel had seen red, and said stuff he shouldn't have. He'd grown up with parents who fought over everything, and he'd sworn he wouldn't fight in front of his child. But he had, and it'd been for Rianne. Who could look into the face of his beautiful child and not think her perfect as she was?

Rianne bit into her toast, and Joel fed Fluffy, then poured himself another steaming cup of coffee. "What I want most in all the world, Rianne, is for you to be happy."

She lifted her eyes as her dad slid into a chair across from her. "So…it's okay if I go see Sylvie? And it's okay if I let her make me a dress? I want a frilly dress, like the blue one with the shiny ribbons and lace."

"This desire to have a girly dress is something new. Generally when we shop for your clothes, you pick jeans and tops with your favorite cartoon characters."

Her blue eyes clouded, and she blinked as if warding off tears. "Maybe Mommy will like me better if we send her a picture of me in a dress." A tear did slid between her lashes, catching on the curve of her cheek.

Joel's hand wobbled so much as he lowered his mug, he spilled his coffee. Lord, was it possible Rianne had tapped into his thoughts? Sliding to his knees, Joel wouldn't allow her to turn aside. He gently brushed away the tear. "I swear, sweetheart, it's me Mommy doesn't like. Not you. *Never* you. You know how messy I let my room get. I don't scrub the shower. Sometimes I wear holey jeans or the same shirt for three days. That's why Mommy got fed up and left."

"But…she left me, too. I make my bed and put on a clean shirt every day. At school, only one girl 'sides me didn't have a mommy. Why, Daddy?"

Joel felt sweat bead on his brow. Maybe it'd been a mistake to send her to an expensive private kindergarten; at the initial interview even the principal had mentioned most of their students came from two-parent households. Friends warned him he'd face this conversation one day. He actually thought he'd be better prepared.

"You were only a baby when Mommy and I found out we were both happier people if we didn't live together. I can do my work here at home, but she had important stuff that took her far away. Out of the country. I'll call and ask her for some tapes." How could he tell Rianne that Lynn had chosen those years as a correspondent in preparation for her current job?

Rianne slowly nodded. "Okay. But I think being mommies and daddies is 'portant. When I grow up, I'm gonna make cookies ev'ry day with my kids. And I'm gonna work at home like you do, Daddy."

Joel hugged her tight, knowing he probably ought to explain that not every parent had the luxury he enjoyed of working at home. He'd save that for another father-daughter talk. Joel stood, and let her go back to her breakfast, all the while thinking he should dig through his boxes for a cookbook and find a cookie recipe.

He jotted a note on an already long list. "We still have a lot of unpacked boxes, but what do you say we play hooky and I take you fishing this afternoon? This morning I thought we'd sign you up for first grade, and then have lunch at a café in town."

Rianne pondered his proposal as she ate the last peach half.

"I never fished except at the school carnival. What if I can't? What if I don't catch any?"

"There's nothing to fishing. When we were at the hardware store ordering the door locks I installed yesterday, I noticed they sell fishing rods. It isn't necessary to catch any fish. The fun is sitting on the dock bobbing your fly in the water."

"Flies! Yuck!"

"They're fake. And I'll bait your hook. Does that sound better?"

"I 'spose. Can I ask Sylvie to go with us?"

Joel almost blurted out that even Sylvie's own grandfather used to confide that women and fishing didn't mix. But what kind of message did that send to his daughter? "Sure," he muttered reluctantly. "After we get back you can invite her." With luck, she'd be busy or gone by then.

RIANNE'S PREVIOUS SCHOOL had been the penthouse suite of a posh high-rise. This school was built of clapboard and stood in the middle of centuries-old towering trees. Joel assumed they were sugar maple and hickory, because a sign along the road said they'd entered Hickory-Maple Gorge. There were hints of red and gold in the leaves, a sure sign that autumn was around the corner. Joel had only ever visited his great-aunt during the summers, but she'd had shown him pictures of the vast wilderness known as the Great Smoky Mountains.

Kicking through crisp leaves to reach the entrance to the rustic school filled Joel with heightened anticipation. He envisioned taking Rianne on weekend excursions to explore this beautiful countryside.

Inside the office they were greeted by a pleasingly round woman. Her name tag read Mrs. Pearson, and in smaller letters under the title *School Secretary,* it said, Ellie.

"Mr. Mercer," she exclaimed before Joel introduced himself or produced Rianne's records. Her knowing his name gave Joel pause, as did her next words.

"I wondered when you'd get around to registering Rianne…isn't it? Moved into Iva's place over a week ago. Took your time getting here. Does that mean we're the tardy type?"

"Uh…no," he said, pulling a thick, cream-colored envelope out of his back pocket. Meeting her unwavering eyes, Joel slid the packet across the polished counter. The room smelled of paper, aging wood and furniture wax. It wasn't pungent, but very different from Rianne's kindergarten, with its modern decor. He shifted his gaze downward when he felt Rianne clutch his leg. "Say hello to Mrs. Pearson."

"'Lo."

"Mercy," the secretary exclaimed. "Her kindergarten curriculum reads like nothing I've ever seen. Cultural Studies? Reading? Beginning French?" Peering over the counter, Mrs. Pearson gave Rianne a thorough once-over, then frowned at the child's father.

"Atlanta is a progressive, multicultural city," he murmured.

Her response to that was simply to pass him a clipboard of forms. "Fill these out on both sides. I'll need to run copies of her vaccination record, if you remembered to bring one. If not, she won't be fully registered for school until you provide us with an original."

Joel produced that from his shirt pocket, feeling as if he needed to gain the approval of this tart-voiced woman.

"Saints be praised. A sensible dad. I'll fire up the copier and give this back for Dr. Randall's records. I expect you'll be taking Rianne to him. Doc Randall is the only pediatrician currently practicing in Briarwood."

Rianne tugged on her dad's pant leg. "Will I get to meet my teacher and see my classroom?"

Hearing her query, Mrs. Pearson turned from the copier. "Angie Wallace is due to get the next first-grader. Students were parceled out between her and Donna Martin at the end of last year. Teachers aren't officially back until a week from next Monday. If you're Baptist, ask at church on Sunday.

Somebody will introduce you to Angie. If you're Methodist, Presbyterian or other, you're out of luck till school opens. I'll lock the office and give you a tour of the classrooms as soon as you finish with those forms," she said, dealing Joel a pointed stare.

"Yes, ma'am. Snooks, have a seat, please. Daddy needs to concentrate." He was grateful she complied without her usual *why.* Maybe Miss Ellie wouldn't consider him a total bumbler. Joel was glad he'd been through this drill once before and knew how tedious it was. If not for an open window behind the secretary's desk, which allowed in the chirp of an occasional bird, the silence in the room would have frayed his nerves.

"There, I think that's everything," he finally announced, pocketing his cheat sheet before spinning the clipboard around.

Ellie rose from her desk, pen in hand. She separated out the first page and touched the tip of her pen to each completed line, one after another. "Nice printing," she noted dryly. "You wouldn't be a teacher, would you?"

"No." Joel let it drop at that.

"I see you're self-employed. What do you do?"

"I work at home. I've listed a cell phone number and my home phone. I can always be reached at one or the other should Rianne need me."

"Huh. The secretive sort, I see." Ellie snorted. "Hope it's nothing illegal or immoral. Nicer woman than Iva Whitaker never lived. If you're up to mischief, she'll be turning in her grave."

"Could we get through this process, do you think? I promised Rianne lunch in town. I'd like to be seated before the work crowd rolls into the café." Actually, he planned to eavesdrop, hoping he might pick up tidbits of local gossip. Not that he'd hear very juicy stuff with Rianne in tow. But he might overhear something to indicate where singles in Briarwood went to hook up with other singles.

"Divorced, huh? For a minute there, I was afraid you might be one of those adoptive fathers of a different persuasion. Especially since you checked nondenominational under religion."

Was she kidding? Joel realized she wasn't. He leaned over and said in a low but firm voice, "Mrs. Pearson. Federal equal opportunity law prohibit establishments that receive federal aid from asking those kinds of questions."

"You work for the government, Mr. Mercer?"

Confused, he shook his head, and she went back to ticking off each line on the form. "Kay Waller, soon to be Kay Ramsey, told her cousin you asked Sylvie Shea if she had a kennel license. If you were a gov'ment man, I figured to call poor Sylvie and commiserate. A finer woman never lived."

"You just said the same about my great-aunt." Joel drummed his fingers on the counter.

"I like Sylvie lots," Rianne piped up from where she sat idly kicking her feet in the air because they didn't reach the floor. "Yesterday, she let me bake cookies with her. Today I'm gonna 'vite her to go fishing with Daddy and me."

"Well, now." At last a smile lifted the edges of Ellie Pearson's lips.

Joel groaned inwardly, recognizing that vulture-sensing-a bachelor look. It was so blatant, Joel felt compelled to state, "Inviting Ms. Shea to go fishing is Rianne's idea. Not mine. Aren't we about ready to see the classrooms?"

"Yes, indeedy." Ellie dropped the forms on her desk and retrieved a big ring of keys. From then on, she gave a running dialogue regarding points of interest in and around the school. Joel was happy to escape some half hour later with no further mention of his career, his religion or lack thereof, or his neighbor.

"So what's the verdict, Rianne? Do you think you'll like this school?"

"It felt comf'table."

That answer produced a smile from Joel. "Exactly how I

recall feeling about the house and the town when I used to come here as a boy."

"Were you my age?"

"Older. I was ten my first visit. I begged to come back every summer, and did for five years. There's the café ahead. Help me find a parking place on the street." He knew Rianne loved to spot parking spaces when they visited the mall at home. This was probably her first experience with parallel slots on a main street. And meters, he saw.

"There's a pickup leaving, Daddy. Oh, oh…you came close to that car." She leaped back as Joel pulled abreast of the vehicle directly in front of the opening. He explained why he had to do that to successfully back in.

"When will I be big enough to drive?"

Her query sent a ripple of apprehension through Joel. Of course he knew the day would come when he'd teach her to drive. As would the day he'd have to deal with boys and dating. Woes for the far-off future. "Chickadee, let's not rush things. You're trying to make your dad old before his time."

"What's a chickadee?"

"A cute little bird. And before you point out that birds don't drive, let me say it's a figure of speech. An endearment. Think about what you'd like for lunch instead of giving your old man heart failure thinking of you behind the wheel, okay?"

"I don't know what this restaurant's got."

Joel pocketed his van keys and hurried around to her side, leading the way into the café after he shut her door. "Hamburgers. Smell them." He sniffed appreciatively and flashed a smile at a busy waitress, who directed them to a booth near the center of an old-fashioned room decorated in fifties fashion. A wave of nostalgia at the pink and white booths, and a soda fountain along the back wall, hit Joel full force. Nothing had changed since he used to come here with Iva or Bill.

"Daddy, she said we could sit here."

"Right. It's just so weird. I feel as if I've stepped back in time. It looks the same as when I came here as a kid."

"Do you remember their menu?"

He threw back his head and laughed. "Fantastic burgers with big fat French fries. That's standard fare for boys. Girls are pickier."

"Says who?"

They both glanced up in surprise at hearing a familiar lilt. Sylvie Shea stood next to their booth, grinning from ear to ear, a pad in hand and a pencil over her ear. She wore a white uniform and a pink apron.

"Don't tell me you have a third job?" Joel found it hard not to show she was the last person he wanted to see. Especially, in the very place where he'd like to gather facts that would allow him to add a comic character patterned after her.

"I worked here through high school to earn money for college, but then used it to pay rent in the New York garment district." Not knowing why she'd revealed that, Sylvie untucked her pencil from her hair, cleared her throat and muttered. "The owner's daughter, Kristi, had an appointment out of town today. Rianne, I heard what your dad wants. A burger and fries." She scribbled on the pad. "The cook does a really great grilled cheese sandwich. If you like those, I recommend sharing your dad's fries." She winked. "That way you can save room for a chocolate sundae. I guarantee it'll be the best you've ever eaten."

"Can I, Daddy?"

"Why not? And I'll snitch a bite of your sundae."

"Just water to drink?"

"Coffee for me. Rianne, milk?"

"If Sylvie thinks water's the best, that's what I want."

Joel noticed the hero worship in his daughter's eyes. He'd have to break that growing bond, he feared. But the next words out of Rianne's mouth made that difficult if not impossible, for the time being at least.

"Daddy and me are going fishing this afternoon. Will you come, Sylvie? Daddy said I could 'vite you."

Sylvie didn't have warning enough to conceal her shock. "Uh, what time are you planning to go? Just down to Whitaker lake, right?" She actually had no plans for the afternoon, except to do a bit of work on the dress.

Rianne nodded, clearly expecting Joel to supply a time.

"Two, two-thirty, I thought," he mumbled, aware that would be cutting it close as far as eating, purchasing poles and getting home. He hoped he'd cut it too close for Sylvie.

She tore their order off her pad and dropped her voice for Joel's ears only. "You said four or four-thirty, Joel?" Bending slightly, she said, "Striped bass surface in the early a.m. after the mist clears off the lake, and they rise to feed again shortly before the sun goes down." More loudly, she said, "Sounds like fun. I'll cook whatever we catch for dinner. If you'd like me to, that is." Clearly flustered again, she grew red. "Uh, my dad has Iva's row boat and canoe stored at his place out of the weather—to keep them from rotting. If you were thinking of using either, we'll all need life jackets. I can phone and have Dad haul the boats to your dock."

"Four o'clock works. I was planning to fish from the dock. Guess I'd better buy Rianne a life vest in any case. Thanks for the reminder. It's been years since I've been fishing. If Mr. Shea made me wear a life jacket, I've forgotten. As for cooking whatever we catch…will we catch anything?"

"Oh, ye of little faith. Unless local kids have sneaked down there recently, the lake's gone unfished for a while. But if you're not a fan of eating bass, we can toss them back instead of cooking them."

"No. Cooking's great, thanks. Rianne's never eaten fresh-caught fish. Your grandpa showed me how to clean and fillet. I hope I haven't forgotten how."

"Locals will tell you it's a skill that comes back, like riding a bicycle. I do it, but cleaning fish isn't my favorite part of the deal, so thanks for offering. Well, hey, I'd better turn in your order or you'll both be gnawing on the table legs."

Rianne giggled, and Joel thought he'd never heard a nicer sound. She laughed aloud so seldom. Now he worried that might be his fault. His and Lynn's. Because they couldn't make their marriage work.

Wanting her laughter to continue, Joel reached across the table and tickled his daughter. "Gnaw away, snooks. That'll leave more fish at dinner for me."

His ploy worked. Rianne laughed long and loud, drawing the eyes of others.

Sylvie quickly introduced the newest additions to town. "I'll leave y'all to give names," she added hurriedly. "I see orders are up, and I'm not here to play the hostess with the mostest."

Rianne giggled again. "Daddy, I thought you said bestest wasn't a proper word. How come mostest is okay?"

Everyone found Joel's predicament humorous. And even more when Sylvie muttered, "Yeah, Dad, explain that." She promptly dashed away toward the pass-through that connected the main dining area with the kitchen.

"Sometimes, Rianne, it's a case of do as I say, not as others do. That means don't follow those who would lead you astray," he called loudly enough for Sylvie to hear. "Lead you astray means steer you in the wrong direction."

"Oh, Daddy, Sylvie would *never* do that."

Joel felt another punch. How could Sylvie have garnered such devotion in such a short time? He thought it wisest to let that subject drop. He stood and shook hands with the local men and smiled politely at the women, some of whom he recognized as the bearers of casseroles even now filling his freezer. He was irked to hear a few whispers that he was divorced. Joel wished like heck he'd written *separated* on Rianne's school form where it asked for his marital status. Sweet Ellie Pearson had obviously lost no time in spreading the word.

The food came then, piping hot and as good as Joel remembered. He was a bit disappointed that the talk swirling through the room had nothing to do with anything suitable for his comic strip. Few lunchgoers, if any, fit his singles profile—except for Sylvie Shea. This might not work out for him, after all. A general topic of discussion among the women appeared to center on what each planned to wear Saturday night to Kay Waller's wedding. The men, mostly shopkeepers from the area, discussed how much they wished their town would quit having so many weddings.

Now that might be fodder for a strip. If he did more with the male viewpoint about weddings and other boring gatherings forced on them by girlfriends, wives or partners.

"Daddy," Rianne said for the third time. "Did you forget we're gonna share your French fries?"

"Oh, sorry. My mind wandered for a minute." He dragged her plate over and scooped onto it the number of fries he thought she would eat.

"Where does your mind go?"

"What?" Joel pulled back from visions of his characters.

"When it wanders, where does your mind go?"

"Rianne, baby, you take everything so literally. When someone says that, it generally means they're not thinking not about what's happening around them, but their thoughts have skipped ahead to planning the future."

"Oh. You plan for a lot of future, I guess. You never hear me when I talk."

That bothered Joel. "I am so sorry, honey," he said. "The last thing in the world I want is to tune you out."

"It's okay."

"No, it isn't."

"You two aren't arguing over who gets the last French fry, are you?"

Joel whirled, feeling Sylvie's breath ruffle the hair above his right ear. His nose ended inches from her bust line. Startled by the tremors it set off within him, he slid a foot across the bench seat, toward the wall. Still, her frothy, flowery perfume wrapped around him, triggering desires long buried.

"We're 'scusing Daddy's mind. 'Cause it doesn't stay where he sits."

"Oh." A frown, indicating that Sylvie didn't understand, puckered between her eyes.

"Forget trying to make sense of it." Joel folded his napkin and laid it beside his plate. "That was great, but I'd forgotten how big these are."

"Would you like me to box the leftovers to go?"

Joel deferred to Rianne, who rubbed her tummy. "I'm full. I didn't save room for a chocolate sundae."

"How about if I give you a rain check on the sundae? You can come in someday after school."

"Is that okay, Daddy?"

"Sure. Thanks, Sylvie. Do I pay at the register?" He wanted to bolt, and found it odd that Sylvie went about the business of cleaning the table so nonchalantly.

"Yes, at the register. So, I'll see you guys again around four? I'll, uh, meet you at the dock. That way if I'm late, you won't be held up."

She sounded suddenly shy, which to Joel was even more unsettling. If he'd been able to conjure up an acceptable out, he'd have done so on the spot. Because there was one fact that refused to be denied: Sylvie Shea played hell with both his body and his mind. He couldn't make tracks fast enough. However, he wasn't willing to disappoint Rianne. And she wanted Sylvie to fish with them. But Joel didn't breathe freely until he and Rianne reached the hardware store and he engaged the clerk in a no-nonsense discussion about fishing.

Sylvie purposely didn't allow her gaze to follow the father-daughter duo as they left the café. She already knew, from the way news traveled, that he was divorced—thanks to Ellie Pearson's call—so she might as well brace herself for the works. *The works* meant tons of unsubtle pressure brought to bear by family and friends who couldn't wait to marry her off.

Margery Franks, part-owner of the café, led the charge, mere moments after she'd shut Joel's money into the cash register. The buxom woman rushed over to help Sylvie. "My, he's polite, and a really handsome man. And his little girl is as cute as can be. Don't you think so, Sylvie?"

"Rianne is sweet. She's in first grade, but Ellie probably mentioned that."

"Kid's gotta be lonely, stuck in that big old house so far from town. And she's 'bout that age where she'd benefit from a woman's guidance. Don't you agree?"

Sylvie picked up the tray of dishes, saying nothing.

"Well, I'm right, aren't I?" Marge demanded of the room at large.

Jim Newsome, seated in the booth adjacent to the one Joel had vacated, spoke up. "Stop pushing her, Margie. She's got a date to go fishing with Mercer and his kid this afternoon. What you need to do is let her off work early so she has time to get a makeover at the beauty parlor."

Sylvie spun. "Stop it, all of you. Joel Mercer and I are neighbors—that's it. And this is not a date. I have no intention of getting a makeover today or any other day. Kristi's shift goes till three, and I'm here until then."

Someone across the room, a woman, said, "Coming from the city and all, he probably owns a tuxedo. He'd make you a good escort for Kay's wedding, Sylvie."

"Riiii…ght," her male companion jeered. "No better way to give a divorced guy the willies than to take him to a wedding first thing."

"Enough!" Sylvie tore the slips for three customers off her order pad and walked around slapping them down on tables. "I have an escort for Kay's wedding. And Mr. Mercer and I have absolutely nothing in common. Zero. Zilch. Nada." That effectively stopped talk. That, and Sylvie's slamming into the kitchen.

Before three o'clock rolled around, she wished she'd kept her mouth shut about having an escort to Kay's wedding. That comment launched a too-frank appraisal of Jarvis "Buddy" Deaver the fourth, which left Sylvie with a throbbing headache.

So, she wasn't in the best frame of mind even before she got home and changed into peach-colored sweats to hike the half mile to Whitaker Lake, with Oscar in tow. When she arrived, Joel promptly berated her for bringing the dog. "Why would you haul that ox to the lake? He'll lumber around barking and scare off our fish," Joel complained.

Ignoring him, Sylvie set her pole on the weathered dock. She hugged Rianne, who'd left her dad putting a colorful fly on her hook. A moment later, the girl threw her arms around Oscar. "I don't like fishing," Rianne said loudly. "Daddy, can I stay over here and play with Oscar instead? Maybe then he won't bark."

"No, dang it. Do that and you'll never get the hang of tossing out a line. Come on, take your pole. All you need is a little practice."

Afraid Rianne would appeal to her next, Sylvie found a shady clump of chinquapin trees, chose one and looped a sturdy rope she'd brought around its trunk. Testing the rope and finding it secure, she knotted it through the leash. Oscar flopped down on his belly in the cool grass surrounding the tree.

Rianne sulked, continuing to pet the dog after Sylvie had left.

"You won't get her to like fishing by forcing her," Sylvie said quietly, expertly attaching a feathery fly to her hook and casting into a deep pool a few yards out from the dock.

"You seem comfortable with a pole. How do you think she'll learn?"

"I developed a liking for the sport over time. It'll help

when she catches her first bass. I see you're up on us by—what, three nice-size fish?"

"Yeah. Rianne," he called. "Leave the dog now."

"If you want, I'll take him and go home." Sylvie reeled in her line and climbed to her feet.

"No. No," Joel objected. "Rianne will have a fit if she thinks I sent you away. Rianne...I said *now!*" Joel extended the girl's pole.

She moseyed back, reaching her father at the same time a large fish surfaced to nibble at a patch of algae off the end of the pier. "Wow, can I hook that fish, Daddy?"

"Maybe. Take the pole and do as I say." Joel handed her the short rod, all the while giving a running list of instructions. Sylvie stepped aside to allow them room.

Wonder of wonders, she thought. The granddaddy fish actually took Rianne's bait. The girl danced around excitedly, having no clue how to reel him in. Sylvie tried to tell her, but Joel rushed in to remove the rod from her hands. He said the fish was too strong.

"Let her do it," Sylvie said. No one noticed, until too late, that Oscar had pulled loose from Sylvie's knot. The big dog bounded across the rough boards, his chain clanking behind him until it tangled in the tackle attached to Joel's pole.

Sylvie watched in horror as Joel stepped back. Oscar tried to stop, but must have gotten scared when his leash whipped up and smacked him in the head. He uttered a surprised yelp and barreled full tilt into Joel.

Man and dog hit the water simultaneously with a huge splat, drenching Sylvie and Rianne where they stood.

Sylvie would never know how she managed to save Rianne's pole and rescue the fish. She'd reached over to catch Joel's sleeve, but the material slipped through her fingers, and she was left grabbing Rianne's pole instead.

Oscar paddled to shore and heaved his soaking body onto a bank as Sylvie unhooked and dumped the little girl's catch into the bucket with those of her dad. The big dog shook himself vigorously, looking for all the world like a drowned rat.

"Sylvie, Sylvie! Oscar swimmed back, but where's my daddy? I don't see him anywhere."

Sylvie froze at Rianne's cry, and spun around, scanning the glassy surface of the lake in disbelief.

Chapter Five

Thinking it couldn't be true, yet with her heart pounding fast and furious, Sylvie dropped Rianne's pole and raced to where the girl was hopping around at the end of the dock. It *was* true; there was no sign of Joel's sun-streaked hair breaking the water.

Whitaker Lake wasn't very deep. But Sylvie knew it originated from an icy stream that ran through her woods, and that the stream was fed by mountain snows. Not only that, the lake was murky. You couldn't see anything below the surface.

Rianne had begun to sob, and that had Sylvie's nerves jumping. "Hon, I need you to go sit with Oscar. Hang on to him, okay? We don't want him taking another swim and maybe winding his leash around me or a pier pole." Speaking as calmly as possible, Sylvie had already begun to strip out of her sweats, down to her underwear.

"Is my daddy drowned?" Rianne's eyes were big, horrified, filled with tears.

"Don't even think it. I'll find him. I know this lake, honey." Dropping her sweatshirt on top of her sneakers, Sylvie took the time for one quick touch of Rianne's chilled face. "I need you to be brave. You'll see me dive and come up, and dive again. Promise you won't move an inch away from Oscar. There's just you and me to help your dad. We don't have time to call anyone else."

Though tears ran silently down her face, Rianne signaled

that she'd heard and understood. She sat with the dog, where he'd stretched out in the sun to dry his sopping coat.

Sylvie trusted Rianne to keep her word. Had to, because she'd already hit the water in a shallow dive before verifying that Rianne had followed all her instructions. The shock of the cold lake water drove the breath from Sylvie's lungs as she tried to pinpoint exactly where Joel had gone down.

In the shadow of the pier the water below was inkier than she would have guessed. She'd fibbed to Rianne about knowing the lake. Kids used to sneak out here from town to swim, until a classmate a few years older than Rianne had drowned, and Iva posted No Trespassing signs. Except for a few rowdy boys, kids always obeyed the postings.

She shivered, coming up for air. Rianne's thin voice, asking if she'd found her dad, rang in Sylvie's ears. Saving her breath, she dived again, refusing to consider that Joel had gone in steeply enough to hit bottom and break his neck.

Her lungs near bursting, Sylvie thought she glimpsed a dark shadow off to her left. A bulky shadow that could be a man. But she had no choice other than to go up to refill her aching lungs. Taking care to dive over the shadow, she felt like sobbing in relief when her fingers grasped fabric that could only be Joel's shirt.

Aware that he wasn't safe yet, she kicked hard with all the strength she could muster, taking them both into sunlight and blessed air. The question remained—how much water did he have in his lungs? How many precious minutes had ticked past?

Rianne's happy cry and Oscar's approving bark gave Sylvie the impetus to swim to the dock hauling Joel's dead weight even though her arms ached. She attempted to heave him up onto the planks, but the dock was too high and Joel was too heavy. He was unresponsive, which added to Sylvie's panic. She refused to consider that he might already be dead. She'd witnessed his fall. Granted, it happened fast, but he and Oscar had just sort of toppled off the pier. At the time she'd almost laughed. Right now, she felt that nothing would ever seem humorous again.

"Sylvie, can I come help pull Daddy up?"

"No! No," she repeated, less harshly. "I'll take him to where the lake's shallower." At that point, she was able to roll him onto the grassy slope. As she climbed up beside him, the sun warmed her icy bones. Every bit of exposed skin was covered with goose bumps.

Careful to move so that her body shielded him from Rianne, she turned Joel on his stomach and turned his head, then checked his airway. She didn't think he'd been chewing gum, but he might have been. Flinging a leg over his hips, she desperately tried to recall remnants from a long-ago life-saving class. The instructor's words flowed into her head. *Place. Press. Release. Rest. Then repeat the process until the victim's breathing.* She went through the sequence several times, but nothing happened. Rising above him to provide greater pressure to his chest, she went through the actions again. For all Sylvie knew, the method was obsolete. What if she should be doing something else? A newer method? All at once, his abdomen convulsed. Joel's eyelids fluttered, then opened. He gagged and spat out a stream of water. Then he coughed three or four times.

"Oh, thank you, thank you, thank you," she chanted, and tears fell.

Those words rained down on Joel. He couldn't figure out why he felt wet, cold and weighed down. Shock, pure and simple, ran through him as his hazy gaze lit on his new neighbor. Something was very wrong here. Her hair appeared lank. Weeds, or he thought they were weeds, dangled above her left ear. As well, she wore…something skimpy and diaphanous. Practically see-through. Except that Joel was squinting into the sun. That did it. His head might feel as big as a barn, but he was darned sure he wasn't hallucinating. Bolting upright, he sent Sylvie sprawling.

At that moment, Joel heard Rianne shout, "Daddy, Daddy, you're okay!" His wind was cut off as her little arms wrapped around his neck and her weight draped over his back. Before his addled brain could assess anything else, Oscar flattened him. The dog loomed above him, licking his face, and Joel gagged again.

"Yuck! Will somebody please remove this beast?"

Sylvie grabbed Oscar's leash. Rianne tugged on the dog, as well. Eventually, they were able to muscle Oscar to within shackling distance of the tree.

Positive they'd resembled a slapstick comedy, Sylvie suddenly realized how few clothes she had on. using two half-hitches to tie the rope, she raced for the sweats she'd shed on the pier. Aware that Joel Mercer's eyes tracked her every move, Sylvie shimmied into her sweatpants and shirt with as much haste and dignity as possible. She lacked finesse, since her skin remained too wet for the fabric to slide well.

"I remember now," Joel exclaimed. "Rianne caught a fish. I went to help reel the sucker in and…" His accusatory glare found Sylvie. "You didn't tie that brute. He broke loose and knocked me off the dock." Sounding indignant, Joel pulled at his dripping shirt and pants. His shoes were missing. *Italian loafers*. Rubbing his forehead, Joel discovered a lump the size of a large hen's egg. "Ow! Damn," he swore succinctly.

Because he'd scrambled closer to Sylvie, she also saw the bump she'd missed, probably because of her worry. "Gosh, I guess that explains why you sank like a rock. You must've hit a railroad tie, or the metal cleats where Iva tied the boats. Man, you're lucky. You actually had a close call, Joel." Sylvie had to sit down, her knees too weak to support her.

"None of this would've happened if you'd left that mutt home. At the very least, you need to learn how to tie a decent knot."

Rianne burst into tears. "It's all my fault," she wailed. "I untied Oscar so he could come sit by me while I fished. I didn't tell you 'cause you sounded mad. Then we saw the big fish and…I forgot Oscar wasn't tied. I'm sorry, Daddy."

The truth hit Joel almost as hard as whatever had knocked him in the head. "Sylvie, I'm sorry I yelled at you. I owe you an apology." Joel actually felt himself pale at what might so easily have occurred. He recalled flying off the dock, but he didn't know quite what happened after he struck the water. That was his last memory until he opened his eyes to a bizarre vision—well, he probably ought to forget some of it.

"You don't owe me anything," Sylvie said through chattering teeth.

"Are you okay?" Joel inquired, continuing to frown. He crawled to her side and sank down next to her, chafing her cold, trembling fingers. "To invoke a cliche, all's well that ends well. Even at that, do you mind if we call a halt to this expedition?"

"Are you k-kidding? We've all had plenty. You need to go change out of those wet things, Joel. And you should have a doctor look at your head. What if you've got a concussion? Oh, and you take the fish home, okay?"

"Fish?" Joel's gaze sought Rianne's. "I'm sorry we lost your very first catch, snooks. That was a really big fish."

"We didn't lose him. Sylvie put him in with yours."

Sylvie blanched. "I did, and I probably wasted time doing it. I swear I had no idea you hadn't bobbed straight up again, Joel. Not until Rianne called out to me."

"No matter, I owe you both." Joel released Sylvie's hand and clapped his own over his heart. "In exchanged, I volunteer to clean and cook the fish tonight."

Grateful for even a semblance of normalcy, Sylvie smiled. "Now I'm *sure* you have a concussion. Have you ever cooked bass?"

"Rianne, hear that? Sylvie's casting aspersions on my cooking. Come vouch for your dad."

The girl hugged him. "I don't know what 'spersions are,

Daddy. He microwaves fish sticks," she told Sylvie in all seriousness.

"Well, then," Sylvie drawled. "How can I refuse?"

Sensing she was moments from bursting into laughter, Joel wrinkled his nose. "At the risk of being tossed back in the lake, I have to ask if those weeds you're wearing in your hair are this year's fashion statement?"

A hand flew to her head. Sylvie combed through her straggling hair, and figured she must look a sight.

"Other side," he said, clambering up to collect the bucket of fish and their poles, and then grasp his daughter's hand.

It wasn't until Sylvie and heard his nonchalant whistle that she was able to see the humor in her disheveled appearance. "Hey, what time is dinner?" she hollered up the path.

Turning, Joel shrugged. "Since bass doesn't come in a freezer package with microwave instructions, I'm not sure. How long does it take to cook these babies?"

Sylvie suddenly conjured up a vision of microwaved bass, heads and all, and tough as boot leather. "Tell you what, Mercer. How about if you clean the fish and I cook as we originally planned?"

"Say yes, Daddy! Maybe Sylvie will let me help."

It was his daughter's enthusiasm that cinched the deal for Joel. He'd already begun having second thoughts about inviting Sylvie to his home. Partly because it wasn't anything he ever did. But more so, he reluctantly admitted, because that unsettling image of her wet, half-naked body rising above him, her long legs hugging his hips, provoked—well, plain lust. Lots of it.

Still, he owed her more than one simple dinner. She'd saved him from drowning. Wasn't there some old saying about saving someone's life and then that person—shoot, he couldn't remember—but weren't they joined forever?

It wasn't until after he'd showered, changed and felt halfway human again, that Joel went to clean the bass and realized the messy state of his kitchen. Unpacked boxes were piled everywhere. Whenever he or Rianne needed something, he'd ripped open boxes until the article came to light. Most women tended to like neat, tidy houses. The last thing he needed, or wanted, was for his well-meaning neighbor to decide he should have help getting his house in order.

"Rianne, we're not ready to entertain. We don't even have three plates unpacked. Nor have I unearthed our frying pan. Will you run next door and tell Sylvie I'll have to clean and freeze the fish? Ask if she minds postponing?"

Rianne carried Fluffy into the kitchen and set her in front of her water dish. "I know which box the plates are in. And that big box is our pans."

Joel knew she was right. "Snooks, imagine how this mess will look to Sylvie. I don't want her telling the whole town we're slobs."

"She wouldn't. Sylvie's nice. And it's not nice to un'vite her after you asked her to dinner. That's what you told me the time I un'vited Corky Blake to our Easter egg hunt."

Wincing, Joel rubbed the back of his neck. "That's different, Rianne. You'd sent Corky an invitation, and his mom had already RSVP'd that he could come."

"It's not different," she said stubbornly. "Sylvie RSVP'd, too."

He started to counter her argument with another, when his daughter marched to the door and said, "I'll go tell Sylvie we haven't unpacked all our stuff, so can we cook and eat at her house?" She was out the door, tearing down the driveway before Joel came to the realization that he was doomed. Whatever happened, he'd have to fumble his way through it.

He'd cleaned the bass and had the entrails wrapped to toss in the garbage by the time Rianne returned.

"Sylvie said okay. She said she should've thought of that herself. Oh, and she said don't worry about bringing anything but the fish, 'cause she's got plenty of potatoes and vegetables. Did you know she picks them in her mama's garden? Sylvie never buys vegetables at the store like we do."

"My great-aunt, the lady who left me this house, had a garden behind the garage. That was when I found out that people grew peas, beans and corn. Being a city boy, I didn't know you pulled carrots out of the ground. My aunt grew pumpkins for Halloween. I always had to go home before they were big enough to carve as jack-o'-lanterns. Iva sent me pictures of some I'd planted." A fond smile touched the corners of his lips. "How about if when we get the house squared away, snooks, I rent a rototiller and turn the ground in her old garden? Come spring, you and I can plant seeds. I'll have to buy a book. I don't know what to plant when."

Rianne climbed on a chair on her knees to inspect the fish. She set her elbows on the counter and cradled her chin in her hands. "I'll bet you could ask Sylvie's mom. I saw her picture at Sylvie's. She's pretty. Sylvie's also got a dad and two sisters. One has kids who are gonna go to the same school as me when they're old enough. They stay overnight at Sylvie's house sometimes. Next time they do, she said I can go over and play. Kendra, the girl, is only four. Roy's two. Daddy, did I play with Barbies when I was four?"

"I think so." Joel was astonished by how friendly Rianne seemed to be getting with their neighbor. In Atlanta they'd barely had a nodding acquaintance with anyone living in their apartment complex. Quite honestly, Joel preferred life that way. But maybe his preferences shortchanged his daughter.

"Did Sylvie say what time she'd like us to bring the fish over?" he asked, feeling a panicky need to stop discussing the apparently close-knit Shea family. His had been the exact opposite. For as long as he could remember, his parents fought over everything.

"She said anytime." Rianne rocked back and forth on her elbows. "I got there when Sylvie finished showering. She's got a pretty robe. It's not fuzzy like mine, Daddy. I think the material is like that white dress she sewed for Kay. 'Cept Sylvie's robe is red. Shiny and red. Maybe she'll still have it on if we hurry and go over there now."

Joel, who was rummaging in the fridge as Rianne babbled, had popped the top on a beer. He'd barely taken one swig when she dropped that bombshell. The picture forming in his mind had Joel choking and spewing beer all over the floor.

"Are you okay?" Rianne studied her father worriedly.

"I took too big a mouthful," Joel muttered, doing his best to wipe up the spill and also dispense with the image of Sylvie in red satin. Maybe if he concentrated on the way her hair had looked earlier—no, that was no good, either. At the time she'd been quite the spectacle in her wet underwear. Pale peach. A color that made her freckles stand out. Unfortunately, Joel vividly recalled the freckles sprinkled across her nose, her shoulders—and the smattering that dipped into her cleavage.

"Would you like a lemonade?" he abruptly asked Rianne.

"Uh-huh. Can I take the cup to Sylvie's?"

"No. Drink it before we go. I plan to finish my beer. We need to give her a chance to get presentable."

Rianne reached for a plastic glass her dad had poured three-quarters full. "What's that mean, Daddy? Get presentable?"

"It means we need to allow Sylvie time to dress, dry her hair and maybe put on makeup. Such things are important to women. Men and kids, we're more apt not to care if people see us looking, well, grubby. Women worry about appearances."

"Oh." Rianne slurped up her lemonade. "Sylvie's robe's not grubby. It's pretty. But we can wait. I still need to find a Barbie. After we eat, if you say it's okay, Sylvie said she'll help me pick material from her scrap drawer for a Barbie dress."

Oddly relieved to be handed the perfect opportunity to make a speedy exit after dinner, Joel said, "No problem, snooks. I'll leave you ladies to your sewing, and I'll come home and try to make some headway unpacking boxes."

Nodding, Rianne set down her glass and ran upstairs.

Joel wandered from room to room sipping his beer. He couldn't explain a sudden restlessness to put his stamp on every corner of this old house. He wanted this home to spell security and a solidity he'd lacked growing up with a stern, military dad and an indifferent mother. He'd been an unhappy child—except for the summers he'd spent here. Someday, he thought, Rianne would bring her children here for the summers and holidays. By then he'd probably be shuffling through the fallen leaves with the aid of a cane and a pipe tucked between what Joel hoped would be his own teeth. Chuckling, he decided that, yet again, he'd let his mind wander too far.

Rianne skipped into the room, crossing the dusty rug that needed replacing, or else a good cleaning. "I'm ready to go to Sylvie's. I've got a Barbie."

Ruffling her fair hair, which was closer to Lynn's light blond shade than his darker tones, Joel drained his beer and crushed the can. "Okay, let me dump this in the trash and pull the fish out of the fridge. I wonder which box has my wine. I stored some bottles in that cabinet the movers set in the corner. It's customary to take a dinner hostess wine or candy."

"Why?"

"It just is. Come to think of it, I don't know whether Sylvie drinks wine."

"She does, I think."

"Oh? You think so…because?"

"She has some in her 'frigerator, Daddy. White."

"In that case, give me a minute to slit a couple of these boxes to see if I can locate my stash." Joel soon found the bottles and chose an excellent Chardonnay his boss had given him for Christmas. He set the bottle aside while he retrieved the fish.

Joel hoped that with the help of a bottle of fine wine, he could get through the awkwardness of dinner with a woman he really didn't know—but felt unwillingly attracted to.

Hearing their knock, Sylvie yelled, "Come in," from the depths of her kitchen.

Joel wasn't sure what he expected to see when they walked in, probably because of Rianne's description of the red satin robe. He'd put on slacks and a reasonably dressy shirt. He did think Sylvie might have chosen something nicer. She'd pulled her dark hair into a ponytail and skewered it with pieces of wood resembling chopsticks. Her baggy capri pants could have come from Goodwill. The logo on her out-of-shape shirt advertised a five-year-old sardine festival, of all things. Joel didn't know such a festival existed.

To top it off, she was barefoot. Joel scowled, remembering his lost loafers.

"Do you intend to hold that bottle of wine all evening," Sylvie teased, "or would you like to give it to me so I can chill it a bit?"

"Uh...here." He thrust the bottle and the plastic container of fish into her hands.

"You'll have to toss this dish, you know? Plastic absorbs the odor of fish. If fresh fish sits in plastic too long, anything you store in it from now on will smell fishy."

Joel rubbed an index finger along the bridge of his nose. "Guess my lack of culinary know-how is showing, huh?"

She shrugged, stowed his wine and crossed to the island counter where she'd already set out bowls of milk, melted butter and cracker crumbs. "You admitted the only fish you cook are frozen fish sticks. How's your head, by the way? Ugh...that goose egg is already turning interesting purples and greens."

"I must have a hard head. I haven't felt any pain."

"You may have a high tolerance. Did it hurt a lot when you got the cut that left the scar running from your lip to your chin?"

His fingers flew to the spot. "You're observant. No one notices. Not even me unless I go a couple of days without shaving."

Solemnly, Sylvie imagined him unkempt. She wondered if his beard was darker than his hair. "The scar really stood out when I gave you CPR."

Without thinking, Joel stroked a finger over his lower lip. "Really, you…uh…gave me mouth-to-mouth?"

Sylvie felt her cheeks heat. "No. Nothing like that. The woman who taught my life-saving class was ancient. In her day they didn't give mouth-to-mouth for drowning victims. I meant your skin was cold from the water, and your scar was noticeable."

Joel quickly buried his hands in his back pockets and nodded. "I got this scar when I drove a car I'd made out of scrap lumber in a soapbox derby. I was twelve or so. The wheels broke off halfway down the hill. I flew out and smacked my face on the bumper of a parked vehicle."

"I never knew that, Daddy," Rianne exclaimed. "Where's your scar? Can I see?"

"It's always been there, honey." He bent down and drew in his lower lip to make the jagged white line easier to see.

"I thought scars were scabby and bloody."

"New ones are. They look like this a long time after the doctor takes out stitches," Joel told her, suddenly straightening self-consciously when she threw her arms around his neck and planted a big kiss on the mark. *What if Sylvie had kissed him at the dock?* She hadn't, but…

"My friend Heather got stitches in her knee when she fell down on the ice. At show-and-tell she said it hurt a lot and she cried. Did you cry, Daddy?"

Joel found a shaky grin. "I probably wanted to. But a twelve-year-old boy doesn't dare shed a tear when he's in pain. He has to suck it up or his friends'll call him a wimp."

Rianne turned to where Sylvie was readying the fish for baking. "That's not fair, is it, Sylvie?"

"No. But it's one of the big differences between men and women, short stuff."

"I'm not so short!" Rianne went into peals of laughter. "I might be taller than you someday. My mama and daddy are the same height. Daddy says that means when I get to be a grownup, I'll be as tall as him."

Sylvie popped the baking dish into the oven, and mentally measured Joel Mercer as she stripped off her oven mitts. "Rianne's mom must be tall. You're what? Six feet?"

"Just. Lynn used to tell everyone I was six feet, but she was only five foot twelve."

"So, she had a sense of humor?" Stepping past Joel, Sylvie removed the makings for a green salad from the fridge. It wasn't until she reached for a bowl that she realized his smile had disappeared, to be replaced by frosty disfavor. "Oops, I should've remembered. Ellie said your marriage is off-limits."

"Pardon?" The frost turned to outright ice.

"Ellie Pearson, the elementary school secretary. She came into the café shortly after you guys left. Ellie said you were closemouthed on quite a few subjects."

"There's why. See how fast she blabbed my business all over town?"

"Hey, I'm with you. But gossip is this town's lifeblood. You're smart to keep anything to yourself that you don't want spread about. I'm going to set the table out on the side porch. There's a nice breeze that comes through the screen this time of day. Rianne, you want to help? Joel, why don't you open the wine? The drawer behind you has a corkscrew. You may have to rummage to find it." Sylvie passed a basket filled with napkins and silverware to Rianne, and she picked up plates and glasses.

Joel watched her bump against a door leading to a porch that faced his living room. If the perimeter of his property wasn't so overgrown with brush and weeds, she could probably see straight into his picture window. The hell she wasn't nosy! She was just sneakier about her questioning than Ellie Pearson.

He dug around for the corkscrew, wondering what she'd

think if he called a contractor tomorrow and arranged to have a block wall erected between their two properties. Then it dawned on him that he wanted privacy for himself that he didn't afford others. For instance, in his work he could be considered nosy and gossipy, depending on how a person took his comic characters. To do research, he lurked in dark corners of singles bars and made notes on how men and women interacted. Then he went home to his drawing board and turned his observations into comic strips that were read in a million homes each day. He tweaked real-life situations into encounters people discussed at water coolers—and even laughed about. But if the couples he spied on ever suspected they'd end up with their private moments revealed by his comic strip, they'd probably lynch him.

"Out of curiosity," Joel said when Sylvie returned to get the water pitcher and to ask what she should fix Rianne to drink, "is there a favorite hangout in Briarwood where singles go to meet other singles?"

That was probably the last question Sylvie expected to hear from Joel Mercer, because he sent out every signal in the book saying he wanted to be left alone. She grinned. "That depends on what kind of action you're looking for."

"Pardon me?" He spilled some wine filling the second glass as he glanced around to see where Rianne was.

"It's okay. I let Rianne put kibble in Oscar's bowl on the back porch. She asked to feed him. I hope that's okay."

"Fine, as long as she doesn't turn him loose. I shudder to think how fast he could destroy a table set with dishes and glassware."

"Poor Oscar. He gets such a bad rap from you. Yet I keep him inside at night and he's never so much as knocked over or broken one thing."

"I'll have to take your word on that." Absently, Joel ran two fingers over the knot on his forehead. "Ah, back to what we were discussing…."

Sylvie lifted her glass and clinked it to the rim of Joel's. "Cheers. So, are you looking to get laid or what, Mercer?"

For the second time in one afternoon, his beverage choked Joel and spurted out his mouth and nose. "*Excuse* me?" he eventually croaked.

She put down her wine and crossed her arms. "Uh…our methods for hooking up in Briarwood aren't as sophisticated as I suspect they were where you lived. Nightspots in and around our town are kind of…specialized. Take Mack's Tavern, west of town. Singles go there for serious drinking after a divorce or separation, or if a significant other has done them wrong. The Lamplighter off Main, a guy takes a girl there if he's trying to impress her. Truckers, motorcyclists and the like wander in and out of a place called Ginny's. I've never been inside, because if you're ever spotted going in or leaving Ginny's, it gets you talked about for months in places you probably wouldn't even imagine." She gestured with her glass. "If you just want to shoot pool, have a beer, listen to country tunes or meet up with friends, that would be Spike Turner's joint. A log cabin. Quaint interior. No food except popcorn and peanuts. Mostly twentysomethings hang out at Spike's." Sylvie twirled her glass and studied the contents. "Now…if you've got marriage on your mind, which I doubt, you only have to meet my mother or my sisters. They're known throughout the valley for linking couples anxious to take a walk down the aisle."

Stopping abruptly, Sylvie knelt to peer in her oven. Seemingly satisfied, she slid a pan of yeast rolls onto the shelf above the fish. "To be completely honest, Joel…if just getting laid is what you're after, you'd be better off making a so-called business trip to Asheville."

Joel remained speechless. He didn't know what to make of Sylvie Shea. Had she been ad-libbing that rundown, or what?

Rianne skipped back into the room. Sylvie promptly sent her into the bathroom to wash her hands.

"What you just said," Joel ventured. "You were pulling my leg, right?"

"Every word's the absolute truth, I swear," she said, solemnly raising her hand.

His jaw went slack as she turned and handed him a salad. "I have three dressings. Blue cheese. Italian. light. Or creamy ranch. Oh, shoot, I'll set out all three." She headed for the porch.

He followed after putting down his wine. "Okay, I'll bite. If your mom and sisters have such a great track record getting people married, why are you still single?"

She hesitated, then sighed. "I'm their one failure. I've besmirched their spotless record. So, here's the tip of a lifetime—if you like your status as it is, Joel, avoid them like the plague. Don't forget these names: Dory Hopewell, Nan Shea and Carline Manchester. Anyone attempts to introduce you, run, hide or otherwise make yourself scarce."

He nodded mutely, still unsure what he'd agreed to. But he felt the urgency of her admonition—and knew that, despite her tone, she wasn't joking.

Compared to the conversation they'd just had, dinner chatter was casual and relaxed. Sylvie knew everything there was to know about Briarwood. She told funny story after funny story throughout the meal, and Joel's mind was reeling by the time the dishes were cleared and arranged in the dishwasher.

"Rianne, honey, did you ask your dad if you could stay a while and cut out a Barbie dress?"

"Yep. He said okay. He's gonna go home and open some more boxes."

"Great. Men and sewing never mix. Well, never say never. Rarely mix." Sylvie waved Joel away as one might a pesky gnat. It shouldn't have made him feel inconsequential, but it did. He stewed over that until some two hours later, when he heard Rianne charge up the steps and Sylvie's low, pleasant voice calling "Good night."

Had he not been knee-deep in the bath towels he was trying to fit into a too-small hall cabinet, Joel would've raced into the darkness to tell Sylvie Shea he'd figured out how she'd managed to avoid walking down one of those church aisles. She had a negative attitude when it came to men. And she was as blunt as a worn nail. For some reason, it irked the hell out of him.

Chapter Six

The clock Joel had unboxed and set on the rough-hewn mantel in his living room chimed ten o'clock. Rianne had long since gone to bed. Joel thought he was making good progress unpacking. Except that he kept tripping over a stack of boxes he'd broken down for the garbage. Rather than wait to take them outside in the morning, he decided to go now and load both of the cans he'd rolled out to the end of his lane for the next day's pick-up. It made sense, since Briarwood had once-a-week collection.

Lights from an approaching car blinded him for a moment as he closed the lid. His was the last house on a dead-end street, so he assumed someone had taken a wrong turn. To his surprise, the car, a late-model compact, entered his lane. The driver probably hadn't seen him. The red car stopped next to his van, and two women got out. When the passenger crossed in front of the headlights, Joel saw she was very pregnant.

"Ladies," he called. "Do you need assistance?"

They turned in surprise, retreating marginally as he hurried to where they stood. The taller, thinner of the two had opened the car's trunk by then.

Joel was pretty sure they weren't the type to siphon gas. He supposed they had the wrong lane, and the wrong house.

"You must be Joel Mercer." The pregnant woman's grin could be described as foxy, but then she grew serious. "We apologize for taking so long to come by, and for calling so late in the day," she added. "Days have a habit of getting away from us, I'm afraid. We hope you'll think it's a case of better late than never."

At this distance, thanks to the light spilling from his un-curtained front windows, Joel could see the women's features. There was something familiar about the speaker's silent companion. Yet Joel was positive he'd never met either one before. At a loss to respond, he pocketed his glasses and waited politely.

The driver thrust a box she'd taken from the trunk into Joel's hands. At last he understood their mission. The box, warm on the bottom, held two hot casseroles. "This is so kind of you," he murmured.

"Sylvie said the day you moved in you were inundated with food. But we've been to plenty of church potlucks with some of the people who brought that food. We figure you already dumped three-fourths of what you got. Since you have a young daughter, we know kids can be picky eaters. You can freeze these dishes if you want. One's spaghetti. The other's macaroni and cheese with ham."

His smile came more easily. "Rianne, my daughter, will thank you from the bottom of her heart. She didn't much like the dish labeled succotash."

The women nudged one another. "Carol Tucker's specialty. Raccoons like it," the woman with the darker hair said with a semi-straight face. "By the way, I'm Dory Hopewell." She pointed to her companion. "My sister, Carline Manchester. My husband is Grant Hopewell. Hers is Jeff Manchester. I think you met them when they repaired our sister's fence. Well, your fence, too." The speaker jerked a thumb toward the fence separating his house from Sylvie's.

That was when the names set warning bells jangling in Joel's head. These were the marriage-broker sisters Sylvie had cautioned him about mere hours ago.

"Someday we'd love to hear your version of the flattened fence. Sylvie told us Oscar knocked it down. But she told Grant she'd climbed up for your cat and the limb broke. Did the limb hit you in the head, by chance? That's a nasty knot you've got there," the pregnant sister noted.

Their formidable scrutiny suddenly made Joel claustrophobic, even though they were standing under a velvet sky littered with stars. "I didn't realize Sylvie had climbed out on that broken limb," Joel said, edging toward his porch steps. "My injury, uh, came from a…a fishing accident today. I hate to seem impolite, but Rianne's asleep upstairs. I haven't installed smoke alarms yet, and anyway, I don't like leaving her alone. Thanks again for the food."

"You're most welcome," Dory murmured. The sister bobbed her head, too. "Of course you have to worry about your daughter. When you moved in, there was some speculation as to whether your wife had stayed in Atlanta to sell your home. Then you registered Rianne at school, and Ellie Pearson passed the word that you're a single dad. We've got a friend who's the school psychologist, in case Rianne's having difficulty dealing with the breakup."

"Hardly," Joel said stiffly. "Lynn and I separated when Rianne was a baby."

A knowing smile passed between the two of them that left Joel kicking himself. Why had he revealed so much? He should've heeded Sylvie's advice to run the minute he heard their names. They were a disarming duo. And potentially dangerous.

"By the way—" Dory slammed the lid of her trunk and removed her keys "—I hope Sylvie invited you and Rianne to Kay Waller's wedding tomorrow night. Six o'clock at the white church on the corner of Thistle and Shamrock. The reception-dance is a block up the street at the Elks' Club. Everyone in town will be there."

"Why would Sylvie invite us to someone else's wedding?

And why would I go when I don't know the couple?" He tried to remain polite, but he was beginning to feel panicky as he sensed a hustle coming.

Carline supplied the very answer Joel didn't want to hear. "Next to our once-a-year all-denominational church baseball game and picnic, weddings are the best place to meet everyone in Briarwood." She waddled by him, opened her car door and sank heavily into the seat. "I know you probably don't want to barge in. Sylvie said you wouldn't. But it's a perfect opportunity for Rianne to meet other kids. Oh, and even though the wedding itself is formal, guests can wear any old thing. You get a free meal for simply showing up." Carline threw out the extra incentive as she shut her car door.

On the driver's side, Dory wasn't in as big a rush to go. "You know Sylvie, so if you'd be more comfortable riding to the wedding with her, I'm sure there'll be plenty of room in Buddy's car. Buddy Deaver is what you'd call a pity date for Sylvie. He's home on vacation, and his mom literally begged Carline to dig up somebody to go with him to Kay's wedding. Our sister's a big softy. But there's absolutely nothing between her and Buddy. Hope we see you tomorrow, Joel. My daughter, Kendra, is really looking forward to meeting Rianne." Her door also slammed, and the engine sprang to life. Two seconds later, the red car backed from his lane—then "poof" it was gone. Joel welcomed the darkness closing around him. Especially as the women's impact left him feeling like he'd been hit by lightning. The hell of it was, they'd dangled the one carrot most likely to get him to attend a perfect stranger's wedding. *Well, two carrots.* The first being the fact that Rianne meet other kids. The other, an opportunity for him to identify the members potential of Briarwood's singles set.

Single women loved weddings, as far as he could tell. Bachelors climbed on board for the simple reason that if they didn't, their current girlfriends would never speak to them again. Then all subsequent Saturday nights would be spent drinking beer and watching sports channels.

Joel's phone was ringing as he walked into the house. He snatched it up, even though it meant juggling the heavy box holding the casseroles. At almost eleven at night, he couldn't imagine who'd be calling, other than possibly Lynn. She'd be leaving the TV studio about now. "'Lo," he mumbled.

"It's Sylvie. I saw Dory's car pull into your drive. What did she want? I'm almost afraid to ask."

"Actually, it was both of your sisters."

"Oh, no! Double trouble," Sylvie moaned. "Whatever they wanted, Joel, I hope you said no. Believe me, I know what I'm talking about."

"I have no doubt you do. First time I've ever been team-roped into going to a wedding."

"Kay's wedding? You barely met her, and you've never met Dave, the guy she's marrying."

"I know. Which makes the whole invitation ludicrous."

"Good. I'm glad you resisted."

"Uh, can I phone you back? Your sisters brought casseroles. I need to go stick them in the freezer."

"That's okay. I'm headed for bed. I'm helping decorate the church in the morning. Those of us in the wedding party are taking Kay to lunch at eleven, then we're all going to her salon to be beautified for the ceremony. Ugh!" She heaved a giant sigh. "That's de rigueur for all weddings in Briarwood. Oh, another thing…if they put the food in dishes that need to be returned, my advice is to transfer it into your own bowls now. Rinse their dishes. Let me return them. Otherwise, you'll give them another chance to have a crack at setting you up with someone. Namely me. G'bye, Joel."

"Wait," he sputtered, and found his protest floating in empty air. Sylvie had indeed hung up. But that was okay. If he told her he was toying with the idea of attending that wedding, she'd do her best to talk him out of it. She wasn't aware that he was capable of holding his own against far more seasoned matchmakers than her sisters. He'd been in the so-called *market* for five years, in a Southern city where the accent was on marriage. Atlanta boasted a hundred times more determined mothers than Briarwood. Joel had successfully evaded the net thus far. It'd take more than two sneaky women to shove him into matrimony again.

Joel could've hit redial and called Sylvie back. But if he told her he was considering the wedding, she'd probably feel obligated to have her date give him and Rianne a lift. Joel preferred to operate on the fringes. Set his own terms for navigating this affair. *Oh boy, was that a bad choice of words.*

Replacing the phone, he continued on into the kitchen. There he took Sylvie's advice about emptying her sister's dishes. That was a no-brainer. He scrubbed the crockery clean and thought about adding the country cousin to his comic strip. He could see her, all right, dragged to town by a family determined to marry her off. Poppy and Rose would sympathize mightily.

He galloped upstairs to his office. There he spent the better part of three hours drawing a dark-haired, dark-eyed, wholesome-looking character with a sprinkling of freckles across the bridge of her nose. The freckles were a nice touch. The perfect contrast to his current characters' sophistication. He wrote a character description, outlined some plot ideas and included sample dialogue.

Rocking back in his chair, Joel recalled being enchanted by Sylvie's golden freckles today.

Giving his new character a last check, he scanned the drawings and e-mailed his proposal to Lester Egan at the paper. Joel knew his editor would get back to him tomorrow morning—well before the wedding.

Shutting off his computer, Joel realized he'd decided to attend the wedding, where he'd almost certainly gather information for his project. But—did he need a gift? What did a guy give a couple he'd never met?

Another issue suddenly struck him. He was in the process of taking off his jeans, when it occurred to him that Rianne would need a new dress. Especially since she'd made so many pointed comments about the pretty dresses Sylvie created. Earlier tonight he'd noticed what a hodgepodge of clothes Rianne had.

Climbing into bed, he turned off his light. He should probably have heeded Lynn's barb about the way their daughter was dressed that day at the studio. He still resented Lynn's public delivery of that remark. So, he was guilty of letting Rianne choose her own clothes at the store. If Lynn hadn't run off to the hinterlands to make her mark on the news world, she would've understood how thrilling it was the first day Rianne came out of her room already dressed to go to the sitter. She'd been three, and he'd worked downtown at the paper. It seemed he'd spent hours every morning packing toys and outfits to cover all weather. Plus changes of clothing, in case of spills or potty training debacles. It'd all fallen on his shoulders.

Yes, he'd encouraged Rianne's independence. But wouldn't that serve her well in her future?

Joel wished Lynn had noticed that he'd been a stickler for manners. Rianne was polite, and never rowdy in public. He also wished his ex had seen how desperately Rianne wanted to please her mom, that mythical figure who'd been little more than a photograph. Or an occasional card, letter or gift arriving from a foreign country. Maybe a phone call now and then, since Lynn was once again based in Atlanta.

He crossed his arms behind his head and stared at the ceiling. Dammit, he did want his daughter to fit in here in Briarwood.

The next morning over breakfast, Joel brought up the wedding idea to Rianne. "Last night after you fell asleep, Sylvie's sisters came by and brought us casseroles."

"Are her sisters pretty, like Sylvie?"

"What? Pretty? I didn't notice. It was dark out. They never came inside. Why do you ask if they're pretty?"

The girl poured syrup on a waffle Joel had just pulled from the toaster. "Sylvie does neat stuff with her hair. She looks different all the time, but she's always pretty, doncha think, Daddy?"

"I guess. Getting back to my point," he said, controlling the amount of syrup Rianne was dumping on the waffle, "her sisters said everyone in town will be at Sylvie's friend's wedding tonight. The upshot of all this—how would you like to go? They said lots of kids will be there, including one of their daughters. Won't it be nice to make friends your age?" Joel didn't expect to see hesitation lurking in Rianne's blue eyes. "Is that a problem, honey? If you'd rather not, we can skip it."

"I wanna go. But how am I s'posed to meet kids?"

"Well, I guess we'll introduce ourselves."

Her smile spread syrup from ear to ear. "I thought you meant you were gonna drop me off."

"What? Didn't I walk you to your classrooms in preschool and kindergarten?"

"Uh-huh. I didn't know how weddings work. I've never been. You and Mommy had a wedding, 'cause you showed me pictures. Why wasn't I there? I mean, I know kids are gonna be in Kay's. Sylvie sewed their dresses."

Joel rose and plucked another hot waffle out of the toaster. "You were born way after your mom and I got married, snooks. Sometimes, like after a death or divorce, children from the first marriage can play a role in the second wedding." He sighed. "Marriage can be complicated, honey."

"Are you gonna get married again? You said you and Mama got 'vorced."

"Rianne, eat your waffle before it gets cold. I promise you, I have no plans to marry again."

"Why?"

Unintentionally, Joel squeezed too much syrup on his own waffle. "Maybe I haven't found a woman willing to answer all your *whys,*" he said, staring with dismay at his swimming waffle.

"Sylvie let me ask as many *whys* as I wanted the day we made cookies. And when she showed me how to cut out Barbie's dress."

Joel knew beyond a doubt he was not going down that winding path with Rianne. "Which reminds me of what I meant to say before this conversation got off track. We need to go out this morning and buy you a new dress."

"Goody, goody!" Rianne paused to swallow a bite of syrup-soaked waffle. "I don't guess there's time for Sylvie to sew me a dress, is there?"

"Definitely not. And if you see her between now and the wedding, I forbid you to ask her. Is that clear? I happen to know her schedule is full right up to wedding time."

"What's she doing?"

"A lot. Delivering dresses. Oh, and the women in the wedding party are taking the bride-to-be to lunch. What else did she tell me? I know…this morning Sylvie's helping decorate the church. Like I said, she's booked up."

"Okay. Maybe I should I ask if she wants me to feed Oscar."

"I'm sure Sylvie's planned for that. But it's good of you to offer. Hey, wanna help me buy a wedding gift? Now, there's a chore I hate. Buying presents. Maybe that's why guys get married," he muttered. Then, afraid how that sounded, he laughed. "I mean…women like to shop a whole lot more than most men, Rianne."

"I like to shop. Can we buy new shoes and socks to go with my dress?"

Joel sat for a moment contemplating future parties, school dances, proms and a myriad of other teenage activities. That would entail dresses, makeup and so on. He'd already had a taste of buying tap and ballet outfits. Odd how easily women handled purchasing soccer shoes, Little League uniforms and football helmets for their sons. Shopping genes had sure bypassed him. Although, he thought wryly as he rinsed off their breakfast dishes, men managed to acquire a lot of know-how about such issues as front versus back bra closures.

"Why are you smiling?" Rianne asked.

Caught, Joel quickly sobered. "You know me, snooks, I just had an idea for something funny for one of my cartoon characters. Which reminds me, if people we meet ask what I do…like what's my job, just say I work at home, okay?"

"Why?"

"How did I know that would be your next question? Because…the paper I work for is in Atlanta. People in Briarwood, North Carolina, won't ever see Poppy and Rose."

"Oh. Mommy saw them somewhere way far away, 'cause she said so."

"She did. My strip is syndicated in some other papers. Big daily papers. Briarwood's newspaper is a small weekly."

She shrugged. "I'm going upstairs to check my Barbie case for a color dress I want us to buy for me."

"While you're up there, straighten your bed so that lazy cat will come down to get her breakfast."

SYLVIE GOT UP EARLY to prepare for her busy day, but found herself stuck on the phone with Dory, who was saying, "Why didn't you invite your studly neighbor to Kay's wedding? I'll tell you why. Because he's available, and you're afraid to take a risk again, Sylvie, after you got burned by that jerk in New York who stole your virginity—and your work."

"Dory, that's private! And…who said Joel's available? Not him. Did he?"

"Aha, I hear interest in that question."

"How can you hear anything, Dor? You never listen. I can't believe you and Carline made a midnight end run around me. You guys hoped I wouldn't see you—that's why you paid Joel a late-night visit."

"It wasn't *that* late. Honey, we love you. Joel Mercer is

new blood. You've dismissed every other single male we've tried setting you up with."

"At least you admit that's why you took him casseroles," she grumbled. "And haven't you forgotten Buddy Deaver? Carline already fixed me up for the wedding. Who knows, maybe tonight I'll discover ol' Buddy and I are soul mates."

"Pu…leese! That is *so* not going to happen. Carline must think you're totally hopeless. I saw Buddy in town yesterday. He hasn't changed. That's why I felt your situation deserved drastic measures, hence the casserole run. Promise me that when Mercer shows up tonight, you'll introduce him around. You are his nearest, dearest neighbor, after all."

"I am not hopeless! And Joel's not going to Kay's wedding. Furthermore, I warned him what you two schemers are up to. If that's your only point in phoning this morning, hang up and let me get ready to go decorate the church."

"There's nobody who loves weddings more than you, Sylvie. You love the flowers, dresses, matching napkin colors to cake decorations, the works. Mom said she surprised you the other night with a visit and you tried to hide the fact that you're sewing on *the dress* again. When will you admit you want to take that walk down the aisle as much as the next woman?"

"Goodbye, Dory." Sylvie hung up, knowing the dress form in the corner mocked her words. She hated the way her sister's last jab had left her trembling. Didn't anyone understand how much the truth hurt?

Wanting to weep, but refusing to give in to the feeling that always overwhelmed her on the day of a wedding, Sylvie hurried out to feed Oscar. She glanced into Mercer's backyard. Thank goodness Fluffy was nowhere in sight. Speeding through her remaining chores, Sylvie grabbed the keys to the Mutt Mobile and loaded the gowns she needed to store at the church. Seconds before taking off, she made one last survey to see that she hadn't forgotten anything, and saw Joel back out of his lane.

He sure was easy on the eyes. Given the slightest encouragement, she could do something stupid like fall for him. For that reason, she was very glad Joel had no interest in attending Kay's ceremony. She was exceedingly vulnerable at weddings.

The bout of blues Dory had instigated with her phone call soon disappeared. Sylvie did love the pomp and circumstance of weddings. Her fascination with them had begun at age ten. Her aunt Gail, her mom's sister, married a man she'd met in New Orleans. They'd booked an historic plantation, and Gail's gown came straight out of *Gone with the Wind.* Nan Shea had taken her daughters to New Orleans for two whole weeks while she helped her sister prepare. If Sylvie shut her eyes, she could still relive every fabulous hour of those fourteen days.

Dory and Carline had whined constantly and begged to go home. Sylvie sat and drew pictures of Gail's gown and her bridesmaids' dresses. She sketched the arch, the candles, the flowers and the cake. And, oh, those glorious hats. Aunt Gail gave Sylvie permission to take home a stack of old bridal magazines. She still had pages from them in her files. Every year thereafter, Sylvie had saved up her allowance to buy the current bridal magazines on the market.

She owed her grandmothers for noticing her interest and encouraging a desire to learn to sew the delicate fabrics. Although most people thought Sylvie's real talent lay in new designs.

But...she still liked sewing gowns designed by others.

"Sylvie, is something wrong?" Kay asked an hour later, midway through the frenzy of decorating the church.

"Nothing. Why?"

"You seem, I don't know, distracted." Kay looked worried. "It's not because you think I'm making a mistake marrying David, is it?"

"Heavens, no!" Sylvie hugged the jittery bride. "You should know me, Kay. I'm always preoccupied on wedding days. I want every detail to come off exactly as I see it unfolding in my mind."

"Knowing you, they will. Hey, do you think it's too late

for me to call and invite your neighbor to the wedding? Carline delivered gifts to the apartment this morning and suggested it. She said it'd be a nice gesture, since he and his daughter would have a chance to meet everyone then. I thought about mentioning it the other day, but I was afraid it would be tacky."

"You were perfectly right, Kay. Carline's hormonal, remember. I'm sorry she added to your wedding-day anxiety."

"And yet, she has a point. I just phoned David and dumped the decision in his lap. All he has to do today is pick up the rings and his tux. He knows where Joel Mercer lives, so there's no reason he can't run out there."

Sylvie frowned. "Surely he won't go."

"I guess it's doubtful. Guys don't do spur-of-the-moment stuff like that. Would it be the faux pas of the decade if he did ask Joel? You act like it'd be terrible. I can borrow your cell and call Dave and nix the idea once and for all."

"Don't be silly. Joel and his daughter drove off right before I left the house. My only concern is that Dave would make a wasted trip across town."

"Oh, well." Kay relaxed enough to grin. "If you think my nerves are shot, he's a basket case. A drive from one side of town to the other could only calm him."

The women shared a laugh at the groom's expense. And Sylvie proceeded to the next item on her lengthy list, which included lunch with Kay and a trip to the beauty parlor.

Late getting home to exercise Oscar before her shower, Sylvie was driven by the ticking clock and Buddy's imminent arrival. After she showered, she noticed that Joel's van was back. Since she had other, more pressing concerns, she dismissed him from her mind.

Her biggest concern at the moment—the car her date arrived in and parked at her door. Not his father's Caddy. That would've been preferable. The car sitting in her drive was bright blue, low slung and possessed a feral growl. Sylvie had to consciously bite back a word she never uttered. But…surely anyone who drove a high-powered sportscar went by Jarvis, rather than Buddy.

Peering out a side window, she saw he wore a tuxedo and carried a plastic corsage box.

Sylvie drew back. What now? Should she lose the corsage that matched all the other bridesmaids'? Wear two flowers? Yikes!

Since Buddy was obviously trying to make a good impression, she opted to wear his flower now and tell him she'd exchange them at the church.

"Hi," he boomed through her screen, standing too close for Sylvie to open it and let him in. "Sylvie…I don't know if you remember me." He fiddled with his skewed bow tie.

"I do. Oh, you brought me flowers. That was sweet. But…did Carline mention I'm in the wedding party?"

"Mother bought the gardenia. You don't have to wear it if you'd rather not."

She forced him back by opening the screen. Lunging toward her, he grabbed and pumped Sylvie's hand up and down until she thought her arm would fall off. His palms were slick with perspiration. Obviously Buddy-Jarvis-Deaver's cool facade was all in his automobile. She finally wrenched her hand free. "Ah…let me grab a wrap for later. I'll, uh, wear your flower until the ceremony, Buddy. That way, if they run pre-wedding photos in the paper, your mom won't feel her effort went to waste."

"That's good of you. I see you know how Mother is."

Sylvie wouldn't touch that remark. Plus, she did remember Buddy after she managed a close-up. He wore the same buzz cut that had set him apart in school. And his stubborn cowlick remained, parting his hair smack-dab in center front. One thing had changed, though—he used to be painfully shy. On the drive to the church, during which Sylvie would have preferred silence, Buddy talked nonstop, boring her with stock market statistics for the entire year.

Every so often, Sylvie glanced his way, hoping he'd run down. Unfair of her? Perhaps. Her eyes crossed when he started probing her finances and that of her family. But when he said, "I'm glad you offered to go to the wedding with me, Sylvie. I haven't seen these characters since high school. I know after you reintroduce me they'll all ask what I can do for them in the current stock and bond market."

"Buddy, uh, Jarvis," she blurted, not caring if she sounded disgusted. "Weddings are social occasions. You can't use Kay and Dave's special day to shove your business ventures down the throats of their guests."

He gunned the high-powered motor petulantly, even though he'd just entered a restricted speed zone that curved into the church parking lot. "I thought you, of all people, would be financially savvy. Mother said you worked in New York City. Practically Wall Street."

"The garment district is not on Wall Street."

Buddy launched another incomprehensible diatribe explaining market growth. Sylvie knew then that it was going to be a long night.

JOEL HEARD Sylvie's date drive in. Actually, he'd been watching at the window. However, he identified the honeyed growl of a Lamborghini seconds before it made the swing into Sylvie's drive. A sportscar aficionado, but forced to sell his Porsche—which hadn't been half the car parked at Sylvie's—in exchange for a van, Joel all but drooled down the glass. This dude obviously didn't have a baby and all the kid paraphernalia to transport to and from a sitter. That was when Joel had kissed his Porsche goodbye.

Gripping the curtain in one hand, Joel pictured Sylvie's previous date. That guy's car hadn't exactly been the vehicle of a pauper.

Straining for a better glimpse of the car, he saw the couple exit the house. Each could have stepped out of a fashion ad. Armani tux, he guessed, having occasionally traveled in exalted circles. And Sylvie appeared très chic in a long, slinky dress reflecting the iridescent colors of the fading sun.

Joel caught the turn of the man's head and jerked sideways so as not to be seen with his nose glued to the window. He hurried to another spot to follow the departure of what he considered to be one of the world's most well-honed automobiles. That tail fin was pure beauty.

"What'cha doin', Daddy?"

Joel jumped guiltily back a second time. He hadn't heard Rianne enter the room. "Hey, baby, don't you look spiffy?" Making a huge show of bowing, Joel extended a hand. "May I have this dance, fair lady?"

She twirled around until her pale-blue organza dress stood out like a bell. "I brought down the ribbon that matches my dress. Will you tie it in my hair like the lady at the dress store showed you?"

"I'll try. I'm afraid my fingers will be all thumbs."

"You only have two thumbs, and so do I. Two's all anybody's got, silly."

"Feels like more when I have to tie these shiny ribbons." He made four attempts and worked up a sweat. "It still doesn't look right," he said critically.

"If I'm careful not to get my shoes dirty, may I run over to Sylvie's and ask her to tie it for me, Daddy?"

"Too late, snookums. She just left with her date."

"What's a date?"

"It's a who. In this case, a guy driving a sweetheart of a car."

"We could've given Sylvie a ride."

"Considering how pretty and dressed up she was tonight, I'm sure she'd rather ride in the hot car, not in our van."

"Why?"

"You'd know if you saw his car. Hey, if you're ready, maybe we'll get to the church in time for me to show you what I mean."

Considering the number of cars in the parking lot and parked all along both sides of the street, Joel thought they wouldn't find a place. He'd forgotten the Lamborghini until lo and behold, the only open spot was right beside it. He squeezed from his seat, taking pains not to let the door of his five-year-old van touch the spit-polished-midnight blue lacquer on the sportscar.

Joel pointed out the various features to Rianne.

She peered inside. "It's got no room, Daddy, and the seats go way back. Sylvie would've been more comfortable, I bet, if she'd come with us."

Deciding his kid just didn't understand, Joel took Rianne's hand. After a last longing glance at the car, he allowed her to lead him into the church. He hadn't realized it was almost six, and they were late. The wedding party was lined up in the hall.

Joel knew the moment Sylvie spotted them. He would've seen her shock even if Rianne hadn't shouted loudly enough to make everyone in line pause. "Sylvie, Sylvie…hi! Oh, you're even prettier in that dress than Daddy said."

Sylvie's face turned five shades of red, and Joel was sure his matched. He didn't need to witness the cat-that-got-the-cream expression lighting the eyes of the two women he'd met last night. They, plus a third, older woman who resembled Sylvie enough to be none other than her mom, began to whisper. Joel suspected he heard Sylvie groan. Or perhaps it was no more than a gleeful chortle among the three.

But Joel would hate Rianne to feel she'd done anything wrong. Nevertheless, he bent and murmured near her ear, "We're in church, snooks. Lower your voice, please. You can talk to Sylvie later. I think we need to find our seats."

Hopping backward on her shiny patent leather shoes, Rianne continued to wave excitedly at Sylvie. If any poor soul at the gathering remained unaware of a connection between the new man in town and Sylvie Shea, they'd surely gotten the word by the time an usher led Joel and Rianne to the bride's side of the satin-roped aisle.

Whispers traveled along the rows like a rolling snowball.

Joel heard his name several times. He heard speculation as to how he knew Kay and Dave. Heard it noted that he was kin to Iva Whitaker. And he supposed it served him right for having fine-tuned a propensity for eavesdropping in his work.

Too late, he saw that it was a huge error in judgment to be here, just as Sylvie had tried to tell him. Sitting heavily, Joel stifled an urge to flee. In reality, he had no expectation of escaping anytime soon. Rianne was too definitely enamored of this whole wedding business.

Chapter Seven

The wedding was grander than Joel had expected. Huge wicker baskets of flowers sat between fan-shaped candelabra. White satin ribbons looped from pew to pew along the center aisle, which was covered with a white satin runner.

With the first chords of the wedding march reverberating through the chapel, the guests' attention switched from Joel and Rianne to the front of the church. A minister, looking resplendent in a gold-and-purple robe, entered through a side door. A nervous groom, who no doubt had been coached to death the night before, came to stand unsteadily at the altar.

Far from bored now, Joel began taking note of small details. The groom, for one thing. The way the guy kept running a finger around the inside of his collar, as if to loosen a strangling tie, for instance. That had Joel seriously contemplating the possibility of writing a few scripts from a male's point of view. He'd already decided Poppy and Rose would get caught up in helping Cousin Petunia find a husband. Almost without realizing it, he started assessing the proceedings with an artist's eye. For a small-town production, the overall effect appeared very professional. Sylvie's doing?

If you discounted the fact that every time she glanced in his direction, she shot daggers through him, Joel actually enjoyed imagining her in his unfolding strip. In that respect, even Sylvie's daggers worked to his advantage.

He hadn't named his country cousin in the pilot he'd sent in for Lester's approval. Now, surrounded by fragrant blossoms spilling from baskets carried by the bride and her attendants, Joel knew he wanted something in keeping with Poppy and Rose. Petunia had been silly and off the cuff. He tested others—iris, violet, lily, daisy. None suited the character he'd drawn. There had to be a name, other than Jasmine, with a southern flavor. Dogwood sounded way too hokey.

Leaning over abruptly, Joel asked Rianne if she knew the name of the big white flowers in the bride's bouquet and in the bridesmaids' corsages.

The girl shook her head.

A large woman seated on the other side of Rianne murmured, "Magnolias. Aren't these glorious? I grow some outside my sun room, but I never would've thought to mix them with camellias or baby roses. Only Sylvie would be that clever, even if she had to get them from a California hothouse this time of year." She nodded sagely. "Before Sylvie came home, our fall brides were relegated to decorating with old standby's like maple leaves and chrysanthemums."

Not having any interest in those details, Joel offered a polite smile over Rianne's blond head. He saw that the ribbons he'd tied were slipping. Discreetly he attempted to adjust the one in the worst shape. Apparently pitying him, the matron on the other side of Rianne calmly shoved his hand aside. Deftly, she retied and knotted the ribbons on both sides so they matched perfectly.

How did she do that? Joel's smile came from his heart. His child sat transfixed throughout the bow-tying, totally focused on the service.

Joel faced forward again, now giving the minister's words his attention. His gaze kept drifting to Sylvie, however, and his mind returned to the name Magnolia. The more he considered it, the more he thought the name would resonate with readers who loved Poppy and Rose. Pleasing them was important. He wanted long-time followers to identify with Magnolia and empathize with her, so they'd be fully involved in any situation Joel landed the poor cousin in. Yes, *Magnolia* might work.

He emerged from his plotting cocoon after the crowd surged to its feet around him. Rianne attempted to tug him to a standing position. He struggled up and saw that the bride and groom were being presented as husband and wife. Their requisite kiss brought applause, chuckles and whistles throughout the church.

Again Joel's eyes strayed to Sylvie's slightly wistful expression. He experienced an odd tingling of his limbs. Why was she wistful if, as she said yesterday, she ran like hell to avoid her family's attempts to match her with a man? He wondered about that as the newlyweds broke apart, beamed at family and friends, and the organist pounded out the recessional.

The happy pair's exit was considerably slowed due to well-wishers and sniffling huggers. Weddings and births ought to be happy occasions. Joel thought people should save tears for tragedies and funerals.

At that moment Sylvie drew abreast of his row. She did her best to telegraph her deep displeasure at seeing him there, all the while responding positively to Rianne's excited babble.

The woman who'd tied Rianne's hair bows zeroed in on the exchange. Once the party moved past, she bent toward Joel. "I'm Freda Poulson, the local librarian. You'd be Harvey and Iva Whitaker's great-nephew, I assume. And this beautiful, charming child is…?"

"My daughter, Rianne. I'm Joel Mercer," he said, accepting the woman's soft hand. "Rianne loves to read. You'll see us at the library as soon as we get completely moved in. By the way, thanks for helping with the bows. They're beyond me."

"You poor, dear man. However do you manage to raise a daughter alone?"

Joel, who'd dropped his hand to Rianne's shoulder to hold

her wiggling to a minimum, felt his fingers tighten. "We do fine on most fronts. I'm a little deficient, I admit, in tying hair ribbons, but basically, we're thriving."

Freda tsked. "There's so much more to raising girls as they mature, you know. If I may be so bold…I don't think you should wait much longer before finding her a stepmother to direct her along the proper path." Freda paused, apparently to let her advice sink in, then said quite matter-of-factly, as if she was Joel's best friend, "Are you aware that the perfect candidate lives right next door? It's a shame you got off on the wrong foot with Sylvie Shea. Such a dear. A finer family than hers doesn't exist."

Floored at the temerity of a virtual stranger, Joel groped for a suitable response, but came up empty.

His daughter had no such problem. "What's she mean, Daddy? Shouldn't you tell her we like Sylvie a whole bunch?"

Leaning backward to see the matronly woman, Rianne said again, and more loudly, "Sylvie's wonderful. She let me help her bake cookies for her Sunday school. We cut my Barbie out a dress. And Sylvie's making me one 'xactly like it as soon as she finds a pattern. Yesterday when Daddy fell in the lake, Sylvie pulled him out and brought him back to life."

Joel considered clapping a hand over Rianne's mouth, then decided that would only make matters worse. Maybe if he ignored the entire outburst, the woman, Freda, might move along. But no such luck. She ran a speculative eye over Joel.

"Really?" The librarian sidestepped her way to the end of the pew. Moments ahead of merging with the other guests flocking down the aisle, she thumped Joel on the arm with a hand still clasping the hankie she'd used to dab her eyes during the ceremony. "Saint's be praised! Maybe now Sylvie can bring out that secret wedding dress she dragged home from New York. Nothing would make Nan and Rob happier." Thankfully, the librarian's bulk was swept toward the exit with the press of jovial guests.

Joel sagged with relief. *What secret dress? And who were*

Nan and Rob? Someone else had mentioned Nan. Joel couldn't recall who or when, he was so rattled. Plainly, people in Briarwood weren't familiar with the term *privacy*. As a result of his hanging back, he and Rianne missed their turn to join the exodus. For a minute they seemed to be stuck in the pew, awash in the battling scents of perfumes and colognes passing them by. He spotted an opening in front of a senior couple plodding slowly along. Joel shoved Rianne into the stream of traffic.

The next thing he knew, they'd emerged in the much fresher air of a balmy southern night. Joel considered going straight home. But that wasn't to be. Men and women began to stop and strike up conversations. Most now knew Joel by name. He was frequently slapped on the back and shook hands until his fingers felt numb. Rianne, he noticed, reveled in the attention. Belatedly, Joel figured out that they were being steadily herded to the next location, the Elks' Lodge. The reception was already in full swing by the sound of it.

In the foyer, Joel saw people deposit gifts on three long tables already laden with wrapped packages. He pulled Rianne out of the shuffle. "I left our gift in the car. Either we'll have to walk back for it and hike up here again, or if you're okay with skipping this part, we can stop by on the drive home and I'll run in with our gift."

"You'll do no such thing," Dory Hopewell said from behind him. "Why drag Rianne all that way?" The woman bent to the child's eye level and said, "We haven't met. I'm Sylvie's middle sister, Dory. My daughter, Kendra's, just inside with her father and brother. How would you like to come along with me and meet her? I'll get you girls some punch. Your dad can come round and find us as soon as he returns."

She straightened, saying for Joel's benefit, "If you'd like to drive and save the hike uphill, there ought to be parking spaces at the rear of this building."

"Can I stay, Daddy? Sylvie showed me Kendra's picture.

Next week she's gonna be five like me." Rianne giggled.
"'Cept the week after that, I'll be six, and we won't be the
same age again for 'nother year. Sylvie figured that out."

"I don't think I can let you stay, Rianne. Anyway, our
van's not far." To Dory, he said, "I'm not in the habit of turning my daughter over to strangers."

Dory batted a hand through the air. "That probably makes
perfect sense where you used to live. In Briarwood, there's
no such thing as a stranger. Look, here's Kendra now. And
the Martin twins. They'll be in Rianne's first-grade class. I
don't envy their teacher, but let's see if I can tell them apart
to introduce them." Dory pointed a finger at a gap-toothed
pigtailed girl. "Nikki. And Nola." Her daughter and the twins
dissolved in laughter and promptly corrected Dory's mistake.

Joel noticed the twins had old-fashioned manners, in that
they called Dory Mrs. Hopewell. She seemed not the least put
out, and hugged all three. Her easy manner with the kids, and
their obvious acceptance of her, went a long way toward per-
suading Joel to give in.

As his original intent in coming here was so Rianne could
make some friends, he capitulated—to Rianne's obvious delight, and also the delight of her newest best friends. "Okay,
but listen up. We're not staying long," he counseled both the
excited kids and Dory Hopewell.

She patted his arm in a familiar manner. Did everyone in
this town assume that if you lived here, you were instantly bos-
om buddies? "Go retrieve your gift, Joel, but hurry back. You
won't be half so grouchy once you're inside and get swept up
in the party atmosphere. The band Dave and Kay booked for
the evening is the best in the area. There'll be tons of food, a
moderate amount of spirits and good company all around."
Winking, she added, "Failing that, you can slink off into a corner and natter on about sports with my husband and brother-
in-law, who are past masters at avoiding the dance floor."

Her engaging grin was so like Sylvie's, it got under Joel's

skin. "Okay, okay. Rianne, you stick with Dory and the kids until I get back. I'll only be a few minutes."

"Yippee!" the twins shouted at the top of their lungs. "Come on, Rianne, we'll show you the table with the pink punch for kids."

Joel watched his daughter dart off. She didn't bother to say goodbye. That upset him. Maybe she was already growing up, as Freda, back at the church, had suggested. Maybe he was already losing his influence.

"Is something else bothering you?" Dory asked. "I promise to keep a good eye on her. Really, I swear she'll be fine."

"I know. It's just…earlier tonight someone remarked how quickly kids begin to spread their wings. I believe this may be my first experience. Now I'm wondering if standing aside is going to be even harder than I suspected."

It was obvious from her expression that Dory Hopewell understood and empathized with Joel. "It helps to have a partner to share half the burden of raising kids."

"Yes, well, sometimes that part of life doesn't work out." Joel backed toward the door. "I'll see you in a few minutes," he said a little more curtly.

"Now I've stuck my foot in my mouth when I didn't mean to. What you said made me stop to think I should march straight inside and hug Grant for all the times he gives me a break from the kids. No one said being a parent is easy."

Joel inclined his chin briefly, but he shot out of the Elks' Lodge like a man possessed. He'd almost reached his van when he acknowledged that he'd probably said too much back there. Telling himself it was too late for regrets over Lynn, he backed the car out of the lot and parked it behind the lodge. Hauling out the gift, a bowl Carline Manchester had wrapped the day he and Rianne had shopped in town, Joel set it on an already full table.

In the main room, the hub of festivities, the lights at one end had been turned low. A multicolored spotlight revolved, raining speckles of light on the heads and shoulders of dancers. More guests sat at long tables covered with pink cloths on the opposite end of the room. Most were partaking of the generous buffet. Some stood in groups, talking. It was at a table near the food that Joel spotted Rianne in the middle of six or more kids.

He worked his way over to her. "I'm back, snooks," he said.

"Daddy, hi. This is Holly and her sister, Ashleigh. Holly's going into first grade, too. Ashleigh will be in third grade," Rianne said with no small amount of respect. "You already met Kendra and the twins. This is Kendra's brother, Roy."

Joel bobbed his head and mumbled that he was pleased to meet the other children. He scanned the area for an empty chair. The three end tables were nothing but a sea of children. The noise made it difficult to hear what anyone was saying. He dropped to one knee to speak directly in Rianne's ear. "I'm going to grab a plate of food and something to drink, then I'll stand right over in that corner. Ask the girls what supplies we need to buy before the first day of school, okay? When we both finish eating, we need to head home."

"Daddy, we can't go before Kay and David cut the cake. Ashleigh said kids get plain toast."

Joel frowned until a melodic voice he recognized, and which always sent shivers up the back of his neck, spoke somewhere above his head. "She's talking about the champagne toast," Sylvie explained with a grin. "I'm handing out glasses now. Adults get champagne, kids get sparkling soda."

Surging to his feet, Joel almost knocked the box out of her hands. The empty glasses rattled ominously. He grabbed for it, but wrapped both hands around the teetering woman. The bare skin of Sylvie's upper arms felt soft and warm, reminding Joel sharply of things he'd missed over the last several years. He soaked up the pleasing sensations, not sure he wanted to let her go. "Here, let me help with that," he said gruffly. "I'll carry the box. You hand out glasses."

She pulled away. "Are you kidding? Imagine what people would say. Why did you come, Joel? And why did Dory make a point of telling me she was looking after Rianne while you ran back to the car after a gift? Oh, and at the church I saw you talking to Freda Poulson, our town crier. I don't have a clue what you two said, but she's practically got us picking out an engagement ring."

"I didn't say anything," he protested. "It was Rianne. You know how kids are."

"Well, you don't know how the women of this town are," Sylvie exclaimed in an irritated voice. "Oh, no," she cried partially under her breath. "I've gotta dash. My mom and dad are headed this way. Be careful what you say," she hissed, and shoved a glass into his hand. She swiftly set plastic cups in front of all the kids, then made tracks out of that aisle.

Joel considered following her. But a beanpole in a tuxedo suddenly blocked his path. "Do you know where Sylvie Shea got off to? I'm Buddy, her so-called date. Someone just saw her talking to you."

"She's distributing champagne glasses for the toast." Joel waggled his. He was interested in meeting one of apparently several men who dated his neighbor. The two Joel had seen both drove hot cars, although the Lamborghini definitely topped the Porsche. While Joel hated to judge, this guy was nowhere near as cool as his car. And Buddy? Only Bubba could be a worse name.

"I'm Sylvie's neighbor," Joel said, when the other man didn't rush right off in search of his date. "Gotta say I envy a guy with a car like yours."

"A birthday present from my father. Oh, I could've bought it myself. I'm a successful stockbroker." Pulling out a handful of business cards, Buddy peeled one off and dropped it in Joel's glass. "Who handles your investments? I can probably double your money." For several minutes, he tossed around facts and figures, all in a monotone.

Joel wondered what Sylvie saw in this dud. "Uh, are you friends with the bride or the groom?" Joel asked as he nibbled on food from the buffet.

"Neither. But I've known them both all my life. I'm home because tomorrow is Mother's birthday. Tonight my parents are busy with clients, so Mother and Carline fixed me up with Sylvie. I thought she'd help me make some valuable business contacts. But she's too busy micromanaging everything at the wedding," he said petulantly. "Just between us…it wouldn't work anyway. Sylvie hasn't invested one cent in blue-chip stocks." Buddy's eyes, which never met Joel's at any time, locked on something over his shoulder. "Oh, hello, Mr. and Mrs. Shea. If you're looking for Sylvie, too, she's not here. It seems she's now in charge of the toast—as well as the bouquets, dresses and catering staff. I wish Carline had been straight about this. My mother expected Sylvie to help me get a foot in the door with her friends. My evening would've been better spent at home checking the Nikkei."

"That's too bad, Buddy. Carline probably had no idea that was your goal. I think she assumed you were attending Kay's wedding because otherwise you would've been alone. Rob and I are well aware of the many tasks Sylvie assumes as wedding coordinator." The woman's gaze moved from Buddy to Joel. She extended a tanned hand toward him. "I'm Nan Shea. This is my husband, Rob." Her gracious smile encompassed both men. "We really came over to introduce ourselves to Joel Mercer, Buddy. He's Sylvie's new neighbor." Adroitly Nan switched gears. She withdrew her hand from Joel's and touched Buddy's sleeve. "Since you have important things to do at home, I'm sure it wouldn't be any imposition to ask Joel if he'll give Sylvie a lift home after the party."

Both men stammered, but Buddy recovered first. "I, ah, don't know what Mother would say. You know what a stickler she is for propriety."

"I certainly do. But if she could see how busy Sylvie is, and how that leaves you twiddling your thumbs, I'm positive she'd agree."

Buddy dallied only a moment longer. "I really need to follow up on today's interest hike. Mrs. Shea, maybe you won't mind seeing that all the guests get one of these." Buddy shoved the fat wad of business cards into her hand, then looking more eager than he had so far, muttered, "Please relay my apologies to Sylvie for abandoning her."

Speechless, Nan said nothing as she fumbled with the stack of loose cards.

Rob Shea promised for her. After Buddy was well out of earshot, he turned to his wife. "What on earth was Carline thinking, hooking Sylvie up with that dork? His father is insufferably pompous. The son is worse."

"Now, Rob. I doubt Carline's seen him since high school. She probably assumed he'd changed."

"Well, he was odd then, too." Rob broke off and clapped Joel's shoulder. "We haven't had a chance to talk, my boy. It'll be a while before anyone gets around to giving you any refreshment in that empty glass you're using as a card holder. What say we find us a beer? I'll deliver the official welcome later, when I put on my mayor's hat. Nan, I know Kay asked you to serve cake. I'll find you again after that ritual's over and done with."

The elegant woman—who, Joel noticed, Sylvie already resembled—rose on tiptoes and kissed her husband's cheek, all while filling his jacket pockets with Buddy Deaver's business cards. "Should I warn Joel you're about to twist his arm to volunteer for a job at our Labor Day Festival?"

"If he plays baseball, I intend to recruit him to join my team. Before John Trent discovers there's a new man in town." To Joel, Rob added, "Those dang Baptists beat us every year. It'd help, of course, if you're a bona fide Methodist. Even if you're not, if you can swing a bat or throw a ball, I'm not above converting you for a single day." Twinkling hazel eyes, very similar to Sylvie's, raked Joel as if measuring him for a ball uniform.

"I've been negligent about attending church," Joel explained. "I hope to rectify that now that we've moved and the pace isn't as frenzied. A lot depends on my daughter. As for baseball, I'm not a bad fielder or batter. I suppose I'm willing to be a Methodist for a day. Oh, Mrs. Shea, before you run off, allow me to introduce my daughter. Rianne may not be your only chocolate chip cookie fan, but I'd lay odds she's the most vocal. I liked them, but years ago I swore allegiance to Mary Shea's oatmeal raisin drops." He raised his voice. "Rianne, honey, come meet Sylvie's parents."

The girl bounced up at once. As Joel had predicted, she spoke first about Nan's cookies and how much she loved them.

"They go fast at my house," Nan said. "I make a batch every week. Next time I do, I'll phone. Perhaps your dad will run you over to sample them hot. You're invited, too, Joel," she said sweetly. "That's the only fair test to see if you still prefer my mother-in-law's recipe over mine."

Rianne piped up again. "Daddy won't switch. He always says those oatmeal cookies are the best. But I bet he'll drive me to your house, won't you, Daddy? Sylvie said her dad makes furniture, and Daddy, you said we need more to fill up your aunt Iva's house."

"Our house now. And I did say that. Listen, snooks, I'm going with Mr. Shea to have a beer to go with my snack. Don't leave this table until I come back. Okay?"

Taking that as her exit line, Rianne dived back between her new friends.

"What a lovely child," Nan murmured. "Please, Joel, call us Rob and Nan. Everyone in Briarwood likes being on a first-name basis."

If Joel felt his feet slipping in the undertow of Nan Shea's charming drawl and equally charming smile, he ignored the warning. Maybe because, as a kid, he'd loved the close-knit ties of Briarwood. He wanted Rianne and him to fit in and become part of it. Wanted it so badly, he forgot to suggest that Rob and Nan give their daughter a ride home, instead.

Sylvie's dad wrenched the caps off two ice-cold beers he pulled from a cooler, one of many lined up along the stage wall. "If we hang around next to the band," the older man shouted, "we not only won't be able to talk about the Labor Day Festival, we'll probably go deaf in the process." He motioned Joel to forge a path through the dancers.

Joel saw that most of the bridesmaids were out on the floor. He strained to see if Sylvie was among them. When he couldn't find her, he searched the room until he did. Their eyes met. She didn't look happy to see him with her dad. Joel thought the you-know-what would hit the fan when she discovered her well-meaning parents had sent her date home and had, just as casually, commandeered him to drive her. It occurred to Joel that this was a perfect situation to use for his comic strip. He anticipated getting some great dialogue if he waited around for Sylvie's reactions to the news.

"I only ever spent a few weeks here over the summer," Joel said when Rob located a quiet corner in the foyer. "Tell me about this festival. Be forewarned that I haven't been here long enough to establish a list of reliable baby-sitters."

"No need for one. The whole town turns out. In my great-grandpappy's day, Briarwood was largely a farm community. Labor Day signaled the end of harvest season and it's still an important event."

"Not too many farms left around here, are there?" Joel gulped down some of his beer and polished off his hors d'oeuvres.

"No. People sent their kids off to college. A good number didn't come back. And who could blame them? It's such a fight, keeping the kudzu vines out. I'm sure you've seen them in the Atlanta area." He shook his head. "Those suckers take hold and kill virtually every plant in the vicinity. Kudzu can kill an entire forest. Farmers around here tried a number of methods to control it, but not all of 'em were good choices. An insect farmers imported also ate soybean crops. Now folks grow only enough to feed their families. They let forestry crews battle the kudzu. The farmers mostly retired or found other jobs. That accounts for so many bed-and-breakfast spots springing up. They cater to tourists driving our scenic parkways." Rob shook his head again and took a swig of beer. "Mountain crafts take less effort than back-breaking, year-round farming. And the money's better in a good tourist year."

While Joel wasn't paying attention, Sylvie sidled up. "Dad, are you boring Joel with Briarwood's history?"

"Oh, I'm not bored. I appreciate knowing the town's background. Rob's about to give me a job at your Labor Day Festival."

The older man bestowed an indulgent smile on his daughter. "Your mother suggested you take Joel under your wing, Sylvie."

"I'll just bet she did." Sylvie's scowl didn't pass by Joel unnoticed.

Apparently, though, it went right over her dad's head. Or else Rob chose to ignore her, saying instead, "Now Sylvie, you need a man's help to carry those heavy boxes of prizes into the booths at the kiddie carnival. I had Jeffery down for that, but as Mom pointed out, Carline's due date falls right on the date of the festival. First sign of a labor pain and you know Jeff will be a basket case."

"Darn, that's true. Still, it's no reason to shanghai Joel. The poor man deserves one year to enjoy the festival with his daughter." Sylvie scanned the room. "I know, Dad. I'll ask Buddy to fill in for Jeff. If I can find him... Mr. and Mrs. Deaver would probably be delighted to have him visit again so soon."

Since Rob seemed not to hear her question concerning Buddy's whereabouts, Joel took it upon himself to interject casually, "Your date went home to download the Japanese stock market reports."

"He *what?* He wouldn't. Not without saying a word to me."

"Well, he felt bad, I think. Although he did seem to indicate that you weren't being much help drumming up prospective clients."

Sylvie rolled her eyes. But Joel felt bad for teasing her.

Rob Shea chimed in again. "I told your mom and Joel, and I'll tell you. That boy is odd. Brags a lot about how good he is, but I hear he's not doing so great. In fact, the kid lost his clients so much money, his dad's stopped referring people Buddy's way. I'm surprised you'd go out with him, Sylvie. Besides, isn't he five or six years younger than you?"

"Three. And you should have this conversation with your youngest daughter, not with me. Carline roped me into being Buddy's date this evening."

"Your mom told me, but why? Carline knows how busy you are during a wedding. What happened to that last young fella? The one Dory had you bring to the house? Chet, that's his name. He's closer to your age, Sylvie. Owns his own company, too. Seemed like he had a good head on his shoulders."

"Yeah, great. Dad…Chet's living with…a life-partner in Asheville." She sighed. "I wish you'd do me a huge favor and tell Mom and the girls to quit trying to marry me off."

"Chet's married?" Rob just shook his head.

"Well, he's in a committed relationship," Sylvie muttered.

Joel understood what she was saying about Chet. That, too, he stored for future use with his Magnolia character.

"Oops…Kay's giving me the high sign," Sylvie said. "And here comes her photographer. They must want to cut the cake. I need to go unhook Kay's train so her skirt shows to full advantage in the pictures."

Joel caught Sylvie's wrist as she gathered up her long dress to navigate through the door. "Name someplace for us to meet afterward. Will you need help boxing up the decorations?"

"Listen, you don't have to stay to the bitter end. I can find someone to take me home."

"Rianne is enjoying every minute here. Plus, she'd never forgive me if I left you in the lurch, Sylvie."

It was obvious that Sylvie badly wanted to refuse his offer. Releasing a breath, she put a hand to her forehead and rubbed away the lines forming there.

Joel could tell when she gave in to the futility of fighting the inevitable tonight. Maybe because he'd already reached the same conclusion during Nan Shea's earlier onslaught.

"You remember the men who came to rebuild our fence the other day? One of them is Grant Hopewell, Dory's husband. He'll be folding and stacking chairs on those rolling carts lined up out in the hall. You can give him a hand. But please keep it low-key. I'd rather not make it too obvious that I came with one man, and I'm leaving with another. You have no idea what wagging tongues in this town can do with a juicy tidbit like that."

"Isn't this much ado about nothing?"

"Ha! You'll wish. Joel, I've lived here forever. I've planned weddings for couples who had no intention of ever marrying. Not until a group I call the marriage vigilantes set its sights on them and got into high gear. You have to see them in action to believe it, Joel. Or better yet…not."

His skepticism might as well have been flashed in skywriting on the ceiling.

"Joel, trust me, you *don't* want to fall into their clutches. And my mom and sisters are their most dedicated members."

He was left pondering her dire warning as he hoisted his beer.

Rob Shea drained his bottle. "Time to mosey back for the grand finale," the older man lamented. "The part I like best about these shindigs is the champagne and the cake. Our bakery does about as good a wedding cake as I've ever tasted. Bad thing about Nan doing the serving is that I won't get to swipe a second slice. Listen, son, I heard part of what Sylvie said. I love that girl to distraction. She is, after all, my first-born. And I guess you'd know there's something extra-special about a man's first daughter. Honestly, I tell you she's obsessed with this idea that the town's out to see her hitched."

Joel nodded. "So, sir, you're saying there's nothing to her concern? You know for certain that your wife and other daughters, for instance, aren't trying to find Sylvie a husband?"

Rob pursed his lips. "Well, I tell them all that just because Sylvie fell in love with weddings from the time she was knee-high to a toadstool, it doesn't mean she's dying to have one of her own."

"You'd know her better than I do on that score. From what I've seen in a very short time, that seems to be true. Although, I have the impression that most women would rather be married than single." That observation was pretty much the cornerstone for his comic strip. And it'd held up through most of his research in Atlanta's singles gathering spots.

"Son, take it from a man who's lived in a household full of females for a good long while. Every time I'm sure I've figured out that something or other is common to most women—one of the women in my family proves me dead wrong."

Rob looked so perplexed, Joel laughed. "It's good talking to you, sir. Since I'm raising a daughter by myself, I'll store your advice for the future. Rianne's only six. But I've already seen that her favorite *anything* today will be the bane of her existence next week."

The older man smiled. "Well, if you ever need a sounding board, I'm a good listener. So was my dad, bless his soul. He used to take me fishing and let me ramble."

His reference to fishing sent Joel's mind straight to his outing with Rob's eldest daughter. Joel couldn't help recalling how Sylvie's wet skin had shone pearly white in the afternoon sun. He remembered again how affected he'd been by her long legs straddling his hips. Joel's mind stalled there, then shut down totally. As if they were acting on their own, his eyes sought her out at the front of the room.

If he'd thought that seeing her amid the wedding trappings would douse the fire licking along his veins, he was very much in error. The flames beat higher. In the pulse at his throat. In his wrists and groin. Joel very much hoped Sylvie had willpower enough for them both. One of them needed to resist these feelings that were overtaking him.

After Rob said he'd be in touch about the festival, Joel wove his way to the children's table, where Rianne now sat alone. He saw the other kids had crowded up to the cake table, to witness the cutting of the cake.

"I'm sorry I was gone so long, snooks. I'll wait here if you'd like to join your friends."

The happy hug she bestowed on him served to remind Joel that he wasn't in any position to be fantasizing about a woman. Any woman.

Quietly, he sat back and watched the crowd. He accepted the champagne an unfamiliar woman poured him. The mood that had come over him passed and Joel began to focus again on eavesdropping, picking up comments and observations to incorporate in his comic strip.

Chapter Eight

It was during the cleanup after the reception that Joel overheard yet another person alluding to Sylvie's secret dress. One of the bridesmaids, perhaps the youngest in the party, trailed after Dory, talking incessantly. "Brian had a great time at Kay's wedding. We danced every single dance. I feel in my bones he's *this* close to giving me a ring, Dory." Swaying dreamily, the girl held her thumb and forefinger a millimeter apart.

Joel took his time stacking chairs. His ears perked up much the same way Oscar's did when humans entered his sphere. The bridesmaid—Joel thought her name was Tracie—reverently brought up *the* dress. She placed the emphasis on *the,* as if only one dress was worthy of such distinction.

Dory continued to fold table linens and pile them on a table. Very close to where Joel closed and stacked chairs.

"Tracie, take it from me," Dory said. "Order a book of bridal patterns and choose one you love. Sylvie refused to sell Kay *the* gown, and you know they've been best friends forever."

"You've seen *the* dress, right? Is it as magnificent as we've all heard? A regular Cinderella ball gown?"

Dory snatched the last pink tablecloth out of dreamy-eyed Tracie's hands. "No one's actually seen the dress, Tracie. But anytime Sylvie wants to avoid doing something Carline and I try to get her to do, she claims to be busy sewing. Even when she's between weddings. So what would *you* think?"

"Somebody we both know well, but who shall remain nameless, got her nose out of joint because Sylvie said she couldn't buy *the* dress. She's spreading rumors in our crowd that perhaps it doesn't exist."

"Ridiculous! I've seen the dress form. She keeps it covered." Packing the last tablecloth in the box, Dory paused to put on the lid. Joel noted her irritated expression. "I can guess who you mean, Tracie," Dory said huffily. "I can guarantee that every dress Sylvie makes is gorgeous. Why fuss over one she's saving for herself?"

"Personally I think it'd be hilarious if there was no dress. Like, what if when Sylvie came home from New York and everybody was whispering that she'd failed or that some guy broke her heart—what if she invented this whole PR strategy around an invented dress? Can you think of a better way to entice customers? It's called applied economics. Mention one-of-a-kind, or for that matter any commodity in short supply, and people line up for blocks hoping to be the one who'll end up possessing whatever it is."

Joel set the fourth of four chairs he'd hauled across the room on the rolling cart, having missed part of that conversation while he was gone. He admitted to being disappointed when the two women finished folding linens and moved on to another chore.

The notion of a Cinderella gown intrigued him. The possibility that this gown might be a fraud, a lie, fascinated him even more. Something like that would add a great twist to the Magnolia plotline. He imagined Magnolia as an expert seamstress—sort of like Sylvie. But not *exactly* like her. That had the potential to cause problems. But—wouldn't it be a hoot to have his character drag a wedding dress to Atlanta? Have wedding dress, will travel to locate a groom. Huh, he'd already decided Magnolia's folks would rope cousins Poppy and Rose into this husband hunt. He'd planned to make Magnolia crafty enough to let everyone think she was playing along—but really had no intention of falling in with their plans. But maybe if she had this secret wedding dress—or claimed to have it… His mind clicked through one idea after another.

Except for keeping tabs on Rianne as she played tag with Dory's children in a near-empty room, Joel's head remained in the clouds as he plotted. This was the part he loved most about working with comic-strip characters. He liked dreaming up funny but plausible situations, based on real life.

In the process he missed a lot that went on around him. Somehow he hadn't realized that Sylvie had changed from her bridesmaid's dress into jeans and a T-shirt until she broke into his trance. "Yo…Joel." Sylvie snapped her fingers in front of his face. "You've just about swept the finish off that linoleum square, " she teased. "Are you asleep at the broom?"

"Wow—some metamorphosis from butterfly to caterpillar. Where's your dress?"

"I always change after the reception. I'll send the dress to the cleaners and when it comes back I'll rip it apart and use the material for another project."

"You only wear it once?"

"No one ever wears a bridesmaid's dress after a wedding's over. Other women can spot a bridesmaid's dress from a mile away. Since I sew, I can at least reuse my fabric. Otherwise it gets costly to keep making fancy dresses."

"I could see that if you were in a huge number of weddings. But how many can that be?"

Dory walked up in time to hear their exchange. "Ha! Ask her how many times she's been a bridesmaid, Joel. A baker's dozen," she answered when Sylvie didn't. "Carline and I say thirteen is unlucky. She should've turned Kay down. After all, Syl, you've been her maid of honor twice now."

"Twelve, thirteen, what difference does it make? Honestly, Dory, you and Carline should get a life. You're too superstitious."

"So? If people say often enough that you're always a

bridesmaid but never a bride, Sylvie, it becomes a self-fulfilling prophecy. Don't roll your eyes at me, Sylvie Shea."

"I didn't roll them, I crossed them. Where's your sense of humor?"

"I don't have one when it comes to the way you create a touch-me-not aura that scares off unattached men."

"I'm sure we can discuss this another time, Dory. I have to make a final sweep of the lodge and then lock up. Joel does not need to hear our bickering."

He leaned on the broom handle, chin nestled in clasped hands, a tiny smile playing on his lips. "Actually, it's fascinating. I'm an only child, so sibling rivalry is foreign to me. This is good stuff to know in case I ever provide Rianne with a little brother or sister."

Dory's head whipped around. "Then you have a fiancée, or at least someone you're seriously dating?"

"Yes, that's it exactly," Sylvie said, abruptly jerking the broom out of Joel's hands.

At the same time, he said dazedly, "No, I'm speaking hypothetically."

Too late, Joel saw the smug smile settle on Dory Hopewell's face.

"Good night, Dory," Sylvie interjected firmly, hooking her sister's arm and dragging her a few feet away. "Thanks to you and Grant for helping clear the lodge. Joel and I will close up, and we'll leave after I collect my dress, plus a couple of boxes of candles and stuff. And Rianne," she added as the kids ran giggling past.

Now it was Dory who blinked in confusion. "I just noticed Buddy's gone. Honestly, don't tell me that little pipsqueak walked off and left you, Syl."

"So you're saying you *weren't* party to our dear mother dismissing my date? She strong-armed Joel into serving as my chauffeur. I figured it was a conspiracy setup by the three of you. I'm actually relieved to discover that my sisters draw a line somewhere in their insane attempt to throw me at any unsuspecting man who has the misfortune of setting foot in Briarwood."

"Sylvie!" Dory burst out. "You're giving Joel a false opinion of your family."

"Oh, I don't think so," Sylvie shot back. "I like Joel. He's a nice man. He's so nice, Dory, he can't fathom the lengths to which my family is willing to go."

"We love you, Syl," Dory responded, spontaneously hugging Sylvie.

"I know." Tears springing to her eyes, Sylvie accepted the gesture. "But, Dory, love means letting a sister muddle along on her own."

"Even if you're making a giant mistake? You're missing out. You should be happily starting your own family," Dory wailed, not releasing Sylvie as she tried to pull away.

"Even if," Sylvie murmured.

Dory's husband, who'd rounded up his son and daughter, sauntered over to where Joel stood apart from the women. "Are they making up after another sisterly spat?"

Nodding, Joel slid an arm around Rianne, who'd skipped up, vainly attempting to hide a yawn.

Grant extended a hand to Joel. "Grant Hopewell. I saw you leaning out your upstairs window the day I repaired the fence you share with my sister-in-law. Rob just told me he recruited you for our Labor Day baseball game. I hope you can play second base. It's a key role against those heavy-hitting Baptists. If Jeff shows up at all, his mind won't be on the game, but on Carline and the baby. He alternates between second base and shortstop. To tell you the truth, our infield's pathetic. Outside of Jeff, we don't have a player who can catch worth spit."

"*Now* you tell me. I should've checked out the Baptists. So you're saying, as ballplayers go, the Methodists stink? Your father-in-law wasn't quite as forthright."

"Well, we have a lot of old geezers. They formed this team ages ago. The younger men can't really kick them off. What can I say—other than that Methodists have incredible longevity?" He grinned. "I consider that a plus. And it *is* only a game."

"But I sense that winning's important." A mischievous light entered Joel's eyes. "Seeing how pious you all are, I doubt you'd consider bringing in a ringer."

Grant glanced toward the women and drew Joel aside. "Who do you have in mind?"

"I've got a good friend, a former frat brother, who plays for the Atlanta Braves farm team."

A schoolboy grin lit Grant Hopewell's face. "Wouldn't I love to pull that off."

"Love to what?" Sylvie asked, walking up to the men. Her sister, too, walked over. Dory swung her son up into her arms.

"Oh, nothing," Grant inserted quickly. "We were discussing the Labor Day weekend. I'll get back to you, Joel, if I may?"

"Sure, no problem. I'm usually home day or night."

Dory, who swayed with her sleepy son, smoothly asked, "So you work at home, Joel? What kind of work do you do?"

Rianne flung back her head. "Daddy draws pictures and puts them on the 'puter," she said, punctuating that statement with another huge yawn.

Because Joel didn't want to get into the specifics, especially now, he lifted her into his arms. "Sorry to break this up, but it appears we've both got tired kids. Time to take them home. I've stayed far longer than I originally planned."

"Mom's fault," Sylvie noted sourly. "But thanks, Joel. If you hadn't stuck around, Grant and Dory would've had to drive out of their way to take me home. They live on the opposite side of town."

"I'm happy to do it," Joel said, lowering his voice because he saw that Rianne had already fallen asleep on his shoulder.

Talk fell off then. Grant hoisted Kendra into his arms, and the four adults shut off the lights. Dory and Grant didn't wait while Sylvie locked the building, but headed for their car immediately.

"They're nice people," Joel murmured, turning to Sylvie as they navigated the dark steps. "If I didn't have my arms full, I'd offer to carry your dress and those two boxes. I hope they're nowhere near as heavy as Rianne. She's fifty pounds of dead weight when she zonks out like this."

"I've draped the dress bag over one arm. And the boxes don't weigh much at all. Rianne seemed to enjoy herself. I saw her with the Martin twins. Another time she was deep in conversation with Holly Johnson and her sister. They're good kids. It's lucky Rianne's not shy."

"No, she's not that." Joel uttered a chuckle that was half despair. "Her mother climbed all over me before we moved here. Lynn thinks kids should be seen and not heard." Joel buckled Rianne into her booster and propped her head on a neck pillow before he gently closed the door. "Lynn, my ex, is a former foreign correspondent recently promoted to TV news anchor. The station threw her a party to celebrate. To make a long story short, she got mad at me for letting Rianne wear jeans to her party. She also said that I let her interact too freely with adults. But I didn't happen to have any friends who had kids."

Taking Sylvie's load, Joel set her boxes on the floor by the middle row of seats, hung her dress on the hook, then held Sylvie's door. He continued to speak after climbing in himself and starting the car. "You asked earlier why I changed my mind and came to the wedding of people I didn't know. It's because your sister said there'd be other kids. I want Rianne to make friends."

"I had no right to take you to task." Sylvie averted her eyes. "I just get so tired of everyone trying to fix me up. Here's a good example—Mother sending my date home. I'm not upset. I'd rather ride with you than Buddy, but—"

"That's a relief," Joel cut in. "I'm afraid I agree with your dad. Buddy's a weird dude. Tell me he has another name. That his parents didn't name him Buddy."

"Jarvis the fourth." Sylvie leaned back against the headrest. "I feel sorry for Buddy. His mother is a control freak, and his dad thinks money fixes everything."

"I guess that explains a lot," Joel muttered. "He seems dedicated to his job. But if your dad's right, he's not all that good at it. Probably because he's obnoxious."

"I agree. Obnoxious *and* antisocial. I think that's his real problem. But I can say for sure I'm not the person to rehabilitate Buddy."

Joel tossed off a hearty laugh. So hearty, he glanced in the rearview mirror to see if he'd awakened Rianne. He hadn't. "Out of curiosity, why did you agree to go out with such a jerk?"

Sylvie rolled her head toward Joel. "Carline caught me at a weak moment."

"It appears you have a lot of those where your family's concerned."

"Sometimes it's easier to give in." She faced front again. "My family's great, don't get me wrong. Here I am, giving you a mistaken impression, just like Dory accused. They have this fatal flaw. They want everyone—friend or relative—to be half of a couple. A married couple."

Joel debated asking the next question, but decided what the heck. "You're against marriage? Isn't that hard, given your business?"

"It's a long story, and we're too near home for me to go into it. Suffice it to say, I don't want to date every unattached male they stumble across."

"Like Buddy, you mean? And the other guy your dad brought up. Mr. Mercedes."

"Chet." She sucked in a deep breath.

"Your dad didn't seem to get what you were saying, about Chet being gay."

Her eyes swung in Joel's direction. "I tried to get Dad to understand that Chet's not available without spelling it out. Chet's company services accounts in and around Briarwood. This is a conservative town. So are Chet's parents from the sound of it. I really don't want the poor man losing business on my account."

"Your secret, or rather his, is safe with me." Joel pressed a hand to his heart. "Obviously your family needs a lesson in screening prospects better."

She swung at his arm. "You love razzing me. Well, laugh now, neighbor. They have you in their sights. Prepare yourself to be inundated with invitations to their various homes—where I'll just happen to be invited separately but on the same nights. Oh, it won't stop there. Joel, you have no idea. I've seen Mom and her wedding vigilantes launch numerous campaigns to marry people off. And guess what? Those very people are all ensconced in wedded bliss. Most are either pushing baby carriages or preparing to buy them."

"Hey, are you familiar with insulation R factors?"

"Yes. Grant owns a construction firm. He's almost as enthusiastic over his field as Buddy is about the stock market."

"I possess an insulation factor stretching to infinity when it comes to people setting me up, Sylvie."

"Wow! Do R factors go to infinity? I think the most I've heard of is thirty."

"New methods let builders blow loose insulation to any depth these days." He flashed a grin, giving her time to digest that fact as he swung into her driveway. She came to life when his headlights reflected off her front window.

"So I can quit worrying about you?"

"Yep. I'm immune. Divorced dads are even more targeted by well-meaning friends than single women are, Sylvie."

She opened her car door and watched Joel leap out and hurry to assist her. It reiterated what she'd told Dory. Joel was nice. And with the exception of her dad and her sister's husbands, Sylvie hadn't met a lot of men who still opened car doors for women.

Joel also collected her dress and the boxes. Sylvie tried to take the lot, but he shook his head. "I'll carry them to the house for you. You didn't leave a porch light on. You'd better use my car lights to find your house key."

"The light by the front door is burned out. I keep forgetting to buy one. It's an odd size and I have to get it at a hardware store. I still have Oscar—hear him? I'm counting on burglars not wanting to go up against a dog with a bark as deep as his. If they knew what a soft touch he is, I wouldn't be so confident."

"I'm afraid after the brute knocked me in the lake, I can't agree he's soft."

"Well, he's rambunctious. Let me just grab hold of his collar, Joel, and we'll avoid the risk of having him knock either of us flat."

"Why don't you own a dog? I'd think a woman living alone this far out of town would want the protection." He waited on a lower step, keeping one eye on Rianne sleeping in the back seat as Sylvie unlocked her door and made a successful grab for Oscar's collar in spite of his leaping up to lick her face.

"I had a springer spaniel named Corky that I got as a pup. The few years I spent in New York City, my folks kept him. Otherwise we were inseparable. I know he died a happy old man, but it's hard for me to think of replacing him. I have a friend who has a springer due to whelp soon. I groom her dogs, and she's offered me pick of the litter. I may get one. I haven't decided." She indicated that Joel should set the boxes inside her door and hang the dress bag over a nearby chair.

"Sorry, I didn't mean to make you sad, Sylvie."

Sylvie nodded as she flicked on the hall light. "I know. Corky's been gone a while. I should get past it." She ran a hand through her hair. "It's more the fact that he died right before I moved home. I had a lot to deal with then, anyway, and his death was…the crowning blow."

Her eyes remained troubled. Remote. Joel wished he'd left well enough alone. Why had he ever mentioned her lack of a pet? "Will you be okay? I, uh, can't continue to let my car run with Rianne inside."

"Of course! I'll be fine. Really!" Sylvie patted Oscar's bobbing head. "Weddings…take a lot out of me. This one was doubly hard. Kay's my best friend. Her former mother-in-law turned Kay's first wedding into a circus. The man she married was a bigger jerk than…well, he humiliated her in so many ways. I wanted this day to make up for everything she'd endured. I think it came off okay. Didn't it?"

"I'm not a wedding expert," Joel mumbled. "But it was as nice or nicer than any wedding I've been to in Atlanta, some of them larger and probably more costly. There I go." He shook his head. "I've got no idea how much a wedding like this one costs."

Her mouth curved in a rosebud smile. "You're kind, anyway, for giving me that vote of confidence. I won't keep you any longer, Joel. Good night. I…do appreciate your staying to the bitter end."

She'd made it plain that she wanted him to leave, so Joel did. Before he did something really stupid—like kiss her. He had absolutely no reason in the world to kiss Sylvie Shea good-night. He'd been her taxi service, nothing more. So why did he have an overwhelming urge to take her in his arms?

Joel recognized that he wanted to wipe away some undefinable sorrow lingering in her big hazel eyes. He clenched his fists, then forced them to relax. As he turned, she stood, still framed in the doorway. They didn't exchange so much as a wave.

He refused to glance her way again, and instead concentrated on backing straight out of her drive until he could pull into his. Nor did he rush to unbuckle Rianne from her child seat. He lamented how the other day she'd asked him to get rid of the seat. Some states had a mandatory six-year or sixty-pound requirement regarding child safety seats; he hadn't checked North Carolina's. But in a week Rianne would meet the age requirement. His baby, a baby no more.

Joel pondered her imminent birthday. Even that didn't completely take his mind off the woman he'd just taken home. Sylvie was his likeliest source of addresses for the girls Rianne had met tonight. Tomorrow he'd order her cake and buy party invitations.

Mounting the steps to his porch, Joel called himself all kinds of a fool, but at the last minute he looked over at Sylvie's house. From this vantage point, a portion of her place was visible, including her front door. By now, of course, he was sure she'd gone inside. But, no. She'd waited, apparently until he'd given in to a masculine need to look back. Slowly, she lifted a hand. He'd hardly call it a wave. More of a see-you-later gesture. After that, she hastily yanked Oscar inside and closed them both off from Joel's view.

He was pleased but also disgruntled to think he'd acted so predictably. Flipping on the living room lights, he carried his daughter up to her room.

Rianne roused when he placed her on the bed and rummaged for her nightgown. Behind him she said in a sleepy voice, "I love weddings, Daddy. Tonight I had the most fun ever. Did you know Kendra says Sylvie is her *auntie?* Auntie Sylvie, she calls her." The girl pronounced the *au* as *ah.* "Kendra has lots of aunties. Do I?"

"No. I have no sisters. Neither does your mom, snooks. You don't have uncles, either." He just didn't consider his father's other son a relative. "Mom and I are only children." He helped Rianne remove her nice dress. As he hung it up in the closet, she dove into the nightie. Her hair ribbons had already fallen out somewhere along the way. Maybe Freda Poulson wasn't an authority on bows, after all.

"Kendra's Auntie Carline is gonna have a baby. Sylvie's taking Kendra to buy the baby a present tomorrow. Kendra asked me to go, too. Will that be okay? And will you give me money to buy the baby something?"

Joel tucked her in and smoothed back her flyaway hair. "Did Sylvie invite you to go along, or was this Kendra's idea?"

Rianne pouted a bit. "Kendra's. But I *want* to get the baby something. They know it's a boy and his name is gonna be Keenan Jeffery Manchester. Kendra gets to hold him after he's born. She said maybe sometime I can hold him." Rianne started to cry. "But prob'ly not if I don't buy him a present."

Joel didn't know how their conversation had disintegrated so fast. "I never said you couldn't buy the baby a gift. Sweetheart, Kendra shouldn't make an offer like that without first asking her mother or her Aunt Sylvie."

"*Auntie,* Daddy. You didn't say it right."

"Excuse me. It's late, baby. Go to sleep now. I'll ask Sylvie tomorrow if it's a real shopping trip. Otherwise, you and I will go and shop for party invitations. Who has a birthday coming up soon?"

"Me! Oh, Daddy, can I have a party? I want to invite Kendra, Nikki, Nola, Holly and maybe Ashleigh. But she's in third grade, so maybe she won't wanna come."

"Tomorrow. We'll talk tomorrow." Joel blew raspberries against her neck and kissed her forehead. "G'night. Sleep tight." He left the room, taking care to keep the door ajar so she could see a bathroom light. It was a pact they'd made at the time of the move.

Joel went straight from there to his office. The first e-mail he opened was from his editor. Les liked the idea of the new character, and the sample strips Joel had e-mailed. He said he'd start running the strip immediately, and further promised a contract by overnight express. He wanted enough strips to run for twenty-six weeks.

Now Joel worried whether he had enough material. He pulled up the previous attachment to take another look at the

frames he'd already sent in. Two weeks' worth, and he liked
to stay four weeks ahead of production.

His phone rang. Late as it was, Joel walked over to check
the readout. He was surprised to see his neighbor's name. *Was
something wrong at Sylvie's?*

Heart tripping faster, he snatched up the receiver on the
fourth ring. "Sylvie? What's wrong? Do you need anything?"

Following a lengthy pause, she said, "For a minute I
thought you were psychic. Then I realized you must have caller I.D."

"Yes. So, you're okay?"

"I am. I found a message on my answering machine from
Dory. On the way home, Kendra told her mom she'd invited
Rianne to go baby-gift shopping with us. Did Rianne happen
to bring it up, or is this Kendra's pipe dream?"

"Rianne did tell me. She's unbelievably excited. I kinda
figured the girls concocted this idea on their own."

"Well, I'd love for Rianne to join us. Dory's leaving Roy
with our folks. She and I planned to take Kendra to hit the
bigger stores in Asheville. But we'll be gone past lunch, into the afternoon. As well, I don't want you to think we'd expect her to buy Carline's baby a gift."

Joel thought how disappointed Rianne would be if he said
no. "You're sure it's all right with you and Dory? I mean, kids
have to learn they need to consult with adults before making
grandiose plans. As far as a baby gift goes, Rianne's dying to
buy a gift for this baby-to-be that already has a name."

"Carline and Jeff aren't anxious to greet their new son, or
anything." There was a smile in Sylvie's voice. "Joel, Kendra will be thrilled to have someone nearer her age on the trip.
She plays with the Martin twins a lot, but it's often two against
one. She spends a lot of time hanging out with adults, too. I
remember you said that about Rianne."

"What you said about the Martin twins jogged my mind.
Rianne's birthday is coming up soon. I hadn't planned on a

party or anything, but…based on her meeting so many kids at the wedding, would I be presumptuous in sending them invitations to a small gathering? It'll be Rianne's first party. In Atlanta, kids at her private preschool and kindergarten were scattered all over the city. Most of them were gone on a last family trip before the start of school, so we skipped doing a party. Her birthday's the week before Labor Day."

"Here in Briarwood she's in luck. Since most families are involved in the weekend festival, just about everyone's in town. And no, it's not out of line. Kids love parties. Plus, it'll be a great chance for you to meet the parents of her new friends."

"I'll make myself a note to get invitations mailed out tomorrow, if I could get the addresses from you."

"Sure. About tomorrow. Dory and I would like to be on the road by nine. She's driving and they'll pick me up. That's not too early for Rianne, is it? Oh, and let her wear shorts or pants. Comfortable stuff. Especially shoes."

"Nine is good. I'll have Rianne ready and see that she has money for a present and lunch. Her teachers always told me she's a good kid on school outings, so I assume she'll be fine. I'll give you my cell number in case you need to reach me. Not that I expect any problems." He paused. "With a day to myself, I may see if I can buy, wrap and hide her birthday gifts. In the morning, could I trouble you for those addresses—the Martin twins and Holly…somebody. I don't recall anyone else."

"There were two boys." Sylvie named them. "Nice families. But maybe you're against co-ed parties."

"No. Include them. I'm not the world's best party-planner. Your dad said the bakery in town makes superb cakes. I thought I'd order one, and lay in a store of ice cream. I suppose I need a game or two."

Sylvie heard his apprehension. "Joel, if you'd like, I'd be happy to help with the party." The minute the words left Sylvie's mouth, she wished she could take them back. Where was her head? Helping him throw his daughter's party was precisely the type of thing that would feed gossip. In fact, she could vividly imagine her family's reaction.

"If you have any ideas for games, Sylvie, I'll owe you almost as much as I do for pulling me out of the lake. No…I shouldn't joke about that. Every time I recall how close I came to drowning…"

"Don't think about it. The accident happened because of Oscar. By the way, you'll be happy to hear I had a second message on my machine. His owners are back in town. They're picking him up early tomorrow morning."

Joel planned to draw Oscar into his script. He had several scenes in mind. "He's not so bad, I guess" Joel admitted. "Oscar kinda grows on you. I know you'll miss him."

She sighed. "I'll probably have to take one of those spaniel pups. I shouldn't confess that I talk to a dog, but Oscar's been great company. The house doesn't feel half so lonely when he's around."

Joel didn't want to picture Sylvie feeling lonely. He knew what she meant, though. When Lynn walked out, Rianne had been a baby, but he talked to her as if she understood. He told her about his work. Sometimes he'd just needed to hear his own voice. Yes, Joel was familiar with the loneliness Sylvie mentioned.

"Uh, Sylvie, I hate to cut you off, but I need to get some work time in. I'd just booted up my computer when you phoned."

"Oh. It is late. I have a row of seed pearls and some faux diamonds to sew on a dress. Sorry I disturbed you. Bye."

The phone clicked in the middle of his farewell. Man, he hoped he hadn't hurt her feelings. What dress? He didn't know much about it, but weren't those seed things used to trim wedding gowns? Joel's fertile mind immediately conjured up the secret dress. But just because Sylvie planned to sew on pearls and phony diamonds, didn't mean it was *that* dress.

What if it was, though? What if she worked on it whenever she felt sad and lonely? That would be perfect for Magnolia. Joel had first thought he'd give her a finished gown to drag around. But maybe one in progress would touch readers more. Hell, it touched him as he imagined Sylvie feeling lonely. *Maybe he shouldn't use her as a model.*

Sylvie wasn't exactly the way he envisioned his character. With her charm and energy, Sylvie was a focus of attention, and she knew everyone in Briarwood. Yet, Joel had picked up on a certain nuance in her voice tonight. What if a different woman lurked below the surface of all that vitality? A sensitive, more tentative woman?

Damn, he didn't want to think about that, either. And Magnolia wasn't really Sylvie. She was a composite of any number of single women, as were Rose and Poppy.

He told himself it was coincidence that Sylvie came to mind as he sketched situations involving Magnolia's arrival in the big city. Sylvie's parents were fixtures in Briarwood. Maybe he'd give Magnolia's parents a summer cottage on the outskirts of Atlanta—they'd be in a good position to stir the pot occasionally. Unhappy with their meddling in her life, Magnolia moves bag and baggage in with her cousins. *Perfect.* The secret dress consumes half of her dinky closet. Joel sketched a frame in which Magnolia feverishly sewed on the dress one night while her cousins slept.

An hour or so before dawn, he e-mailed six weeks' worth of strips.

When his machine confirmed that the last one had safely arrived, Joel stretched and yawned. He needed to find out more about Sylvie's dress. Not that Magnolia's would be like Sylvie's mysterious gown, of course.

Anyway, Sylvie had her head screwed on straight. She didn't need a man. Joel pictured Magnolia as more…vulnerable. The dialogue he chose for her would let readers know her protests were pure defense.

Joel wanted readers to see that deep down, Magnolia, like her cousins, dreamed of having a house in the burbs, a white picket fence and two-point-five children. Unlike Sylvie Shea, his characters all longed to be married. Magnolia, especially, ached for a husband.

Well, maybe "ached" was too melodramatic.

He was pleased with his night's work. However, he needed to get some information from the gossips in town about how *the* dress had come into existence, even though all the stories would be exaggerated out of all proportion. Somebody had probably fabricated the tale about a guy in New York dumping Sylvie. Who'd be such an idiot? In fact, hadn't Sylvie said she came back home when her Grandmother Shea died?

He was pretty sure she had.

Joel set his alarm for eight, then fell into bed. Better get some sleep. He dared not let Sylvie and Dory leave without Rianne. If he did, he'd never hear the end of it. Nor would he deserve to....

Chapter Nine

In the morning, Joel made the mistake of telling his daughter he'd confirmed her baby-gift shopping expedition with Sylvie, Dory and Kendra. Rianne shrieked with excitement. The girl was even more ecstatic to hear her trip wasn't just a matter of going to downtown Briarwood, but all the way to Asheville. Joel had difficulty getting her to sit down and eat breakfast. "Eat," he directed for the hundredth time, "or I'll change my mind."

She began to stuff her cheeks with pancake, all the while wiggling and kicking her feet. "Maybe I'll see school clothes to buy, too. Will you give Sylvie 'nuff money in case I do?"

"Snooks, I think Sylvie's got plenty to do. If you see something you really like, maybe Sylvie or Dory will jot down the name of the store. You and I can go back-to-school shopping another day."

"But we'll already be there. And some other girl might buy the dress before you take me back. 'Sides, Sylvie knows more about what little girls wear to school than you do, Daddy."

She had him there. "I'm sure that's true. However, school-shopping is a job for parents."

"Why?"

"Rianne, eat!"

"Ashleigh said moms hafta buy dresses for girls. 'Cause dads don't care if stuff looks nice or colors match. Like hair bows and socks and sweaters and—"

"All right," he broke in. "Who walked around the store the other day until we found a hair ribbon the exact shade of the dress you wore to the wedding? Not you, little miss. Your dad pointed out that the blue you first found clashed with the dress."

"Mommy looks nice on TV. Her colors always match. Do you think she might come and take me school-shopping?"

Joel almost dropped the spatula and the pancake he'd just lifted to flip. He'd shown Rianne plenty of pictures of Lynn. This was a new wrinkle. To his knowledge, it was the first time she'd ever asked to do anything with her mother. Awash in sudden panic, Joel floundered for a suitable response. Lynn hadn't returned his call when he left a message to let her know they'd arrived in Briarwood. She had his cell number, and he'd left their home number, too, specifically saying it was in case she wanted to contact Rianne.

If ever anyone was saved by a bell, Joel was. By the front doorbell. His watch said eight forty-five. He still needed to comb Rianne's hair and send her in to brush her teeth.

She ran to the door and returned with Sylvie in tow.

"Is my kitchen clock slow?" he asked. "I show we have fifteen minutes to spare."

"We do. Uh, I needed to catch you before Dory arrives."

Joel could see that Sylvie's thoughts were turned inward. "Rianne, scoot upstairs and brush your teeth. And do a good job, because I'm planning to check them. Bring your comb down, okay? And the yellow barrettes that go with the shirt you have on." Maybe he made that point to show he did have color sense.

"What's up?" he asked, collecting the dirty dishes from the table. "Is taking Rianne going to be a problem?"

"Oh, heavens, nothing of the sort." She bit her lip, then blurted, "Mother phoned this morning. She said Dad's calling a committee meeting for the Labor Day Festival. It's this evening. Hot dogs and chips at their house at five o'clock.

Mom suggested Dory and I come straight there from shopping. She also suggested you meet us there, so Rianne and I can switch from Dory's car to yours to ride home afterward."

"Sounds fine. What's the problem?"

"It's started, Joel. The finagling to throw us together. Did you mean it last night when you said you have a built-in immunity to being hustled toward the altar?"

She looked so genuinely upset, Joel tried to take her seriously. Really, he thought her folks were probably just being nice in including him. "Sylvie, did you ever stop to think that if you resisted less, they might give up faster? Sometimes the fun for matchmakers is more about the challenge. If you play along, suddenly their challenge is gone, and they move on to someone who provides a greater test of their ability."

He read total disbelief in her eyes. "Trust me," he said.

"I don't know. I haven't put up a lot of resistance in the past. I can't seem to tell them no, so I go out with the guys they dredge up."

"Have you dated one of these guys more than once?"

"Sometimes. Until it's obvious we're both miserable."

"But I heard you arguing with Dory. I'm telling you, don't do that."

Rianne thundered down the stairs, Fluffy slinking along behind her. "Daddy, does Fluffy have water in her bowl? She was in the bathroom sink."

Sylvie laughed. "The porcelain in the sink is cool. That's a common thing cats do when the humidity gets this high."

"You're smart," Rianne said happily. "Sylvie, will you put my hair in braids? The way you fixed yours that day at the lake?"

Sylvie took the brush and asked Rianne to sit in the chair. She made such short work of fashioning two braids, Joel watched in silent admiration.

"Daddy, did you ask Sylvie if she minded helping me pick out some school clothes today?"

"No, Rianne. I thought we settled that issue. If you see

something you like, I said maybe Sylvie will write down the name of the store. I'll take you back another day."

"But, Dadd…eee!" Rianne's lower lip protruded a mile, and she flounced out of her chair.

"It wouldn't be any trouble, Joel," Sylvie remarked when Rianne was making the journey back up to her room to return the comb and pick up a sweater in case it got chilly later at the committee hot dog fest. "We'll be in the baby departments of clothing stores and they're adjacent to departments carrying her size. Dory may want to buy some stuff for Kendra. She goes to kindergarten this year."

Joel dug out his wallet. "I'm not going to object if do you run across something. One of the hardest things to do when you're a single dad is buying clothes. I can't go into her dressing room if she needs help. And yet, when I see some of today's teens at the malls, I'm sure I'll do a better job of helping her choose stuff that's appropriate."

Sylvie glanced at the ceiling and hummed.

"What? I see skepticism written all over you."

"Well, fortunately you have six years or so until she's a teen. I suppose you can burn candles and pray in the interim that the fads change." She smiled. "Briarwood is conservative compared to New York. I lived and worked in the garment district, and I can tell you that designers sit in coffee houses and dream up wild, outlandish fads to set the fashion world on its ear. Who's most susceptible to buying the rage of the age? Pre-teens and teens, that's who. Believe it or not, they have the most discretionary money to spend, at least according to surveys."

"It's a parent's job to set limits."

"Make that *try* to set limits. Show me a parent who doesn't want his or her kid to fit in. I remember my mom complaining about the gross things Carline's crowd all had to have. In the end Mom said a few items of silly clothing were the lesser battles."

"You're the third person in the last few days to give me a reality check about the teen years—the school secretary, the librarian and your sister, Dory." Joel turned as Rianne skipped into the room. She looked so sweet and wholesome in her blue shorts, yellow T-shirt and twin pigtails. A car horn honked outside, and Sylvie said it was her sister.

Joel hugged Rianne. He issued the standard lecture about being good and minding her manners. Part of him wanted to scoop her up and lock all doors and windows against the inevitable growing-up process.

"Catch you again at five o'clock. Before I forget, here are the addresses you wanted. Shoot, I forgot to write down my parents' address, Joel. Oh, it's in the phone book. In two places. Under Rob Shea and again under Briarwood's mayor."

"I'll find it. Have a good time. I did list my phone numbers. I gave it to you along with the cash."

"Right. And Joel," Sylvie said with a mischievous smile. "Take heart. We won't be bringing home any leather or Goth outfits."

That promise sounded so ridiculous it restored his good mood. Joel stepped out on the porch and waved to Dory. Kendra and Rianne had already met at the entry to his lane, skipping and chattering excitedly.

Joel was slow to close his door, choosing to linger in the opening until Dory's car disappeared. It crossed his mind that Lynn's career couldn't hold a match to everything she was missing in not seeing these milestones in her daughter's life.

DORY HAD BARELY driven off when she nudged Sylvie in the ribs. "I'm surprised to see you coming out of Joel's house instead of yours, big sister. What gives?"

"As if you don't know about Mother's trumped-up festival committee meeting this evening. I went over to deliver the invitation in person. Anyway, I knew he'd probably want me to carry Rianne's money today."

"Is he going to the meeting? What is it he actually does for a living, Sylvie?"

Sylvie knew she'd have a hard time revising her opposition to her family's unabashed probing, as Joel had suggested. "He's going to the meeting. I haven't the foggiest idea what his job is, Dory. He works nights. Maybe he makes book, for all I know."

"Is he paying a lot of alimony?"

"Dory, for pity's sake!" Sylvie darted a glance over her shoulder at the girls talking and giggling in the back seat.

"Words like alimony go right over their sweet little heads, Syl. Maybe Dad will find out today. He's going to run over to Joel's to see if he wants to fish for a while this afternoon."

Sylvie sank back in the seat. From experience she recognized that there was no putting brakes on the Shea machine once it got rolling. Maybe she should sit back and see if R-to-infinity insulation was as powerful as Joel claimed.

"No comment to that?" Dory inquired.

"What's to say? Who'd listen if I objected? Besides, Joel's a big boy. I trust he's not going to get drawn into anything he doesn't want to do."

"Oh-ho, do I detect a difference in your attitude, big sister?" Dory half snickered. "Does that mean you're the tiniest bit interested in him, Sylvie?"

"What were you planning to buy Carline's baby?"

"Quit trying to change the subject. You always argue when anyone in the family messes with your love life. When you stop, it means something's up."

"That's rich. I have no love life, Dory. And you know what's funny? He's the first guy you've shoved in my path who has a built-in obstacle. A kid," she said, lowering her voice. "You're the one who's forever saying that kids have a way of putting the skids on your love life."

Her sister remained quiet for so long, Sylvie decided she'd scored a point. "Baby gift," she prodded, satisfied with her success. "Jeff hasn't left much for us to buy, has he? Outside of a cradle—which Dad's carving for them like he did for you and Grant—there's not a whole lot they need other than clothes. And even that's iffy."

"I thought a nice handmade quilt. The craft shops in Asheville ought to have some beauties."

"Oh. So, you're not planning to shop in the big department stores?"

"I'd want a gift that's one of a kind. We can go to a mall if there's something you need. We have all day. Or most of it, anyway."

"Rianne asked if I'd help her find a few outfits for school. Joel forked over enough money to buy her a whole wardrobe."

"He did? Wow. That's significant."

"How, Dory? His child expressed interest in looking for school clothes. We're going to a town where there's more choice. He's not. And guys dislike shopping, while women love to poke around. Don't make more of it than that."

"Okay, okay. But it goes to show how much he needs a wife."

Sylvie nearly took a chunk out of her tongue, she bit it so hard to keep from exploding at her sister with the one-track mind. Sylvie decided not to ask Dory for any game suggestions for Rianne's birthday party. Imagine what a mountain she'd make out of *that* molehill.

JOEL CLEANED UP the kitchen after the women and kids had departed. He drove into town and bought the few toys he knew Rianne wanted. A kind clerk took pity on him and wrapped the gifts. That was a bonus. He didn't wrap gifts any better than he tied hair ribbons.

From the store he headed for coffee at the café. This time, instead of going to a booth, he sat at the counter. These were folks who'd worked with Sylvie when she went to high school. And after she'd returned from New York. If anyone had the lowdown on *the* dress, he figured they might.

Three coffees later, he left in disappointment. The conversation was easy to work around to Sylvie and her incredible talent with needle and thread. An iron-haired waitress, the most talkative, said flatly, "If anybody knows how Sylvie came to have one dress left from an entire collection we all know she spent years dreaming up, I don't know who it'd be. No one in her family. Or if they do, they haven't spilled the beans in five years."

"Are you saying she's worked on one dress that long?" Joel assumed he looked as stunned as he felt.

The woman scowled and scrubbed the counter until it shone. "You seem like a smart fella to me. Ask yourself why a sweet girl with Sylvie's talent would suddenly up and leave the hub of her industry, and come back to bury her light under a bushel in her hometown?"

"A man, I suppose," he said, hoping to coax out more details.

"Yes, we all think she got her heart broke."

"Personally or professionally?" Joel murmured, then experienced jab of guilt for prying.

"If you knew our Sylvie, it's pretty much one and the same thing." The waitress clammed up then as the lunch crowd began to file in.

Joel dropped his money on the counter and went to buy party invitations and paint. Then he ordered Rianne's cake. All the way home, he considered other possible reasons for Sylvie's actions. He had a good imagination, so he decided it'd probably be better if he didn't know the truth; his own version might well be more interesting. Not that there was a snowball's chance in hell anyone in Briarwood would ever see his comic strip. And if they did, he doubted they could connect him to the scrawled *J. Mercer* near the bottom of the last frame. He'd worried about being found out when he'd first begun collecting data in Atlanta's nightspots. He'd been afraid that people who saw him hanging around singles bars might accuse him of exploiting them. No one ever did. Readers never seemed to link cartoons to real-life situations.

He swung into his lane and stopped behind a green pick-up truck. To say he was surprised to see Rob Shea crawl out from behind the wheel was an understatement.

"There you are, young fella." Rob tugged on an earlobe. "I was fixin' to leave. Earlier I got to thinking maybe you'd be at loose ends with your little girl off to the city with my daughters. Wondered if you had time for a little fishing. Tell you the truth, after we talked at the wedding, I've had a hankering for it. I guess I mentioned I haven't done much fishing since my dad died."

"Just let me grab a pole. I bought some paint for a couple of bedrooms after I shopped for Rianne's birthday gifts. Fishing sounds a whole lot more enjoyable than moving furniture and getting out a paint roller."

"I knew you were a man after my own heart. Here, let me give you a hand hauling that stuff into the house."

Joel handed Rob a light sack of presents. He picked up all four gallons of paint. A courier's envelope was stuck inside his screen, and he set it on the hall credenza, knowing it was his contract. "Do you have a pole?" he asked the older man after he'd run upstairs to hide the gifts.

"Sure do. In my truck. Hand-tied flies, too. And beer. I'll get my stuff and meet you on the trail."

Joel dug out his pole and grabbed an ice chest for storing fish. They met at the fork in the path. Talk ceased as they strode side by side through dappled sunlight. Both men chose spots to sit on the dock. Their hooks were baited, and each had an open beer at his side when Rob cleared his throat. "Got a call this morning from Orville Thatcher. He's our baseball team's third baseman. Orville's arthritis is acting up bad. Claims he can't play in our Labor Day game. My son-in-law Grant mentioned you might have a friend from down south, willing to fill in."

Waiting for Rob to ask more about his friend, Joel was surprised when that seemed to be the extent of the older man's speech. "Uh, sure. I'll give my buddy a call when I get home. Can I let you know at the meeting tonight if he's free to drive up here? Did Grant tell you—"

"Don't wanna know any particulars, Joel. Any friend of yours is okay with me. I'm taking your word, understand, that he knows which end of a bat is which."

"I'll vouch for that," Joel said, stifling a grin. So that was how a staunch Methodist got around the thou-shalt-nots? The subject was dropped.

Joel asked about Rob's work. His handmade furniture and fishing was all they talked about for the better part of two hours, until they put their catch in the cooler and headed up the path. "That was pure relaxation," Rob said, sliding the parts of his pole into a bamboo container he'd left in his truck.

"You take this string of fish, Rob. I'm sure someone in your family's better at cooking them than me."

"That's right nice of you, son. Oh, and tonight at the meeting, I see no need to say anything about your friend to the group. If he shows up to visit you over the holiday, it'll just be the neighborly thing to let him play on the team. Anything else stays in the family."

Rob was long gone before his words fully sank in. Joel had to say Rob Shea was a sneaky bastard who played hardball in more fields than a ball diamond. Calling him *son,* tacitly suggesting he was part of the Shea brood, referring to family…

He phoned Brett Lewis and delivered his request before he got busy filling out the invitations to Rianne's party, all the while mentally shaking his head.

Joel arrived at the Shea home a few minutes after five, not knowing what to expect. A tightening in his gut loosened the instant he spotted Dory's car parked in the wide drive—because it meant Rianne was back.

The house itself was probably fifty years old, but immaculately kept. Joel thought the four upper dormers with their slate-blue shutters added a homey effect. He wondered what effect colored shutters would have at his place, and made note to check into it.

Rianne launched herself at him seconds after Nan Shea answered his knock. "Daddy, Daddy! I got four pretty dresses, and socks to match. And…and new jeans and two shirts. And I picked out the cutest baby shirt and pants all by myself. Auntie Dory called it an outfit. Come see. Kendra's Grandma Nan's been 'specting all our stuff. She said we're some good bargain shoppers. Me and Kendra, she meant." In a hushed tone, Rianne pulled Joel's head down. "She said I can call her Grandma Nan. Is that okay, Daddy? Kendra said she'll share, 'cause when the baby gets here, he'll call her Grandma Nan, too."

Doing his best to take everything in, Joel let Rianne waltz him around in a dizzying circle. "Whoa! Let's start with looking at what you bought. We'll work through the remainder of your list from there."

He saw Sylvie across the room. The indulgent smile she wore had the tension drawing his stomach tight again.

In the center of a group of mostly older women, Sylvie stood out like a vibrant long-stemmed rose in a patch of fading blooms. She caught him watching her, excused herself and hurried over to his side.

"Hi. Glad you found us. Are you on your way to see Rianne's purchases?"

"I'd better, otherwise I don't think I'll have a moment's peace."

Sylvie led him to a back bedroom, her mom's guest room, where she said the clothes were laid. "While Rianne gives you the fashion show, I'll go commandeer you a drink. What'll you have?"

"A soft drink. Cola or root beer is fine. You seem none the worse for wear after a day of being dragged around the big city by this shopping machine." He yanked Rianne's braid, a single plait down her back now, different from the two she'd left with this morning.

"Hurry, Daddy! And let go of my hair. Sylvie French-braided my hair and Kendra's 'xactly alike. Auntie Carline says we're some kinda cool. Oops," Rianne clapped a hand over her mouth. "Well, she *said* we could both call her Auntie."

Sylvie laughed. "Oh, for their boundless energy. Show your dad the dresses before you burst with excitement, Rianne."

Joel noticed that Sylvie slipped out, but returned to hand him a soda. Then she huddled anxiously near the door. "Come on in," he said. "You remind me of somebody about to take flight."

"Do you like the clothes?" Digging through her jeans pockets, Sylvie eventually pulled out a wad of cash. "This is all that's left of the money you gave me. I hope we didn't overspend. They're all really cute on her, and they're well-made."

"Hey, you did great. I'm amazed you got all of this and had money left." He took the bills and their fingers touched. Pleasantly, Joel thought. She had nice hands for someone who didn't pamper them, but worked with a needle every day.

Sylvie apparently didn't share his reaction, based on the speed with which she withdrew.

"So, you're saying you think we did okay?"

"Sylvie, quit fretting. Rianne's happy, aren't you, kiddo?"

The girl nodded vigorously, holding up first one treasure, then doing the same with the next.

"Her happiness is all that matters to me," Joel said, again tweaking the end of Rianne's braid. She pulled free of his fingers and flung an arm around Sylvie and another around Joel.

"See, Sylvie? I knew Daddy would love everything."

Nan Shea poked her head into the room. "Here's where you all are. Grant's finally here. Rob's throwing hot dogs on the grill as we speak. Everybody's breaking out into their committees, Sylvie. Oh, and Kendra's looking for you, Rianne, honey. Kendra's dad swung by their house. He brought

Kendra's doll case, and she wants to show you some of the dresses Auntie Sylvie sewed for her Barbie."

Rianne squealed and tore out of the room, leaving Joel and Sylvie standing close together at one end of the big bed. "Should I make her come back and fold these dresses into their bags?" Joel asked.

"I'll fold them," Nan, said, shooing the couple out the door. "Sylvie, introduce Joel around. Be advised, Joel... Harv Jensen's going to ask if you'll judge floats at the parade. Be firm in telling him no if you'd rather not. Harv's a high-powered salesman. He gets pushy, but we're all used to him by now."

"Judge floats?" Joel whispered to Sylvie as he followed her from the room. "What's that about?"

"The parade. They're home-built, anything from kids decorating their doll buggies to the school teams constructing elaborate floats they'll use at the homecoming game. We have categories." She covered her mouth and murmured near his ear. "Everybody ends up with a ribbon. The judging's all in the spirit of fun, and I'm surprised the kids never seem to catch on. Fun's the aim of the whole festival."

As they stepped through the back door onto the Shea's massive, extremely comfortable patio, a breeze whipped a loose lock of Sylvie's hair across her cheek, where it caught on her upper lip. Joel slid a finger under the strand and made three attempts to dislodge the fine hair. She blushed, and then they both laughed at his effort.

A very pregnant Carline waddled out the door, and saw them with their heads together. "Okay, you two. Break it up," she teased. Her voice carried loudly enough so that many of the people already seated at tables stopped talking to check out the commotion.

The interest they garnered did not please Sylvie.

Joel, who'd gone at once to get a cushioned chair for Carline, missed all the interest.

Carline's husband, Jeff, walked over, and thanked Joel for helping his wife.

Sylvie used that opportunity to begin Joel's introductions. She deftly maneuvered him around the whole patio, trying to keep a circumspect distance between them. Soon, Joel's head spun as he struggled to keep all the names straight. "I hope there's no test later in the evening," he joked with an elderly man whose name tag said Jaime Blodgett—pronounced Hymee, Joel learned.

Sylvie moved on to the next committee chairman, but as Blodgett continued talking and seemed hard of hearing, to boot, Joel draped his arm casually over Sylvie's shoulder. He drew her against him, and pinned her to his side.

She tried twice to escape. "What are you trying to do?" she demanded in an undertone when it became clear Joel wasn't budging.

"I don't want you cutting me adrift in this crowd. Your mom said I'm on your committee. I know if I keep you in sight, I'll eventually find out what's expected of me Labor Day weekend. Lose you, and who knows how many chores I'll end up inadvertently agreeing to do."

Rob Shea gave a piercing whistle, and a production line began as people passed around paper plates heaped with chips, baked beans and hot dogs. People not already seated bickered jovially over favorite tables and chairs. Joel searched for Rianne and found her at a small table filled with kids. Her laughter reached him, and for a moment, contentment stole over Joel. It struck him just how very long it'd been since he'd felt like this.

The next thing he knew, Sylvie's warm, soft hand closed over his and pressed every so slightly. "Is something wrong?" she asked. "Do you need a condiment for your hot dog? Another drink? Tell me what, and I'll go nab it before we begin."

"No. There's nothing missing. As a matter of fact, I was sitting here thinking how very right everything is." Giving her a satisfied smile, Joel flipped his hand over and clasped hers more tightly. In the fading daylight that had begun to cast shadows through the big old maple trees, he moved their joined hands off the tabletop, to his knee, hidden from the sight of others by a colorful tablecloth.

Sylvie attempted to discreetly dislodge her fingers from his grasp. Her eagle-eyed mother missed so little, Sylvie really didn't want to draw attention to the fact that she and Joel Mercer were holding hands like a couple of teenagers. It seemed so juvenile in one way. But in another, she couldn't remember when such a simple act had felt so…so comfortable.

That might be the wrong word. Old shoes were comfortable. Favorite bras were comfortable. Was *comfortable* a good way to describe stingingly alert nerve endings running from her fingertips to her palm, and out to every major pulse point in her body? How long, she worried, until some astute person in her family noticed her trying to eat with her left hand?

Oddly, no one seemed to. People ate, drank and discussed the festival. At last, when Joel figured out he was wolfing down his baked beans, but Sylvie couldn't get hers to stay on her fork with her left hand, he untwined their fingers.

The meeting broke up too late for some, who complained about having to get up early for work the next day. And too soon for others, like Joel. He abandoned his seat reluctantly and sought his hosts.

"Rob, Nan. Thanks so much from Rianne and me for including us in a great evening. I have a clearer picture of what goes on during Labor Day weekend now. And you've treated Rianne to one of the best days of her life. This—" he waved an encompassing hand "—is everything I had in mind when I decided to move into my aunt's house. I wasn't sure I could recapture the sense of harmony I experienced when I came here as a lonely, confused kid. You've shown me tonight that it's possible."

"You may get bored with our slower pace." Nan hugged his arm as they wove through the tables toward where Sylvie and Dory, with Kendra and Rianne's help, were tossing paper plates into a huge garbage bag. "I've visited Atlanta. It's frenetic."

Joel heard more behind Nan Shea's statement than the words themselves implied. But he wasn't altogether sure what… "Get bored around vital, stimulating people like your family?" he teased. "Frankly, I don't see that happening anytime soon."

"Really?" Nan beamed.

Joel, who considered himself a past master at double-speak, waited for a punch line. None came. Instead, the girls dropped what they were doing and skipped up to hop around him. "Daddy, Kendra's mama 'vited me for a sleepover with Kendra tonight."

"Isn't that splendid?" Nan slipped in oh-so-casually. "Girls, I have extra chocolate chip cookies, potato chips and soft drinks you can take with you. For a midnight snack."

Joel sputtered a bit, feeling things suddenly swirling out of his control. "Tonight? Snooks, I don't know if that's a good idea. You've already had a full day. You don't have a nightgown, even, and it's quite a drive back home to get one."

"Kendra has lots of nightgowns," Rianne said. "Please, Daddy? Sylvie can pick me up in the morning. 'Cause she's going next door to Kendra's, where some woman's dog is having puppies. If they get born tomorrow, like Mrs. Wiley thinks, me'n Kendra get to see the puppies."

Sylvie and Dory both converged on Joel and began talking of one accord. Dory prevailed over her sister. "Joel, I said she had to get your permission to spend the night. And if the puppies are born, then they can go and see them *maybe*. If they're good. That's the deal."

Sylvie denied knowing the plan included a sleepover tonight. Dory tied the garbage bag and handed it to her husband, who'd just walked up. "There aren't many days left until school starts. Sleepovers are more scarce after that. Really, Joel, the girls are getting along so well."

Because they were displaying the kind of ties he'd envisioned Rianne forming here, Joel gave in. He gathered up his daughter's purchases, shook hands with Grant and Rob, and in about a minute, found himself alone in his van with Sylvie.

She buckled up. "My family engineered this," she said bluntly when they'd backed out of the Sheas' driveway.

"Engineered the festival meeting tonight? Don't worry. I enjoyed myself."

She snapped forward. "This!" Sylvie gestured between them. "Us. You and me driving home together. Without Rianne." Flinging herself against the seat, she crossed her arms in disgust. "Honestly, they are so transparent."

"So," he said slowly, as if he'd finally grasped her point. "What shall we should do about it?"

"Do?"

Joel hesitated briefly, and flexed his hands nervously around the steering wheel. "Well…it seems a darned shame for two adults to waste a perfectly good, carefully engineered kid-free night."

Sylvie gaped, but gnawed at her upper lip, saying nothing. She had to admit, however, that she had all sorts of thoughts running through her mind. And what her mind conjured up had her heart pumping blood lickety-split through her veins.

"Am I alone in thinking there are sparks flying between us, Sylvie? If I'm off base, say so, and the whole idea of spending an evening together will be forgotten."

"You're, uh, not alone." Her admission came out sounding squeaky.

He took one hand off the wheel and in the dark, found her cheek. He brushed it softly, then clasped her fidgeting fingers. "It's been a long time since I've felt attracted to anyone, Sylvie. What about you?"

"The same," she said, unable to meet his searching gaze.

"I believe you said there was a man who hurt you." Again he let silence engulf them. "Just thinking if you're still hung up on him, this probably isn't a good idea."

She bit her lower lip. "I—someone made a fool of me, Joel. Please…I've lived in the city, so I know that hooking up for…sex…is handled like a business transaction by some people. Basically, I'll always be a country girl."

"Well, now." He expelled a ragged breath. "I'm uncomfortable with what you called it—hooking up for sex. Just so you know, I don't do that, Sylvie. All I'm proposing is that we take advantage of my having a free evening. To get to know each other better. Hell, I like being around you. But you seem really prickly, like at times you'd rather not be in the same room with me." He broke off then, his voice letting him down with a gruff cough.

She burrowed into the seat again. A soft smile, one that wasn't the slightest bit forced, teased her lips. "You're a fine one to talk, Joel Mercer. We didn't exactly start off well, what with your cat and Oscar causing trouble. And I explained about the wedding vigilantes. I know, I know." She held up a hand. "You're immune—that R factor thing. However, if you like popcorn and old movies, I think we may actually have a place to start over."

Joel couldn't explain it if he tried, but all of a sudden he felt as if he'd dropped about ten years. He started to turn into Sylvie's driveway, then slammed on the brakes, backed up and pulled into his own lane. "I'll have you know I love popcorn, provided it's slathered in artery-hardening butter. And I'll stack my closet full of old movies against yours. I mean, when you're single in a big city and you have a kid, late-night movies become a way of life."

Laughter filled the interior of Joel's van. As they climbed from the vehicle, Sylvie said, "So, are we indulging in this movie fest at your house or mine?"

"Yours," he said, pocketing his keys to grab her hand.

"This short jaunt to my house is insurance. If your nosy family takes it upon themselves to do a drive-by," he said, sounding smug, "they'll see both cars in their proper spots. Who's to know where the drivers are?"

"Brilliant, Mr. Mercer. I'm definitely beginning to like the way you think."

Chapter Ten

"Give me a minute to close all the drapes," Sylvie said when they got inside. "Let my sisters speculate, if they do come by to check on us. It's something I can see Mom doing, frankly. Carline's probably too miserably pregnant. And Dory took the kids home, so it's pretty far for her. But I wouldn't put it past her to send Grant out for milk, and then make him promise to take the lo...ong way home. I guess you're beginning to see what I meant about my family, Joel."

He rattled change in his front pockets. "In spite of that, I like them. They care about you, Sylvie. Every last one. They're happy. Any fool can see they want the same for you. Your mom likes me, but she seems worried that I'll get bored living in Briarwood. She doesn't like me enough to have me start a relationship with you if I end up going back to the big city."

Sylvie just listened to what he had to say. Joel followed her into the kitchen, where she now emerged from the pantry with an electric corn popper. "Mom said all of that tonight?"

"She's subtle, yet at the same time, you get the picture. I've give Nan that. So, when's your sister's baby due? Your dad said something about Labor Day weekend? Did they plan that? A fitting time to schedule the arrival of a baby."

"Carline thinks she might go early. She had a lot of phantom pains tonight."

"My wife had those. Braxton-Hicks contractions, they told us."

"Was your divorce civilized, Joel? So many aren't." Sylvie plugged in the popper and passed Joel two unopened beers. "I assume you didn't drink at the barbecue since you were driving home," she said, turning to measure out oil and corn.

With a twist of the wrist, he wrenched off first one cap, then the other. "I guess you could say Lynn's and my divorce was civilized, although it came as a shock to me. Rianne was a baby. We were saving, or so I thought, for a house. Lynn worked as a junior reporter for a local news channel. She came home one night and over dinner announced she'd accepted a post as foreign correspondent—a stepping stone to bigger and better jobs. After I got past the initial blow, I asked about us. Me and Rianne." He took a swig and motioned with the bottle. "She pointed out that I'd wanted a baby. I wanted the house. She said she wanted more. More money. More excitement. More freedom."

Sylvie watched the steam bead inside the popper lid. "At least she didn't stab you in the back and run off with another man."

"Is that what happened to you?"

Sylvie didn't immediately speak. She tensed, then said curtly, "This popcorn will be done before you know it. My movies are stored in a glass-front cabinet on the east wall of my living room. Why don't you go see if there's something you like. Or at least can sit through. According to Grant and Jeff, men and women will never see eye to eye on what makes a good movie."

Figuring Sylvie didn't want to talk about herself, Joel headed into the other room.

"Holy cow! Okay, I take back everything I said about my movie supply competing with yours." She had her DVDs and videos alphabetized and neatly stored with the titles facing out. That was another difference between men and women. His collection was thrown in boxes without any order whatsoever.

Joel settled on a 1940s swashbuckler, *The Black Swan,* starring Tyrone Power and Maureen O'Hara. It was probably a grade B adventure-romance. But for now, it gave him reason not to go home to an empty house. He liked the idea of sitting on that couch with Sylvie. Maybe they'd even cuddle during the racy scenes, he thought, slipping the cover off the movie. Not that those scenes were likely to get too racy.

The smell of fresh popped corn filled the room as Sylvie entered carrying a large bowl. "Good, you found something, I see. Ah, and one I haven't watched in a while. Pop it in the player, and then come and share some of this while the butter's still hot." She dropped a stack of paper napkins on the center cushion of the corduroy-covered couch. As Joel sat, near enough to reach the bowl but not so close as to crowd Sylvie, he wondered if she'd covered the sofa herself. Other crafts scattered about the room contributed to a pleasingly warm atmosphere.

The initial credits rolled. Neither Sylvie nor Joel were squeamish about diving right into the buttery mix, to the point of batting at each other's hands. "Quit hogging," they accused almost in the same breath. After that, they both had the grace to look guilty, and ended up laughing as good friends might.

Joel spent as much time watching Sylvie enjoy her snack as he did on the movie.

"You chose this film," she finally muttered. "If you're staring at me hoping I'll get so self-conscious I'll hand you the whole bowl, forget it. My sisters tried that trick at the theater. I don't distract easily, Joel."

"Izzat so?" he drawled, studying her from sleep-lidded eyes as he inched nearer, not really having a plan to go farther. "It's a rare man who can resist a dare like that."

Sylvie stopped munching popcorn and swallowed hard. There was something about the glitter deep in his eyes that said he had more than stealing popcorn on his mind.

Joel didn't make any sudden moves, nor did he rush. He caught her hand, which had gone still holding two pieces of popcorn. Lifting her hand to his lips, he nibbled the kernels out of her fingers, then methodically licked salty butter off each fingertip.

A shaft of passion stabbed through her, connecting her tingling fingers with a quivering seizure in a wholly unrelated part of Sylvie's body. She didn't notice when Joel slipped the bowl off her lap and reached around her to set it on the lamp stand. A range of sensations seemed to paralyzed her. As if detached, Sylvie heard voices from the movie soundtrack. Swords clashed in the background. Having steeled herself for so long against any feelings of desire, Sylvie honestly believed she'd lost the capacity to suffer this sharp, immediate need that gripped her.

But she hadn't...

Joel felt the quiver that ran through her and excitement pumped through an out-of-practice body. He loved the effect his touch had on the woman he was with. It'd been so long, Joel actually feared he might have lost the ability to evoke such a response. So it was humbling and gratifying to feel Sylvie's lips soften beneath his. To watch her body become pliant, responsive...

She felt a hot flush sweep over her the minute Joel's fly pressed against her most sensitive spot. She wanted more than that erotic friction. She wanted oh, so much more. But with his kisses inflaming her addled brain, she felt powerless to do anything but *feel*.

And damn Joel Mercer—he was in no hurry to end her frustrations. In slow motion, it seemed, he dispensed with her blouse and his shirt. He didn't even rush to free her aching breasts. Rather, he nipped his way down one side of the V formed by her bra, and up the other. Her nipples throbbed, and Sylvie chased his lips, fusing them against hers.

During one steamy kiss, Joel unfastened her bra. Though he fumbled a bit, he helped her out of her capri pants. Necessity forced them to surface for air before he'd managed to do more than unsnap and unzip his slacks.

It crossed Sylvie's mind that she ought to suggest moving to her bed. But it became obvious that comfort wasn't high on either of their lists. They used precious minutes just determining that Joel had a couple of crushed but usable condoms tucked deep in his wallet. After that, giving each other pleasure took top priority. It'd been a long time since either of them had engaged in love-making, so when Sylvie began to rock her hips, he growled deep in his throat. He reversed their positions, settling her above him.

Being on top was a first for Sylvie. Touching him intimately, exploring his many textures, his shape, his hardness, filled her with a power like none she'd ever experienced. She gloried in knowing that she alone was responsible for Joel's arousal. *She* had the privilege and the means to bring them both incredible pleasure. The ultimate primal satisfaction crashed over her in waves.

Afterward, Joel couldn't move. Didn't want to move. He loved the feel of her pressed fully against him. When he was finally able to command his muscles, he lifted an arm and stroked Sylvie's smooth back.

Her answer was to kiss his chest. She realized that what she'd feared most about ever putting herself in this position again, in making herself vulnerable to another man, hadn't occurred. Sylvie knew Joel didn't love her, either, any more than Desmond had. But he'd made her feel cherished all the same. With Des, it'd always been about *his* pleasure. She could see that clearly now.

"Thank you," she whispered against Joel's hot skin.

"You stole my line," he said, rolling to the outside of the sofa, enough to slip a hand under her chin and tilt her head so he could see her eyes. It pleased him immensely to find them clear and free of any shame or recrimination.

"I suspect our popcorn has grown cold," she said, not sure exactly what was expected after such a cataclysmic coupling.

Laughter rumbled from Joel's stomach up through his

chest, shaking them both. "My ego will really be hurt if you point out that we missed the best part of the movie, too."

She raised herself and peered at the television, leaning her chin on his naked shoulder, "I don't know about the best part. I'd say we missed all of it."

Joel felt an erection building again, just from her casual touch. Kissing her hard, he murmured, "I wouldn't have thought I'd be able to suggest a repeat performance so soon. I'm willing, if you are, to call our last run-through a damned good dress rehearsal."

What surprised Sylvie most was that he didn't have to ask twice. "If you think we didn't get it right the last time." Her soft smile teased him.

"Oh, we got it right. But now we'll improve on perfection," he said, crushing her mouth with his.

Their second time was less rushed. They knew things about each other now that they'd had to guess at before. Ways to touch. Spots to linger on. They clung together for a long while afterward. Neither felt the need to budge or say a word.

When Sylvie did speak, it was lazily. "I'm sure glad I closed the drapes."

"I agree."

"Do you think tomorrow, when I go pick up the kids, that Dory or anyone will…figure it out?" She swung her legs over Joel's, and finger-combed her tangled hair with one hand, while reaching for her fallen shirt and pants with the other.

Joel sat up to give her more room. He studied her, a half smile lurking at the edges of his mouth. "If they walked in right this minute, the answer would be a definite yes."

Sylvie swatted him with her blouse. "That's a given, you dope. It's that…Dory has my mother's eyes. Eyes that can see right through you."

Easier with his nakedness than apparently was she with hers, Joel stood and stepped into his briefs and slacks. He couldn't say for sure how he'd divested them both of shoes.

Or how his loafers and her sandals got wedged so far under the couch. On his hands and knees, searching for them, he asked, "Does it matter that Dory knows? We're not kids, Sylvie. And this *is* the twenty-first century."

Dressed again, she crossed the room to hit the rewind button on the movie that had gone to waste.

Her obvious silence matched the pinched expression tightening her lips. Lips still swollen from his kisses.

Joel found her hesitation troubling. "I was going to suggest making more popcorn and letting you choose the next movie. But considering how long it's been since either of us engaged in the activity we just engaged in, I should probably amend that idea so you can go soak in a hot tub. Otherwise, tomorrow you may have aches and pains that are hard to hide. That could be a giveaway."

"I hadn't thought of that, Joel. You're right." All business now, she scooped up the bowl and the nearly full bottles of beer. "I could…uh…make coffee, if you'd like."

"What I'd like to do is spend the night," he said, pausing to skim his hand along the slope of her cheek. Withdrawing, he lightly rubbed the first shadow of a beard. "But since Rianne could call me at home at any time, we'd better hold off on that. At least until her next sleepover, when I have time to tell her to call my cell if she needs me."

"You, uh, want to do this again?" Sylvie asked, stopping at the kitchen door.

Shoving his hands in his pockets, Joel chewed on his upper lip for a moment. He fought a rush of heat creeping up his neck. "To be honest, yes. But if all you want is a one-night stand, I won't make a pest of myself."

"No…no," she rushed to say. "I…just never thought about down the road." Sounding panicky, she said, "Really, Joel, nothing's changed. Despite this evening. We can't let Dory, Carline or my mom see the slightest hint. I swear they'd have our church booked, flowers ordered and a minister on tap."

He turned after he'd disengaged the front door lock, deciding to throw caution to the winds. "If that's the case, shouldn't *I* be the one to worry? According to rumors, you're the one who has a secret wedding dress waiting for…what? The right man to come along?"

There was a look of shock in her eyes. "Who…said such a thing?"

He shrugged. "I don't recall. Several people in town. Is it true?"

"The dress they're talking about is no one's business, Joel. It's…just…not!" She was so flustered, Joel held up his hands, palms out, to deflect further discussion.

"Okay. Okay! Calm down. I've got no problem keeping our relationship a secret. I like you, and I think you like me. Whatever comes next, I'm fine with playing it by ear, if that's what you'd prefer."

"Yes. That'd be best all the way around, Joel. Tomorrow, we'll both go about our normal lives and see. Uh, good night."

He slipped out then, wondering at her sudden switch in—in what, exactly? She'd said all along that she didn't have marriage in mind. Jeez, neither did he. Or *did* he? No, they were just neighbors. Neither had made a commitment of any kind tonight.

Joel stomped down his lane and up onto his front porch. He didn't have the slightest idea why he was so bothered by something most men he knew would leap at. A pretty neighbor willing to engage in casual sex. But bother him it did.

Restless, yet filled with energy, Joel ended up pacing the floor in his office. If Sylvie didn't care to tell him the story of *the* dress, he'd make up his own version. That was better anyway. Magnolia wasn't Sylvie, and his strip was always a mix of truth and fiction.

Besides, Sylvie was someone he'd come to care for—a lot. God, when he saw her eyes tonight after he'd brought up that damned dress. Unguarded pain. Grief. Maybe the guy in New York had died. Death wasn't something he did in his strip.

He spent some time concocting a reason for Magnolia to be carting around a half-finished wedding dress. She was healing from inner wounds inflicted by a thoughtless lover—someone she'd trusted. Someone who'd left her for the clichéd other woman. Or maybe…the guy had used her in another way? What if he'd sponged off her? Off Magnolia's hard work as a dressmaker.

Rocking in his computer chair, Joel wracked his brain. What if the asshole had talked Magnolia into sewing a batch of wedding dresses, then sold them and pocketed the cash? Oh, yeah. Readers would be totally sympathetic. So, say this guy used the funds to elope with a real bimbo? His readers could relate to that, he'd bet.

Before he shut off his computer, turned out the light and meandered bleary-eyed to bed, Joel had scanned and e-mailed three-fourths of the strips his boss had asked for. As well, he signed the contract and got it ready to return by courier the next day.

SYLVIE DUMPED their uneaten popcorn, hand-washed and dried the glasses and bowl and generally tried to wipe out any sign that Joel had spent the evening there. She plumped the couch pillows on her way in to take a bath. Soaking until her hands and feet shriveled, Sylvie finally crawled out After donning her nightgown, she pulled the cover off her last masterpiece. The last of her dream collection. Tonight, she sat and stared at the half-finished garment and cried. This dress represented so much, including the most beautiful of her sketches. And yet there it stood, the symbol of her failure. She hated that even after so long, town gossips were still speculating about her humiliation.

She sobbed until she was drained. Until she fell asleep. These weren't the first tears she'd shed over Desmond Emerson's betrayal. *The spy. The thief.* Sylvie knew in her heart that she'd never heal until the memory of that last awful week in New York stopped making her cry.

She awakened to light, noise and a blinding headache. The dress sat in the corner of her bedroom in all its icy beauty. Yards of silk tulle in a long train sprigged with lacy appliquéd branches, and leaves studded with seed pears and faux diamonds guaranteed to sparkle as the bride walked down the aisle.

Once the previous night flooded back, Sylvie realized she'd ōverslept. What had awakened her, someone banging at the door? Grabbing a robe, Sylvie called, "Just a minute." She stopped long enough to zip the cover over the mocking gown.

Flinging open the door, she threw an arm over her eyes to ward off the blast of sunlight. She saw Rianne running up the Mercer drive.

Her sister, Dory, waltzed into the house followed by Kendra and Peg Wiley, Dory's neighbor and Sylvie's client, whose spaniel was due to have puppies.

"Are you sick?" Dory asked.

"A headache is all. I took some aspirin last night," Sylvie fibbed, tying her robe around her waist. She saw Dory circling the room, and was very glad she'd taken the time to restore it to rights.

But she'd missed putting away the video. Dory's sharp eyes pinpointed it, and she swooped to pull it from the VCR portion of Sylvie's combination player.

"My sister has a whole evening to entertain her high-voltage neighbor, and what does she do?" Dory wailed. "She watches a boring old movie." Slapping the case back on the TV, she followed her diatribe with a sound of disgust.

Sylvie did what she always did—she laughed at her sister's feigned outrage. And at the moment, was glad she'd forgotten to put away the movie. If Joel managed to act cool today, maybe they could keep her family in the dark.

She hugged her niece hello, then greeted Peg Wiley.

The woman could no longer contain her excitement. "Sylvie, Trixie had her babies last night! The vet helped deliver five of the most beautiful pups you'll ever see. The kids, especially Kendra and Rianne, are dying to see them. Dory insisted we come and ask Rianne's dad if she can stay longer. And I came to see if you still want one of the pups."

"Yes, I've decided I do. Just give me time to throw on a pair of jeans and a T-shirt. Oh, Dory, while I dress, would you make us some coffee?"

Kendra ran up to her mother. "Is it okay if I go next door to see why Rianne's taking so long? She said she was only going home to tell her dad she wants to stay at our house until after lunch."

"Wait a minute. Sylvie," Dory called, "instead of Kendra going next door, you can trot over there in your sexy red robe. If that doesn't wake up Mr. Mercer's you-know-what, then he's a walking corpse."

Sylvie blushed; she could feel it. "Dory, he's a nice man. And a good father. But he's nothing more than a neighbor. I wish you'd stop this."

"Dad or not, Joel Mercer's *hot*. Carline thinks so, too." Dory had followed Sylvie to her bedroom.

Sylvie shoved her sister out.

"Hey, wait a minute." Dory's expression was uncharacteristically sober. "It's not just his looks. He could be the right guy for you. Plus he has a kid—a ready-made family. And considering how much he adores her, he'd probably want another kid if he got married again." Dory shrugged lightly. "You know, Sylvie, I really wouldn't trade a moment of motherhood. It's the most fulfilling experience in the world. And you're going to wait until it's too late."

"Too late? Granted, I'm older than you, but I'm only twenty-six. I recently saw a woman on TV who had twins at fifty."

"Believe me, sis, you don't want to wait *that* long. You want to have your children while making babies is fun. Sylvie Shea, you're a coward."

"Dory, I'm shutting my bedroom door so I can get dressed in peace. I do not, I repeat, do *not* need lectures from my kid sister." Sylvie did close the door then and leaned against it with a sigh. Dory would never let her hear the end of it if she ever discovered how her older sister had spent part of last night.

Dory was banging around in the kitchen when Sylvie emerged. Her eyes drawn to the girls seated on either side of Peg Wiley, she didn't immediately notice Joel propped in her kitchen doorway, one shoulder against the frame. He held a steaming mug of coffee. "Oversleep?" he asked, mischief sparkling in his eyes.

"I must've forgotten to switch on my alarm," Sylvie admitted, trying her best to douse another blush.

Rianne glanced up. "Daddy forgot to set his alarm, too," she announced. "I had to ring the doorbell lots of times to wake him up."

Sylvie loved the fact that he turned red as he mumbled, "I worked in my office until almost one a.m., snooks."

She would've loved to ask what was so fascinating about his job, but Dory came over carrying a pot of coffee and three travel cups. She topped Joel's, and after handing cups to Peg and Sylvie, Dory filled them.

"Okay," she said, "let's load up and go see those pups. I'll run home and collect Roy first, so Grant can head off to work. Sylvie, guess what? Joel's taking all us out for breakfast afterward."

"Why?" Sylvie scalded her tongue on her coffee.

"Oh, call it a celebration," he said, looking smug as he let his gaze sweep her from head to toe.

Sylvie's mouth fell open and once again she felt heat flood her face. Last night he'd agreed to keep quiet about what had happened between them.

Aware of exactly what Sylvie was thinking, Joel straightened to his full height before clarifying his earlier statement. "You don't want to celebrate choosing a new pup? I thought that called for at least an orange-juice toast."

Kendra and Rianne flew off the couch and danced around

and around. "I want a clown-face pancake with strawberry eyes and a chocolate chip smile," Kendra shouted.

"Whoa. Lower the volume," Dory said, stilling her daughter's frantic movements. "Since Rianne's daddy's buying, he gets to choose where we eat."

Kendra stopped. She glanced up and up and up at her friend's tall father. "'Cept for my grandma Nan's Mickey Mouse pancakes, Bettyanne's clown pancakes are the best."

"I want a clown pancake, too, Daddy." Rianne added her plea to Kendra's.

"Who's Bettyanne?" Joel turned helpless eyes on the women in the room. "If I agree, will I be putting some poor neighbor of yours on the spot, Dory?"

She laughed. And it was Sylvie who supplied his answer. "Bettyanne Carmichael runs a Bed-and-Breakfast about two miles out of town. During the winter when tourist season slows, locals can make reservations to have breakfast there."

"Is tourist season over?" Joel inquired of the room at large.

"Not until after Labor Day," Sylvie said.

"Not to worry." Dory hauled out her cell phone. "I heard Bettyanne and Mick's oldest daughter, Brandy, just got engaged. She'll want you to make her dress, Sylvie. You guys run on ahead to see Peg's pups. Here—" she pulled three of Sylvie's pattern books out of the book shelf "—take these. I'll phone Bettyanne."

Dory shoved everyone out the door. It wasn't until Sylvie found herself seated next to Joel and on her way to Peg's home, that she wondered whether or not this was another elaborate setup hatched by her family.

"Peg, did Trixie have her puppies early?"

"Maybe a day. I alerted Doc Weber last week. He said he'd drop in as this was Trixie's first litter. Why did you think she delivered early, Sylvie?"

She turned to smile at Peg. "Just confused, I guess. It's nothing," she added.

Joel glanced at her. "I know what you're thinking, Sylvie," he said in a low voice. "This is the marriage vigilantes' work. But it's gotta be coincidence."

She bobbed her head. "You're right. They couldn't anticipate exactly when Trixie would give birth." Shifting closer, she murmured, "Watch what you say at breakfast, Joel. Especially if we're discussing weddings. That's when they're at their sneakiest."

"I get you. You mean talking about weddings begets more weddings?"

"Exactly."

"Are you two getting married?" Peg leaned excitedly toward them.

"No, no, and *no!*" Sylvie pounced on her poor unsuspecting friend.

Joel caught Peg's eye in the rearview mirror and shrugged.

She arched a narrow eyebrow. "Ah, I understand. Nan's wearing her matchmaking hat again, and this time you two are in her sights, huh, Sylvie?"

"You hit that nail square, Peg. Oh, Joel, turn in the driveway by the dark-green house. That's Peg's."

"I live in the white house next door," Kendra said from the far back seat. "Mama beat us home. I guess Daddy left, 'cause Mama's got Roy."

They could all see that Dory stood at the end of the drive holding Roy. The minute Sylvie opened her door, Dory came up to explain that eating at Bettyanne's was out. "Brandy does want you to make her dress, Syl, but she'll have to come see you. The bed-and-breakfast is full. So it's breakfast at the café in town, kids, or *nada.*"

They groused a bit, but the prospect of seeing the puppies for the first time made them forget about clown pancakes.

Peg led them up a cobblestone walk and into a pristine house. They followed single file into a den that had obviously been given over to the dog, who lay on her side in an elaborate doggie bed. The five puppies were tumbling over one another to eat. Trixie raised her spotted head when the visitors walked in and slapped her tail several times against the pillow.

"Which puppy do you want, Sylvie? I promised my husband I'd only keep one," Peg added, gazing lovingly at all five squirming little creatures.

"I want one," Rianne said. "Daddy, Peg said they won't be big enough to leave Trixie for eight whole weeks. But that could be my birthday present."

Kendra hugged Rianne. "Two look 'xactly alike. We're getting one, Mama said. If you take the other one with black spots, our puppies can be twins."

Joel touched Rianne's shoulder. "What about Fluffy? She didn't like Oscar."

"Oscar's big. A puppy's little. I've got a calendar that shows kitties and puppies who are friends. I bet they can be friends," Rianne insisted stubbornly.

"Pup'ies," two-year-old Roy gurgled, struggling to climb out of his mother's arms.

"No, you don't, tiger. We're going next door. Yell when you're ready to go eat. About the puppy, Joel—you may as well give in. Kids don't let up on something like this."

Feeling sorry for him, Sylvie volunteered to help train the dog. He said okay, and the girls got down on hands and knees to discuss the merits of each puppy as they named their new pets Curly and Spotty. Sylvie selected the runt of the litter, and named him Peanut.

"I'll talk to Jake when he gets home from work. Maybe he'll agree to keep the remaining two pups," Peg mused.

"Serve his favorite meal," Sylvie suggested.

"Now who's being manipulative?" Joel snorted.

Sylvie had the grace to look guilty. "It's a good thing the dogs won't be ready to wean until well after the Labor Day Festival, Peg. I don't think I'd want to be training a new pup with all the running around I'll have to do."

"Daddy said my birthday will be over before the festival. Kendra, guess what! I get to have a party. Daddy mailed 'vitations yesterday." She named the children he'd sent them to. The girls left the pups then and began talking birthday party.

The subject was still being discussed after they were seated at the café.

"Sylvie's helping me with the party, girls," Joel said, as he handed around menus. "Don't forget," he reminded Sylvie.

"I won't. What's the date? I'll mark my calendar when I get home."

Rianne shouted out a date a week off. Joel gave the time.

Dory, busy helping her young son decide what he'd eat, let the conversation slide by without comment. That stunned Sylvie. She said as much when breakfast was over and Joel had driven her home.

"Maybe it means she's decided to back off," he said. "Hey, looks like you've got company." He pointed to a car pulling into Sylvie's driveway.

A young woman Sylvie didn't recognize exited the car and went to knock on her door.

"Just let me out here at the end of your lane," Sylvie told Joel. "Maybe that's Brandy Carmichael."

He stopped and she got out of the van.

"Can I help you?" Sylvie called after a wave at Joel. "This is my house."

"Uh, do I have the right place? I'm looking for Sylvie's Bridal Creations."

"That's me. Are you Bettyanne's daughter?"

"No. Melanie Fitzhugh. My older sister, Lacie, lives in Boston. She bought her wedding gown at a small boutique in New York City. I loved that gown so much, I phoned the shop to get the name of the designer. The owner said it was you and told me you'd moved here. That seemed like a stroke of luck, since I live in Asheville."

"I remember your sister. Her dress was the first one I ever sold to someone who wasn't a friend or relative. But…I no longer design gowns. I have books of patterns, though, if you'd care to see them. I'd be happy to make the dress."

Joel, who listened unabashedly at his car, found that news interesting. He noticed Sylvie didn't mention her secret dress. *The infamous dress.*

In spite of the young bride-to-be's wheedling, Sylvie remained adamant. When the girl finally said she'd peruse the pattern books, Joel shut his car doors, took Rianne's hand and they went in. He wondered if Sylvie and the girl ever came to an agreement. Not wanting Sylvie to know he'd eavesdropped, he never brought up the subject.

And as the days flew past, he forgot about the woman's visit. Possibly because he'd decided he wanted the interior of the house painted before he opened his home to the parents of Rianne's friends.

Sylvie got tied up, too, cutting and sewing gowns for Brandy Carmichael and Melanie Fitzhugh. Although a day rarely passed that she didn't dream about Joel at night and think about him during the day.

It wasn't until she turned the page on her desk calendar and saw the circled date that she realized Rianne's party was the next day. She hadn't bought a gift, nor had she asked Dory about games. In fact, most of the week she'd been out making calls in her Mutt Mobile. Having just come in, she showered and dashed out again to hit town before the stores closed. Her first stop was Carline's shop.

"Wow, Carli, I think your baby's expanded a lot since I saw you at the festival meeting last week. Does your doctor say it's okay for you to be toting boxes and wrapping gifts for customers?"

"If I stay home, Sylvie, I'll go nuts worrying whether or

not my delivery will go okay. I'm better off here—even Jeff says so. My part-timer is already working full-time, and she does all the heavy lifting. She ran down the block to get us milk shakes. That's probably the extra weight you see," Carline admitted wryly. "I crave one every day lately. Anyway, what brings you to town again? You were here this morning."

"Tomorrow is Rianne Mercer's birthday. She'll be six. I need a gift."

"A token she's-my-neighbor kind of thing? I took some darling frilly hair clips on consignment. Circles of lace, dotted by tiny silk roses. A satin bow in the middle holds them together around the metal clip. They come in several colors."

"Joel asked me to help with the party, Carline. So I'm thinking of something more than just hair clips."

"When did all *this* happen? Do Mom and Dory know? I'm sure they don't. I can't believe they'd keep quiet if they knew."

"Dory does know. And I'm only helping with games. Being neighborly."

"Yeah—a role for a moms or potential stepmoms."

"Carline, stop it. Do you want my business or not? I haven't seen Joel or Rianne in over a week. This is a simple favor. One I'd do for anyone in town if they asked."

Carline nodded sagely. "By the way, Kendra said Joel brought you and Rianne over to see Peg Wiley's new pups. And you all went to breakfast together."

"We did. So what?"

Carline leaned on the counter and grinned at Sylvie, who was extremely glad to see her sister's employee return with their shakes.

Sylvie wandered around the store, lingering in the kids' section. She found a pink-and-white jewelry box that, when opened, played a tune. A dainty ballet dancer popped up and twirled around. Sylvie loved the box. As she had it wrapped, she chose a card, and happened to see a book of children's games. She was so relieved. It meant she could skip putting herself through the same grilling or worse by phoning Dory.

That was wishful thinking on her part.

When she got home, the phone was ringing and she grabbed the receiver. "Hi, Mom. What can I do for you? If you're calling to see if the prizes came for the festival, they have. So relax. My back room's full of cartons."

Her mother didn't comment on the festival prizes. "I understand things are getting serious between you and Joel Mercer."

"Carline told you, right? If she gave you that impression, then pregnancy is making her delusional."

"Not ten minutes ago, she said you were in the store and spent thirty dollars on Rianne Mercer's birthday gift. Dory already told me he asked you to host his daughter's party."

Sylvie closed her eyes and fell back against the wall. "I'm not hosting. This is the first birthday party he's given for her, Mom. The poor guy's in the dark when it comes to kids' games. I offered to assist."

"Well, that's significant, because when it comes to kids' games, you're equally in the dark, Sylvie. Carline said you just bought a book of games."

"I did. And do you want to know why? So I won't have to ask Dory for ideas. And do you know why I don't want to ask her? I'll tell you. I knew she'd make a huge big deal of it and call you. After which you'd be on the phone giving me the third degree. And you *are* on the phone giving me the third degree. I thought better of Carline, the little beast. I rest my case."

"Honey, I'm just so excited and happy for you. Dad and I both think Joel is such a nice man. And he plans to make Briarwood his permanent home."

"Mo…th…er! I'm hanging up. Talk to my sisters all you want. Plot all you want. None of that's going to make Joel and me fall in love. Goodbye." Slamming down the phone, she slid her back down the wall until she sat cradling her head in her hands.

Sylvie didn't believe for one minute that yelling at her mom would end her family's interference. They'd go right ahead planning Joel's and her wedding. Forging ahead planning their lives. And she'd given him fair warning. Sylvie was oh, so tempted to sit back and watch him wriggle off the same hook both Grant and Jeff had found firmly implanted in their backsides not so long ago.

Chapter Eleven

Sylvie's day began with a frantic phone call from Joel. "Help!" That was his greeting. "It's Joel. I discovered by accident that my freezer quit. Who does repairs? And do you have freezer space for two big cartons of ice cream that're getting softer by the minute?"

"I can probably fit two cartons in my chest freezer. Call Mullins Repair. Maybe Hank or his son can come out right away. What about meat and other perishables?"

"I didn't have a lot stocked yet. I'll put the ice cream in a plastic bag, and let Rianne run it over while I mop up. I walked barefoot through water, which is how I noticed the problem."

"Okay, I'll go meet her." Sylvie said goodbye.

"Daddy's saying bad words," Rianne announced when she arrived on Sylvie's doorstep. "He stayed up last night to make the house ship-shape for my party. 'Cause he's been painting walls all week. What's ship-shape, Sylvie?"

"It means he wanted everything to look nice for when people come to your party. Is painting's what's kept you two so busy? I wondered, since I hadn't seen either of you in days. You want to come in and make sure I have room for this?"

Rianne skipped along, following Sylvie out onto her porch to a chest-type freezer. "These cartons fit fine, Rianne. Your ice cream will be nice and firm by partytime."

"Fluffy got sick on my bed yesterday. We hadda take her

to the vet. The vet said she might be 'llergic to the paint smell. So till the smell goes away, she has to stay on our back porch with the screen. She doesn't like it."

"Gosh, you and your dad have had some week. Other than storing ice cream, what can I do? Fluffy's welcome to stay with me for a few days."

"I'll tell Daddy. He's worried Fluffy might run away if one of the kids accidentally let her out. Sylvie, will you braid my hair for my party? I'm wearing the dress Daddy bought me for the wedding. I wanted to wear one I had in Atlanta, but it's too short. Daddy said I grew a foot since we moved. He didn't say my foot or his and his is way bigger."

Sylvie smiled. "I've got a surprise you might want now. I worked hard this week, too, and I made you two dresses. I need you to try them on so I'll know where to run hems. If you'd like to wear the fancy one today, I'll hem it now. It's okay, though, if you'd still prefer to wear your other one. It's very pretty."

Rianne fell madly in love with the flocked pink dress. The other was a school jumper, but she could hardly stand still long enough for Sylvie to pin the hem on the pink party dress, which she'd put on first.

"If you were my mommy, Sylvie, you could make me new dresses all the time. Kendra said you sew her pretty clothes even when it's not her birthday or Christmas."

"I like to sew. Some people don't. I'm sure your mom does other nice things for you, Rianne. Honey, can you stand? I don't want to stick you with one of these pins."

"Daddy doesn't know I heard him talking to Mama this morning on the phone. He yelled, 'cause he said it's the second time she forgot my birthday. I don't 'member the other. Should I tell him it's okay? Last year she sent a dorky coat and hat that's still too big for me."

A heaviness invaded Sylvie's chest. How could a mother forget the day her child was born? Her phone rang, jarring

Sylvie out of her sadness. "Stand there for a minute while I see who's calling. Then I'll take this off you, and we'll fit the jumper."

It was Joel. "Is Rianne still there bugging you? I told her to come straight home."

"It's my fault. I'm having her try on a couple of dresses I made, Joel. Do you need her now? She wants to wear one of them at her party, and I thought she could wait while I hemmed it. I already have that color thread on my blind stitcher."

"You made her dresses? Sylvie, that's...well, I don't know how to thank you."

"It's really nothing, Joel. I had the fabric left over from some wedding or other. She also mentioned trying on a dress that's too short. If it fits her otherwise, maybe I can figure out a way to let down the hem and sew lace over the old hem mark."

"We have a box full that are too short. She seems to have shot up, but not out."

Sylvie laughed. "Kids do that. Can you bring the box over? While she's in the mood to try things on, we may as well fit those. Oh, I hear Fluffy's under the weather. If you like, I'll keep her until your paint odor dissipates. That's weird about her being allergic. Although people have allergies, so why not pets?"

"I'll take you up on both offers. Besides, I've missed seeing you this week." His voice dropped and grew husky. "Every once in a while, I noticed you dashing in and out, but I was usually on a ladder with a paint roller in hand."

"I've been busy, too. Sewing. I can't wait to see the changes to Iva's house," she said, feeling the rise of a flush. "Oops, *your* house."

"I still think of it as hers, too. If you have coffee made, I'll be right over. Otherwise, I'll fix some here first. I got hold of Hank Mullins, by the way. He'll try to be here by noon. He didn't give me much hope—said when these new freezers die, that's it."

"He'll be reasonable if you have to buy a new one. A lot

of people are going to Asheville to buy appliances, and his business is barely surviving. I wish people would support our local merchants."

"Okay, I'm sold, Miss Briarwood Chamber of Commerce advocate."

"I did sound preachy, didn't I? About that coffee, Joel. I still have some."

"See you in a few minutes," he said, and hung up.

"Your dad's bringing over the dresses that are too short for you. I'll see if I can add some length so you don't have to toss them out."

Rianne impulsively flung her arms around Sylvie. And the unexpectedness of the gesture left Sylvie recalling Carline's remark about motherhood passing her by. Would it? she wondered. She'd like a child of her own. The tight feeling in her chest came back.

Joel arrived with the dresses and Fluffy. Sylvie settled the cat before she poured Joel coffee, then set to work checking dresses. She discussed ways to fix them with Rianne while Joel wandered around the room, scrutinizing her family photos.

"You look a lot like your mom."

"I'll take that as a compliment. I think Mom's very pretty."

"She is. I meant it as a compliment. These pictures are great. I should dig around and find some I have of Rianne and get them framed. Seeing yours, I realize I haven't been good about keeping up with photos. I wonder if there's any place in town that sells disposable cameras. I should take pictures at Rianne's party today."

"I have film in my camera, Joel. I don't mind taking charge of photos *and* games. The games are easy, and you're not having that many kids."

"Let Sylvie take pictures, Daddy. You cut off people's heads."

Joel grinned sheepishly. "She's right. You're going to start thinking it's a miracle Rianne's managed to survive my parenting this long."

"Not so." Sylvie cut the threads and shook out the finished pink dress. "There, Rianne. Oh, hey, Hank's pulling in your lane, Joel. He's early. Take the mug with you. I promised Rianne I'd braid her hair for the party."

"You can come earlier and provide moral support." Joel surprised her by dropping a kiss on her lips before he headed for the door.

"What was that for?"

"It's because I thought about kissing you all week. That reminds me—Dory phoned. She and the Martins are sharing a baby-sitter at Dory's house Saturday night, for the street dance. She suggested Rianne come over for the night."

Sylvie walked him to the door. Rianne again skipped on ahead, so Sylvie said, "Joel, Dory's so obviously setting us up for another night together."

"Yeah. If you want the truth, I'm counting the hours. Let's *not* watch a movie this time." Grinning cheekily, he loped off then, without giving her a chance to respond.

Sylvie thought she ought to tell him about her mom's last phone call. She would've followed him out, but a shiver of anticipation shot through her at the prospect he'd broached.

Party time came. Sylvie, who'd shown up an hour early, retreated to the kitchen when the doorbell announced the first guest. She intended to stay in the background, and would have managed fine had Nan Shea not bustled in with Dory and Kendra. Nan barged straight into the kitchen, catching Sylvie off guard as she misted a window ledge filled with sad-looking African violets. "Mother," she gasped. "Why are *you* here?"

Nan popped a large dish of whipped Jell-O into Joel's fridge. "I've come for the party. Where else would an adopted grandmother be today? Sylvie, you heard Rianne ask to call me Grandma Nan. A nincompoop can see that poor girl is starved for extended family. Here, let me take over kitchen duty. You go on out and help Joel run the party."

"He doesn't need my help." Sylvie dumped the faded blooms she'd picked off into a garbage can under the sink.

"Quit pouting, and don't forget your camera. He said to send you out, that you're taking photos. Anyway, I can see how things are—how familiar you are with his kitchen." Nan yanked the misting wand out of Sylvie's hand and replaced it with the camera. She gave her daughter a push toward the door. "I hope you plan to have your hair cut before the festival."

Rather than waste her breath saying she knew the house because of time spent with Iva Whitaker, Sylvie shouldered her way out the louvered doors. Later, she'd have to admit that Rianne and Joel, too, seemed to enjoy having her mother serve as faux-grandmother.

And Nan's gift couldn't be beat. Rob Shea had made Rianne a wooden kitchen set. Child-size, to fit a playhouse. Shortly after Rianne had flung her arms around Nan, exclaiming over and over how much she loved the sink and fridge and stove, Nan pulled Joel aside. "Last year Rob made Kendra a darling playhouse. He still has the plans. You've got loads of space in your backyard. All the kids love Kendra's house."

"I'll talk to Rob next week. That sounds like a project I'd like. I love woodworking. Rob's dad helped me build that old treehouse down by the lake one summer. I loved hiding out there to read or think about life. I noticed the floor's rotting. Rianne's not old enough to go there alone yet, but I'd like to restore it. Make it a place a growing girl might one day go to do her dreaming."

"Our girls had a treehouse Gramps built, too. I sewed curtains and pillows. Sylvie will remember. She could do something similar for Rianne. Make it homey."

Joel had a sudden vivid picture of domestic bliss that included him, Rianne and Sylvie. At the successful conclusion of the party, after everyone had left, he wandered around feeling alone. But he supposed that image—of family life—was exactly what Nan Shea had intended to invoke. Even after he lay in bed, the image persisted.

Throughout the week, he puttered in the house, content to watch Rianne play with her birthday gifts. She'd been given quite a few, but had yet to receive the card or present Lynn had promised to mail. It frustrated Joel, although Rianne seemed to take it in stride.

Sylvie called him on two separate occasions to ask for his muscle in setting up the kiddy carnival booths; she'd wanted to get started early. Both times Rianne rode along, as did Kendra. The girls were fast becoming close friends. Joel was glad.

Late in the week, he got a package of the first tear sheets from his new strip. Lester had included a fat check and a note saying initial reports indicated readers loved the changes he'd introduced. This was the first time he'd seen the strips in their proper format. Spreading them one above the other in the order readers would've seen them in the paper, he was shocked to see how closely he'd patterned Magnolia after Sylvie Shea. He drew back and rubbed his jaw, suffering more than a little guilt.

He knew Sylvie far better now. And also her family. Caricatures, which in the beginning had seemed amusing, now felt too much like he was belittling a woman he'd come to admire. A woman he liked, maybe even loved.

Gathering the strips, Joel stuffed them out of sight in a drawer. He was probably so bothered because *he* knew Sylvie had unknowingly served as a model. If anyone in Briarwood read the comic strip, unlikely though that was, he doubted they'd pick up on the resemblance. He clattered down the stairs, glad that Atlanta was as far removed from Briarwood as it was.

"Rianne, what are you doing to that doll buggy?" Joel skidded to a halt outside his still-empty dining room. Nan had said Rob had a dining set in his shop that would go perfectly in this house. Joel needed to find time to go and see it. Just now, his daughter had the hardwood floor—which he'd waxed by hand—covered in crepe paper, glue and glitter.

"I'm making my buggy into a parade float, Daddy. Kendra's fixing hers, and Nikki and Nola Martin, too. Sylvie gave me crepe paper and told me how. 'Cept, I can't get the paper to stick around the inside of the buggy wheels." Tears filled her eyes.

Joel saw the problem. She'd used so much glue it'd disintegrated the paper.

"Will you call Sylvie and see if she can teach me again?" Rianne wailed.

Joel's inclination was to take over himself. But, on second thought, he hadn't seen Sylvie all day, and his day always improved when he did. Pulling out his cell phone, he hit speed dial for her number.

She came without offering any excuses about being busy. Yet, Joel knew she was in the middle of preparing prizes for the festival and finishing two wedding dresses. He opened the door and on this unseasonably warm fall day, watched her pick her way barefoot down a lane he'd recently had graveled. She wore denim shorts and a sleeveless tank. Her hair had been pulled into a floppy sprig atop her head. Escaping tendrils framed a face smeared almost as badly as Rianne's, which was streaked with coloring leaked from wet crepe paper. Sylvie looked like hell, and at the same time beautiful enough to make him instantly hard.

She must have seen the way his eyes raked her body, because she shot a hand to the floppy topknot. "I should've warned you how awful I look. Mom was by an hour ago, and you should've heard her lecture me, because I didn't book an appointment to have my hair done. Or my nails," she said, hiding her hands behind her.

Joel cast a quick glance over his shoulder and ascertained that Rianne was in the dining room. He reached out and pulled Sylvie into a prolonged, satisfying kiss. When he let her go slowly, they were both breathing fast.

Sylvie studied him out of sexy, heavy-lidded eyes. "Now wouldn't that greeting put my mother in a tizzy? She's absolutely positive my lackadaisical attitude about my appearance is guaranteed to drive you straight into Melody Pritchard's clutches at the street dance."

Joel licked his lips and leaned in for a second kiss. "Who's Melody Pritchard?"

"Briarwood's permanent beauty queen. But I have it on good authority that her current 38-24-34 figure is surgically enhanced." Pulling back, Sylvie lightly smacked her cheeks. "Meow! That was totally not nice. She's gorgeous. And rich, because Lyman Pritchard passed on six months ago, leaving Melody loaded. Word is, she claims she married for money the last time. *This* time, she's looking for a red-hot lover."

"Phew, that lets me out."

"I wouldn't say that," Sylvie muttered, darting past him. "Rianne's in the dining room?"

"Yes. Hey, you make an ego-inflating remark like that and walk away?"

He wore such a hit-by-a-brick expression, Sylvie laughed.

"You're laughing at my buggy?" Rianne wailed. "It's awful." Her little chest rose and fell as she cried harder.

"No, honey. It's fine, truly. I was laughing at your dad. Hey, you have the right idea. Your problem is too much glue. Maybe it'd be better to use tape."

"Daddy has some upstairs in his office. My hands are sticky. Will you go up and get it, Sylvie?"

"Sure." She hurried into the hall and started up the stairs.

Joel emerged from the kitchen carrying two beers and a soft drink. "Hey, where are you going? I'm just bringing everyone refreshments."

"To your office. Rianne said you have tape up there. Is it in a dispenser on top of your desk, or do you stick it in a drawer?"

Joel did keep it in a drawer. He recalled seeing the tape this morning—in the drawer where he'd shoved the tear sheets. "Don't…go to my messy office. Here, take the drinks, Sylvie, and stay with Rianne. Let me fetch the tape. I know exactly where it is."

"Okay, sure." Shrugging, she retraced her steps. "I don't know why you'd get your shorts in a twist at the thought of me seeing a messy office. You've been in my workroom. It always looks like a cyclone hit it. Anyway, I like to see where people work. It helps define them, don't you think?"

"In my case, no. Humor me in this."

"I said okay." She fumbled a bit as he handed her the three bottles. "People are always asking me what you do for a living, Joel. All I know is that Rianne said you work on a computer. Once she said you draw stuff. Are you some kind of architect? Or engineer?"

"Graphics," he proclaimed from the first landing. Not precisely true, but he'd minored in graphic design at college. As he dashed into his office, Joel reflected that he didn't like lying to her about his job. He didn't even need to continue working. With the syndication of his early strips, his financial advisor had said he could afford to retire. So why had he jumped at expanding an already syndicated comic? Maybe because that last visit to Lynn at her TV studio had left him with a dissatisfied feeling—that she was somehow showing him up with her success. Maybe because he needed something to fill his time. Maybe because he *liked* his work.

His gaze fell on the latest strips when he retrieved the tape. Joel spared a few seconds to return the stack to its original envelope. Twenty-six weeks wasn't that long, he told himself.

Recognizing his growing attachment to Sylvie, then and there Joel began thinking of finding a husband for Magnolia. He could wind down, and in his last frame he could draw a full-blown wedding party. He envisioned family and friends standing around, crying with joy as Magnolia and her groom—hey, he could have the guy resemble himself—dashed from the church in a hail of rice.

That would spell the end of country cousin Magnolia.

On the ground floor again, Joel took a seat on the floor in the dining room and continued to plot the end of his comic strip as Rianne's buggy project slowly took shape. Perhaps he'd come up with another comic strip later on, six months or a year from now.

That night, he stayed up roughing out all the remaining frames. He went to bed pleased at having salvaged his integrity. He faxed the strips, and started thinking about all the time he'd have to work on the house. All the time to devote to being the kind of dad he'd never had himself.

FESTIVAL DAY began with a huge sense of relief, and also expectation. Joel practically had to tie Rianne down in all her excitement.

"She's not looking forward to this or anything," Sylvie said with a grin when the girl yammered nonstop on the drive to the park. "I stayed up till midnight baking three cakes for the cake-walk. From my kitchen window I saw a light in your corner office until quite late. You must enjoy working during the witching hours."

Joel swung toward her with a frown. "Are you often up that late?"

"Heavens, no. As a rule I'm snoring away." Now she frowned. "Do you work in the nude or something, and you're worried I might see you?"

"What's work in the nude?" Rianne interjected.

Sylvie glanced into the back seat. "Nude is when a person doesn't wear clothes."

"Oh. The people Daddy draws all have clothes."

"I thought you said you did graphics. You draw people?"

"Cartoon people, yes. Where shall I park? You should've said we needed to leave earlier."

"Let me out here, Joel. That section is the food booths, so I won't have to carry a box with three cakes too far. You may have to park in the field across from the baseball diamond.

Remember, Dad showed you? And speaking of baseball, he's anxious to meet your friend, Brett. Too bad he's flying in this morning and out again right after the game. But you still could've met him at the airport instead of giving me a ride and making him rent a car."

"He wanted to do it that way." Joel squeezed Sylvie's hand and murmured in a much lower voice, "I have plans for tonight. Driving Brett to Asheville after the game would have severely curtailed our...free night."

Sylvie knew she turned flaming red. She should be getting used to Joel's outrageous remarks. But maybe she never would because she was beginning to like him too much. She was starting to wish he wanted more than a rare night culminating in great sex. "I'll meet you at the start of the parade route," she said after he stopped and passed her the box of cakes. "Sure you can carry this?" he asked.

She nodded and took off straight away.

During the parade, Rianne and her pals passed the judging platform, where Joel and Sylvie stood. He cheered, and Sylvie snapped photos. "There are kids with pets in their buggies," Joel said. "Dogs, rabbits, cats. I'm still glad I nixed Rianne bringing Fluffy. The band music would've driven that cat nuts. Next year I can see Rianne and Kendra wanting to haul their new dogs."

"I told Rianne to start giving the pup buggy rides from the time she gets him home. These kids' pets have grown up being wheeled around."

"They're cute. The kids *and* their pets. Happy," he added, returning Dory's wave. She and Grant were directly across the street. Grant held their young son, Roy, on his shoulders, and Joel felt a little jealous. He'd always wanted more than one child. "I don't see Carline or Jeff. Did they decide not to come until the game starts?"

"Yes. I called their house earlier. Jeffery said Carline's in a cleaning frenzy. According to Mom, that means she could start labor anytime."

"Then it's good I'm playing his position at shortstop today." Seeing his friend Brett Lewis on the bench, Joel told Sylvie he'd see her later and jogged off across the field.

As things turned out, it was better than good. The first inning had barely gotten underway when Carline's water broke.

Word circulated around the field. It seemed the whole Shea family, with the exception of Rob and Grant, piled into cars bound for the hospital. Sylvie sent Joel a note via the catcher to say Rianne was going along to keep Kendra occupied.

"Nan's going to call me," Rob told Grant and Joel. "I hate to miss being there when I become a grandpa for the third time. But I am team captain."

"Carline understands. Even Jeff was feeling torn about abdicating," Grant said. "Who-eee, will you look at that. Your friend Brett knocked that ball clean out of the field, Joel."

The men high-fived all around. Joel knew Rob felt smug; it was written all over his face when his arch rival from the Baptist team grudgingly congratulated them on Brett's three runs.

By inning eight, the Methodists were so far in the lead, that the Baptists had no hope of overtaking them. This was largely due to Brett, but also Joel, who was a better-than-average player. Rob, in a surprising gesture, motioned both teams to the backstop. "I've got a confession folks. The guilt's killing me. The reason we're slaughtering you this year is because Joel's pal, Brett, is a minor league player. Since I cheated, I propose awarding you Baptists the trophy anyway. According to my wife, if I leave at once, I can make the hospital in time to hold my newest grandson with a clean conscience."

The Baptists' team considered Rob's joke great fun. They acknowledged that with Joel alone, the Methodists might have won. They agreed to save the trophy for next year and not award it to anyone. Everyone came to shake Brett's hand. And to Joel's relief, Brett could tell that Joel wanted to go with Rob and Grant. "Hey, buddy, go on. It was good seeing you even briefly. I said I'd hang out here a while and sign autographs for the kids. If you don't get back from the hospital before I have to leave, thanks for the free ticket out of the city. I wish I could stay. This is grand country." Brett looked envious.

"It sure is." Joel clasped his hand, they parted, and he ran to catch up with Rob. Grant had jogged ahead to get the car. The trio squeaked into the hospital birthing center five minutes after Keenan Manchester had made his appearance.

Kendra and Rianne stood at the door to Carline's room, holding their hands over their ears. Joel walked up behind them in time to see the bundled baby passed into his Aunt Sylvie's arms. He was struck by the tears standing in her eyes and the longing on her face. He knew then that he wanted her to play a larger role in his and Rianne's lives. But how to convince her? He rubbed at his tense neck.

A nurse came in and suggested they all leave and let the Manchester family get acquainted with their son. On their way out, the Sheas met Jeff's sisters rushing in. Rob and Nan stopped to rave about the baby.

Dory turned to Sylvie and Joel. "Grant and I will drop you two at the park. We'll collect Rianne's backpack from your van and meet you later at the street dance."

Sylvie said tiredly, "Maybe it was the added stress of waiting for Carline to deliver the baby, but I'm wiped. Would anyone mind terribly if I skipped the dance this year?"

Dory's expression could only be described as suspicious. "Nonsense. You'll get your second wind once the band warms up. You have a good hour to relax during the barbecue. And aren't you in charge of leftover prizes?"

"There are never leftover prizes."

"We didn't get to play any games or win prizes this year," Kendra complained.

Sylvie affectionately ruffled her niece's hair. "You two girls got the best prize of all, seeing Auntie Carline's brand-new baby."

Rianne launched into a list of reasons why she wanted a baby brother.

"Roy's not so great," Kendra said. "He always messes up my Barbies. Rianne, we're gonna be able to bring Curly and Spotty home soon. Dogs are better than brothers."

"Young lady, tell Roy you're sorry, or no sleepover for you tonight," Dory put in. Kendra quickly made amends.

"Sylvie, I'm not all that big on dances," Joel said. "How about if we go to the park just long enough to eat? If you still want to leave after that, I'll take you."

"I can't ask that of you. This is your first Labor Day Festival."

Dory nudged her sister. "Honestly, Sylvie. People don't offer to do things if they don't want to do them."

Sylvie sent her a dirty look. "What's made you so grouchy tonight, Dory?"

Dory rolled her eyes toward Joel, and significantly lowered her voice. "Mom said she told you Melody's on the loose."

But Joel heard what she said. "Ah, yes, the beauty queen." He deliberately reached for Sylvie's hand. "If you have an ounce of compassion, Sylvie Shea, you won't leave me alone to fall into her clutches."

Dory's jaw sagged. "You *told* him about Melody Pritchard?"

"Sis! Give it a rest." Sylvie shook herself loose from Joel's fingers, which effectively ended the discussion. She did agree to sample the barbecued chicken and roast corn they could smell the minute they stepped from the car.

Her melancholy mood returned, however. She didn't have to beg Joel to drive her home; he volunteered, after making sure Dory had Rianne in tow. "You blue over your sister's baby?" He hadn't said anything during the drive, so when he asked, he'd already parked in his lane. His observation surprised Sylvie.

"No," she said, throwing open her door. "Yes." She changed her tune as Joel rushed around the car. "Envy's an evil emotion, Joel. I hate myself for it."

He ambled toward her house, sensing he had to tread lightly. Joel let her brood silently until they went inside. No dog greeted them. Even Fluffy was back in her own quarters. Joel watched Sylvie drop her purse on the kitchen counter. Stepping up, he wrapped her in his arms. "I don't find your reaction surprising, Sylvie. You're the eldest sister. Something I rarely admit…my dad remarried right after he divorced my mom. He had a second son. We've never met, but sometimes I wonder about him."

Sylvie rubbed her face over Joel's shirtfront. "Why did your dad cut off his relationship with you just because he divorced your mother?"

Joel swayed her from side to side. "Their divorce was bitter. Dad ended up hating her, and I look a lot like Mom. It took me years to realize it wasn't my fault. I didn't figure any of this out until Lynn walked. I'm determined not to set up any blocks between Rianne and her mother. In case you wondered, Lynn's the one not making an effort to reach out to our daughter."

"I picked up enough from the things Rianne said to see that." Pressing closer, Sylvie steadily began to unbutton Joel's shirt. Only a single light burned in the living room, and it was turned low. "Maybe you'd feel better if you had a talk with your half-brother."

He stilled her fingers and made her meet his eyes. "No pity sex, please," he said, the words a growl in his throat.

"I really need someone tonight, Joel. I need you."

The shakiness of her voice touched something deep inside him. "Where?" he whispered tightly, scooping her into his arms.

"My room. Down the hall past my workroom. I left the light on. I didn't know what time I'd get in tonight. You can turn it off if you'd like."

"I want to see you, and I want you to see me. I don't think you have any idea how much this has been on my mind. Since our first night together." No added confessions or comments passed between them for the next while. They lost themselves in a world of sensations, feelings and long kisses.

Joel explored every inch of Sylvie's soft, exposed skin. He kissed every inch.

She responded, happy to stroke and be stroked. Already familiar with each other's bodies, they could dedicate the night to pleasuring each other.

Together, they lay in the middle of Sylvie's big bed, and nothing broke the silence shrouding the room but the tick of the bedside clock. Little by little, their rapid breathing slowed to normal.

Eventually, Joel's lightly seeking hand felt that the skin on Sylvie's back and upper arms had grown cool. He found a quilt folded at the foot of the bed. After shaking it out, Joel shoved their pillows together so they could snuggle better.

"We can't make a habit of this, Joel."

"Why?" he asked, at the risk of sounding like his daughter. Tucking Sylvie against his side, Joel let his eyes study her face as she scrambled for an answer. "*Because* isn't allowed," he murmured. "After two earth-shaking nights, Sylvie, I deserve an honest answer, I think."

"The truth is, Joel, I feel myself falling for you."

He played with the ends of her hair. "Forgive me if I fail to see a problem there."

"The problem is, I fell once before. Hard."

Feeling her shudder, Joel tightened his hold.

"I fell for a fellow wedding-gown designer in New York. Desmond Emerson. He wasn't a big name in the industry…then. But he had contacts, and he lavished me with attention. Des shared one or two of his contacts with me. Various boutiques expressed interest in my designs. One of them sold several gowns and requested more. Also Des had a loft apartment. The light there was great for sketching. He moved me in, and…I thought he loved me as much as I loved him. I was wrong. He loved my designs. I worked night and day building a collection he promised to display for me at a major showing where he'd booked space."

Joel felt Sylvie's tension mount. She needed to get this story out, or he would have stopped her. Because he could guess the rest. After all, it was eerily like the fate he'd plotted for Magnolia. Joel's heart thudded erratically, sinking more with each word Sylvie so painfully spoke.

Emerson had presented her original designs, all right, but as his own. The crowning blow—her collection had brought Desmond Emerson acclaim and big bucks, leaving Sylvie with nothing to show for an entire year's worth of labor.

"One dress," she murmured, her eyes straying to a covered shape standing in the corner. "I had no collection anymore. No interest from name stores. Des had it all. Plus, he up and married our bubble-brained design assistant. I saw pictures of their wedding. She showcased my second-best design. The dress hanging in that corner is my favorite." She took a deep breath. "It's the gown I'd planned to wear at my wedding to Des. If he could've found a way to take it, I'm sure he would have." Pain and sorrow wracked her admission.

Joel felt for her. "He's the reason you quit designing wedding gowns?"

She nibbled a fingernail. "The fire went out, Joel."

"You have a lot of fire," he said staunchly. "And tons of talent with a needle and thread that I'll bet old Desmond doesn't have."

"That's the worst part. He doesn't need to sew. My patterns shot him to the top. He made a fortune selling them to knock-off gown-makers."

"But he has nothing to fall back on when people want something new."

"It doesn't matter, Joel. I've lost all my connections in New York. Even the few I had took time to build. I'm sure Des spread lies about me, too. It was all so humiliating."

"And it has nothing to do with me, Sylvie. Nothing to do

with *us*." He picked up her left hand and kissed each finger. "I love you as you are, Sylvie. I think I've known for a while. Say you'll marry me. I have a solid stock portfolio. I can give you freedom and money to rebuild your dream."

"You'd do that for me, Joel?"

"Sylvie, I believe in you. You *can* make a comeback."

She started to cry quietly. He kissed away the tears until at last she dried her eyes and whispered, "Yes, I accept. I love you, Joel—and not because of what you've offered me. Because you're *you*." Throughout the too-short night they alternately made love and made plans, again and again.

Joel woke Sylvie with kisses shortly before dawn. "I have to go now, sweetheart. Dory's bringing Rianne home early. The church is having a breakfast, and Grant and Dory are going. I'll be glad when there's no need to leave your bed. When can we tell Rianne and your family the news? I'd like us to pick out rings next week."

"Oh, Joel. I need some time to let this sink in. It doesn't seem real." She paused. "Give me a week?"

"One week. I'm holding you to that promise," he said, tying his shoes before slipping out of her room and out of the house.

Chapter Twelve

Light, filtering through Sylvie's bedroom curtains and across her pillow, woke her suddenly from a deep sleep. She grabbed the clock and saw she had twenty minutes to shower, dress and get to church. The whole family had agreed to go and present a special offering in baby Keenan's name.

It wasn't until she stood under a hot, stinging shower and discovered a few pleasant aches that the scope of everything that had happened last night rushed back in a flood of happiness. She'd said she loved him. That was true. He said he loved her. She prayed that was also true.

With no time to waste on reliving the best details, Sylvie stored the lovely reflections to savor later. She pulled a comb through tangles, drew her hair into a reasonable twist at her nape and hopped toward her car, putting on her shoes as she went.

She dashed into church seconds before the service started. Feeling her family's scrutiny, she assumed a blasé expression and opened her hymnal.

At the end of the service, amid the rush of well-wishers converging to ask about the baby, Freda Poulson, Briarwood's librarian, elbowed her way up to Nan and Sylvie.

"Sylvie, dear, have I found out something interesting about your neighbor." That, of course, claimed Sylvie's immediate attention, and also Nan and Dory's. Rob and Grant continued talking with others about the new baby.

"Really? What?" Sylvie asked politely. Freda, the town's biggest gossip, wasn't her favorite person.

Freda sniffed, but bent closer to address Sylvie's mom. "Nan, do you remember how the library committee authorized me to purchase more out-of-state newspapers? Miami, Dallas and Atlanta were the ones we chose. Well, Atlanta sent six back issues for our archives." She paused for effect. "I…discovered your Joel Mercer is none other than the J. Mercer who draws a comic strip called 'Poppy and Rose.' It's a syndicated satire about single women."

Sylvie smiled. "He's very modest. I'm sure that's why he hasn't told anyone his occupation. Wow, maybe he's world-famous."

Freda clucked her tongue. "He hasn't told anyone his occupation because he's spying on you, Sylvie. If you don't believe me, follow me to the library, all of you. I'm going there now to catch up on some work."

Watching her walk away, Sylvie was torn. "Freda's a busybody from the get-go, Mom. She loves stirring up trouble."

Dory pulled Sylvie and their mom aside. "I agree. But what did Freda mean by *spying?* A comic strip about singles sounds innocuous. Except that Freda was positively gloating."

Nan cast a troubled glance at her daughters. "It's no secret that Freda loves the spotlight, but she's not given to outright lying. I admit, I'm curious. Aren't you?"

Dory cast the deciding vote. "We're headed to Mom and Dad's for lunch, and after that we were going to the hospital. I say we send Grant and Dad on with the kids while the three of us swing past the library."

Freda saw the trio at the door. She ushered them into her private office, where she had six comic sections laid out. "Start at the top," she instructed. And they did.

At first no one spoke. Dory broke the ice. "That creep! Freda's right. Magnolia is Sylvie, or I'll eat every last one of these pages. He's good, I'll give him that. Don't you all recognize

Chet and Buddy? And Oscar." Dory tapped the last sheet. "This whole café scene with chitchat over coffee alludes to *the* dress Magnolia has hauled around until she finds a husband. It has to be yours, Sylvie. Aren't you just furious?"

Hurt beyond speech, Sylvie felt a sickening hole opening in her chest. And another in her stomach. The others didn't know about last night. Didn't know about the words, the promises she and Joel had whispered in bed. She wasn't furious. She was betrayed. Once again! Oh, how it hurt. So many feelings clustered together that she couldn't begin to explain that the humiliation she'd undergone in New York was happening all over.

Nan slipped a bracing arm around her eldest daughter's waist. "This is a blow for all of us, honey. We took that man into our homes and our lives. I think you also took him into your heart, Sylvie. Am I right?"

Lifting her head, Sylvie experienced the first jab of anger. "I deserve an explanation," she said abruptly. "Dory, Mom, I'll drop you at home. Tell Carline I'll see her later. I'm going straight home and I'm going to confront Joel."

Nan murmured. "Sure you don't want backup?"

Sylvie shook her head. "I'm the one he played for the fool. I prefer to do this alone."

Saying little, her family nodded, but withdrew. Not even Freda spoke.

JOEL OPENED the door to Sylvie's knock, and she was glad Rianne didn't appear in his wake. In other circumstances, Sylvie might have reached up and brushed aside the hair falling in Joel's eyes—over the glasses he so rarely wore. Her heart lurched painfully as she stared at him in faded jeans and a paint-spattered, close-fitting T-shirt. He had an endearing smudge of paint slashing the cleft in his chin.

Joel broke into a smile. He shifted the can of paint to the hand holding his brush and leaned toward Sylvie, clearly intending to kiss her.

She crossed her arms in a defensive pose and moved aside. "I've come to ask if you're the J. Mercer who draws a comic strip called 'Poppy and Rose.'"

A series of emotions ranging from shock to uneasiness to guilt flitted across his suddenly tight-lipped face. Joel averted his eyes and began to stammer incomprehensibly. His only clear statement was "Forgive me, please?"

Tears Sylvie had been holding in by force of will started to trickle down her cheeks. "Even Desmond Emerson had the human decency to admit his duplicity." She took a step back before spinning to race blindly down his steps. "Stay away from me, Joel. I don't want to ever speak to you again. Not ever!"

"Sylvie, wait!" He chased after her, slopping paint out of the bucket. "I agreed to do twenty-six weeks with the new character. When I added Magnolia, I barely knew you. I've sent in everything. I gave her a happy ending. Sylvie, dammit, listen to me!"

He remembered he was barefoot when he landed squarely on a jagged rock that halted his flight and left him limping. Sylvie was wearing shoes today and she ran like a rabbit heading for the safety of her lair. Joel swore viciously and hobbled back to his house. He should've told her about the strip last night. He should've come clean about the whole works and maybe invited her to see the strips Lester had sent.

Stomping into the bathroom he'd been painting, Joel discovered he was leaving a trail of bloody footprints. He banged down the toilet seat and sat to take care of damage done to his heel by the rock. After his initial panic had passed, he decided in a more rational fashion that it was best to let Sylvie cool down. Maybe on Tuesday, after he took Rianne to her first day of school, he'd take some coffee next door and apologize again. He loved her. She said she loved him. Sylvie wasn't someone to give her love lightly. And neither, dammit, was he. Joel held on to that fact.

At least he did until right before supper, when he was paid

a visit by a host of town matrons. Many were the same ones who'd delivered gifts of food the day he moved in.

This time they called him a cad, a scoundrel, a fraud.

Rianne apparently heard the commotion. She skipped downstairs. "Daddy, who are all those ladies? Why are they yelling at you?"

"I'm taking care of it, snooks. Go back to your room." Stepping out on the porch, he pulled the door shut. "Please," he entreated. "Don't let my bad judgment affect how you treat my daughter."

"Huh," Ellie, the elementary school secretary, snorted, "I thought you were sneaky the day you came to register that poor tyke. But the residents of Briarwood aren't ones to visit the sins of the father on the child. Isn't that right, ladies?"

Joel was greatly relieved to see a round robin bobbing of heads. "Look, I want to set things right with Sylvie and her family. This mob scene will not help my cause."

"How do you plan to set it right, sonny?" asked a woman Joel recognized as a waitress from the café. "You done our Sylvie dirt. And you drank coffee in our restaurant, pumping us to help you do it. We know how important *the* dress is to her. I told you something awful must've happened in New York. Never expected a nice man like you would exploit a neighbor's broken heart."

"I'm a satirist. I show problems in a humorous light."

"Broken hearts aren't funny," a thin, colorless woman stated.

"I can vouch for that," Joel shot back. Indeed, since Sylvie's visit he'd suffered a terrible ache in his own heart.

A woman Joel had met at Kay's wedding reception turned up her nose. "Maybe poking fun at other people's problems is what people do in a big city like Atlanta. That's why none of us want to live there." The woman shook her head. "Iva bragged on you, too. She said you were a country boy at heart. If so, you'll be making amends with our Sylvie. No finer woman exists."

As if that summarized the feeling of the delegation, the women marched off to their separate cars, following a last group glare.

Joel watched them go, beset by a sinking sensation in his stomach. He didn't realize Rianne hadn't obeyed his directive until she said from the doorway in a small voice, "They don't like you, Daddy. What did that woman mean, make amends with Sylvie? Does it have to do with how she makes dresses?"

"Rianne, baby." Sighing, Joel trudged back up the steps. "Daddy didn't mean to, but he hurt Sylvie's feelings. To make amends is to right a wrong. They want me to make her feel good again."

"Can't you tell her you're sorry? That's what you always say I hafta do if I hurt somebody's feelings."

He turned her back into the house. "Kids are better at accepting apologies than adults. Big people take more convincing. I need to figure out some extra-special way of showing Sylvie I'm sorry from the bottom of my heart."

Rianne gazed up at her father with wide blue eyes. "Then do it, Daddy. I love Sylvie a whole lot, and I don't want her to be mad at me like Mama is."

"Snooks, your mama's not mad at you. She's busy with her new job."

Rianne ducked out from under the big hand he'd rested on her shoulder, scooped up Fluffy, who meowed at her feet, and stalked off. "Fix it with Sylvie, Daddy."

"That may turn out to be a very tall order," Joel muttered, lowering his chin to his chest as he shut his eyes and pinched the bridge of his nose.

The evening passed. The most constructive thing Joel did was fax Lester a letter asking for a break before offering anything new. He'd lost his taste for the job.

Monday morning slid by in a haze of loneliness. Tuesday emerged in a flurry of trying to get Rianne fed and dressed for her first day of school. She wanted to ride the bus, then changed her mind, asking her dad to drive her. They finally settled that he'd take her today, check out the bus and she'd ride it on day two.

Joel didn't know what Rianne's reception would be from the Martin twins and Holly Johnson, as their mother's had been part of Sunday's lynch mob. The girls ran up and gathered Rianne into their midst, apparently untouched by the uproar Joel had caused.

He couldn't wait to leave the school. Not knowing what to say to Sylvie, he nevertheless drove home, got out and strode right up to her door.

She didn't answer his knock, even though her car and her Mutt Mobile were both parked out front. He knocked until his knuckles were raw, and pleaded with her to talk to him until he grew hoarse. Her door remained firmly closed.

Retreating, Joel phoned. The first time she picked up. But she slammed down the receiver the instant he spoke.

As discouraged as he'd ever been, Joel did nothing but sit and debate what approach to try next. A knock at his door about noon roused him from his useless deliberations. Joel didn't much care to see whoever might be standing on his porch, considering the blistering his ears had taken from his last visitors.

Looking out the window first, he felt his heart somersault. Sylvie's dad stood there, hands buried in his front pockets, rocking back and forth.

At least Rob Shea wasn't carrying a shotgun. Never the cowardly sort, Joel jerked open the door. "Want to come in, or were you planning to tear me limb from limb in public?"

Rob, who'd been whistling off-key, stopped. "After listening for two days while the women in my family and those in town set themselves up as judge and jury, I came to see if you'd like to go fishing. Told myself, Rob, if ever a man's in need of setting his mind adrift for a few hours, it's Joel Mercer."

"Fishing?" Joel stumbled a bit on that. "I get it. Sylvie must've described how I almost drowned that one time and sent you to finish the job."

Rob roared with laughter. "Son, you do have it bad. Grab your pole. I'll meet you at the fork in the path like before."

Sylvie, having just ventured forth to open her front drapes, saw her father drive into Joel's lane. She pressed her forehead to the window, waiting to see how long he stayed. In short order she saw him heading back to his truck. The fact that he was there at all made her mad. She stormed out of the house.

"Dad, honest to Pete! Don't you think I'm old enough to fight my own battles? Fifty people have phoned to tell me how half the ladies in town shredded Joel yesterday on my behalf." She clenched a fist and hit herself in the chest. "I can handle this. I want everyone…*everyone* to butt out. Is that clear?"

Rob calmly removed the case with his fishing pole from his pickup, all the while taking in the pain-ravaged face of the daughter who most resembled her mother. "I'm too old for fisticuffs, Sylvie-girl. We're just a couple of fellows with time on our hands, who are gonna do some fishin'." He left her gaping after him.

"You're kidding!" Her hand slowly uncurled, and she sputtered ineffectually at his back. Out of the corner of her eye, she saw Joel emerge around the side of his house. He looked so good, a physical pain ricocheted through her. "Dad!" she said in a low, ragged voice. "Last time I fished with Joel, he lost his footing and fell in the lake and nearly drowned. Take care of him, okay?" She flattened herself against her dad's pickup as Joel half turned. Rob continued walking. He did toss a casual wave over one shoulder, so Sylvie went home pretty certain he'd heard her.

"Was that Sylvie?" Joel asked. It was the first comment out of his mouth.

"Yep. Still has a care for your well-being, son. What do you plan to do about it?"

Joel shrugged miserably. "I haven't the foggiest idea, sir."

Rob fell into step with him. "A man needs a plan. When it comes to women, it helps to have a backup, as well."

"I'm open to suggestions," Joel declared as they assumed their spots on the dock and settled down to fish. "I really screwed up with her."

Rob hooked a fish right off, a beauty. He played it carefully, speaking as he did. "Over the years, the thing I've noticed about all my girls, they're marshmallows inside. Women seem to be more complicated now than in my day. Back then, flowers, candy, wine were all a man needed to show he was sorry. Now I hear the young women talking when they don't know I'm listenin'. Seems a fellow needs to come up with a unique romantic gesture nowadays. A special kind of apology."

"Like what?" Joel hooked a smaller fish as Rob landed his. "I asked her to marry me, but maybe you didn't know that. I also assured Sylvie I'd make her dream of becoming a designer possible. I told her I believe in her. My job caused our rift, so I asked for a break. In case you think I can't support her, I can. I made a lot when my comic strip syndicated. And Iva left me more than the house. Mining stocks she thought were worthless. My lawyer tells me they were converted in a big railroad merger recently."

Rob nodded. "Iva and my grandparents. Same stocks. Haven't decided whether to upgrade the family furniture company or retire early. Money's not everything, though, son."

"I know. But Sylvie refused to listen when I tried to tell her I quit my job."

"I don't think she dislikes your job. But it'll take more than talk. Jeff, now, he asked Carline to marry him seven days a week for a month. Didn't work. Then he invited her to a special dinner he cooked. Word is, he spread rose petals from his kitchen to the patio where he'd set a table with white linen and candles. Those rose petals led straight to an open velvet box holding a sparkler of an engagement ring. Did the trick for him."

"Wow, impressive. What about Grant? He doesn't strike me as a romance kind of guy."

"Maybe not as a rule. He's been crazy over Dory from fourth grade. They went steady all through high school. She was on the verge of breaking up, saying they'd fallen into a rut. It was during the ball game at one of our Labor Day Festivals that he hired a friend with an airplane to sky write 'Grant loves Dory' right above the ballfield. Pilot made a trail of hearts off into the clouds. Grant left the game, found Dory in the bleachers and proposed over a loudspeaker. Method worked."

"Hmm. I can see this may take some heavy-duty thinking."

Rob reeled in a second fish. "Sylvie and the others can use a cooling-off period. Don't let it go too long, though." He clambered to his feet. "Well, my boy, no sense over-fishing this spot. Maybe I'll mosey home with this fine catch. Tonight I'll clean 'em and cook 'em myself, and break out a nice bottle of Nan's favorite wine. Best I can do for you is to soften her up some. It's up to you to convince Nan you didn't draw those pictures with malicious intent. But between you and me, folks are amazed by how clever you are with a pen. The likeness between Magnolia and Sylvie took talent."

"I ended the series with a grand finale, Rob. A wedding," Joel said. "And after that, I'm taking a break. Actually, I have a hankering to try my hand at woodworking. I understand you built Kendra a playhouse and you still have the plans. I may build a bookcase after that."

They were halfway up the trail when Rob clapped Joel on the back. "For the past couple of years, Nan's been bugging me to take more time off from my business. I've kicked around the idea of locating an apprentice. Tell you what—I will dig out those playhouse plans. Why don't you come to the shop tomorrow, after Rianne goes to school. We'll talk some more. I'll see if you have a feel for working with wood."

Joel felt the first surge of hope in two days that things might work out, after all. Except there was still the matter of a unique romantic gesture. That weighed heavily on his mind all night. The next week he spent every day puttering happily in Rob's shop. And Rob beamed over how quickly he picked up a feel for woodworking. However, a call from Lester Egan that evening left Joel realizing that his talent lay in cartooning. They ended their conversation with Lester leaving the door open for Joel to return anytime.

A week later, Rianne unwittingly handed her dad a possible avenue to take with Sylvie. His daughter had gotten in the habit of stopping next door after school, either for milk and homemade cookies, or just for girl talk. This particular afternoon, she came running into the house, bursting with news.

"Daddy, Daddy, you know what? Sylvie showed me the most beautiful dress I've ever seen. It's white and shiny and glittery with diamonds. And pearls. Only she said they're fake. It's a wedding dress, Daddy. Sylvie's never showed it to anybody. Only me. And you know what? She's gonna work day and night to finish it to raffle off at the church bazaar. 'Cause she said the choir needs new robes, and this dress will fetch 'nuff money for all the robes they need."

Joel sorted through Rianne's excited, tumbled words. He came to the conclusion that it had to be *the* dress Sylvie planned to get rid of.

He paced back and forth in front of the living room window, staring at Sylvie's house. The news didn't bode well for him or for his chances of making amends. Sylvie was giving up on her career and giving up on ever walking down the aisle herself.

"Snooks, change into play clothes, will you? I need to go talk to Grandma Nan and Grandpa Rob." Joel needed some serious help here. He was so thankful for the generosity of Sylvie's parents. He and they had gotten past his horrid blunder. Now he was about to request their cooperation in a plan he'd discarded once but had decided to reconsider.

Nan listened as Joel repeated what Rianne had said. "Oh, Joel. I'm sorry. I assumed she'd eventually see, as we all have, that you didn't draw that cartoon strip to hurt her. I hate to say it, but you should probably just move on with your life."

"I'm not ready to do that, Nan. Hear me out," he said. "I have a good friend, Julie Kerr. She married my college roommate. And she used to head the fashion section of the Atlanta paper. I did some ad work for her. They moved to Chicago about the time my marriage fell apart. Julie got this great job as editor of *Bride's Delight*."

"I've seen that magazine at Sylvie's house. Her clients often choose gowns they feature. I don't know what you have in mind, Joel, but I'm beginning to see possibilities. Why don't you hold off telling me a minute. Let me bring in the troops. Kendra misses playing with Rianne. Maybe Dory will swing by with her and pick up Carline and Keenan. This sounds like something that calls for a Shea family summit. After I call, I'll fix fresh coffee while you fetch Rob from the wood shop."

Joel wondered hours later if Sylvie's ears were burning. Until this afternoon, he'd been unable to win the hearts and minds of Sylvie's two staunchest supporters, her sisters.

"Joel, your idea is totally devious, but I love it," Dory burst out in the silence that followed when Joel had outlined his plan.

Carline wasn't as quick to embrace the scheme. "Joel, are you prepared to have the whole thing blow up in your face? Not only are you proposing to lay out some big bucks, but you risk public humiliation, if she walks out on you."

The man gazed at the sleeping bundle Carline bounced

gently in her arms. "Did you see your sister's face the day she held Keenan in the hospital for the first time? Sylvie wants what you two have. A home, children, a man to love her unconditionally. I am that man. All I'm asking is one last chance to prove it as publicly as I can. I'm willing to risk becoming a laughingstock in a community where I intend to live for the rest of my life. I also run the risk Julie and her photographer might record my embarrassment and turn it into a feature article…. But if Sylvie chooses to throw my love back in my face because of what I did, it's no more than I deserve."

Nan leaned over and impulsively hugged Joel. Rob stuck out his hand. Dory rubbed hers together. "Joel, can you get your friend on the phone? You'll need her commitment before we can go to work. The church bazaar is mid-November. That's not much time to pull off something as involved as this."

Finally, Carline joined in, "This will require the help of people in town. We'll need to pick folks we trust to keep this quiet. And Sylvie's sharp. What if she smells a rat?"

Dory brushed aside the possibility. "Tomorrow I'm picking her up to shop for material to make Kendra and Roy's Halloween costumes. She asked me to find out if Rianne needed a costume, as well. Sylvie already loves Rianne, and it's a very good sign that she's looking out for your daughter's welfare. I have no problem selecting the three hardest costume patterns in the book. Between sewing them and finishing *the* dress, and with the choir starting to rehearse for the Christmas production, I predict Ms. Sylvie will be far too busy to ferret out our plans."

SYLVIE ARRIVED HOME from her shopping trip to Asheville with Dory. Her arms were filled with bolts of black and orange fabric. Kendra and Rianne both wanted to be witches. Roy, Dory insisted, had his heart set on being the lion from

The Lion King. That pattern might challenge even her expertise with needle and thread, Sylvie thought, as she paused to scoop up her ringing phone.

"Is this Sylvie Shea?" asked a female voice. Sylvie braced herself for a sales pitch and prepared to hang up, even though she said, "Yes, I'm Sylvie."

"Fabulous! You're a difficult woman to track down. My name is Julie Kerr. I'm editor in chief of *Bride's Delight* magazine. We're located in Chicago."

Sylvie dropped the bolts with a bang. "I love your publication. You feature the most beautiful wedding gowns!"

"I think we do, too." Julie chuckled. "Glad to hear you agree. That's actually why I'm calling. I'm putting together a special issue featuring Christmas brides. I recently returned from New York where I gathered names of promising new gown designers. Two boutiques placed your name high on their lists. Trudy Levine explained what happened with your partner, Sylvie, but I'd like to see anything new you might have."

"I have nothing, I'm afraid. I moved home and quit designing."

"What a shame. You have nothing original at all? I'm prepared to fly to…where is it you are…North Carolina? I'd bring a photographer. My aim in this issue is to simulate actual weddings. I've already done two. The designers wore their gowns themselves and rounded up friends to play the groom and attendants. I provide any necessary props like flowers and candelabra. The Christmas issue boosts careers almost as much as our June bride collection. But…if you have nothing made up, I'll keep you in mind for next June."

A silence ensued. Julie eventually said, "I'm sorry to have taken your time, Sylvie. Jot down my number why don't you? Perhaps you'll have something for our June issue. We shoot that in March."

"Wait. I have one dress. An original. My best work, I've always believed. How…how long would I have before you need to shoot photos? The dress still requires some work. I am toying with maybe trying to break into design again...."

"Let me grab my calendar. How much work, Sylvie?" Julie named a Saturday afternoon in mid-November. "Sorry, but that's my last possible weekend to fly a whole crew in and still make my deadline."

Sylvie stretched the phone cord around the corner so that she, too, thumbed through her calendar. "That date's okay. I plan to raffle this dress off during our church bazaar. It's the following week, in our church basement. I'm fairly confident no one's booked a wedding for that Saturday, since I spoke with our pastor about displaying the gown in the chapel starting on the Friday, in fact."

"Even better," Julie purred in Sylvie's ear. "Having a minister in the photos, holding an open Bible, adds so much authenticity. So, we have a verbal agreement? If we do, I'll get back to you after I firm up all arrangements on my end. Can you supply people to be in the shoot? I require signed release forms to allow their pictures to appear in *Bride's Delight*. Parents need to sign for any kids. Like a ring-bearer and oh, say, two little girls to act as flower girls?"

"I have two in mind," Sylvie murmured. "I—how can I thank you enough, Julie? You've called me at a time when I've reached a crossroads in my life. Do you provide information on designers? I mean, if potential brides express interest in your featured gowns?"

"Absolutely. We run a page at the back giving designer names and how to contact them. Be prepared to have your phone ring off the hook in January."

Sylvie laughed. Her heart lightened for the first time in weeks. After hanging up, she hugged herself and waltzed into her bedroom to inspect the gown. Unable to contain her joy at this sudden windfall, she raced back down the hall, picked up the phone and called her mother. She made similar calls to Carline and Dory. "I need your help, guys," she pleaded. "This may be my last chance to see if I have what it takes to break into a very closed field. I think I'd be able to work from home." She took a breath. "Dory, I'm thinking of Kendra and Rianne as flower girls. But…Joel would need to sign a release to have her appear in the magazine. Please, would you ask him?"

"Syl, how long are you going to make that poor man grovel?"

"I don't know what you're talking about. He hurt me, Dory. I loved him."

"Don't you still? A little bit, at least? Come on, Sylvie, I've seen how often you look at his house when I come to pick you up. Didn't Sunday's sermon on forgiveness move you at all?"

"He could've told me. I'd have forgiven him if he'd done that, Dory. I thought what we had was special. Joel encouraged me to dream again—something I couldn't do after New York. I feel so much more for Joel than I did for Desmond. Can't you understand how much I hurt, Dory?"

"I understand you just used the word *feel,* not *felt,* to describe what's in your heart for Joel. We know he hurt you, Sylvie. The family believes it's the last thing he ever wanted to do. All I'm suggesting is that you consider giving him a second chance." Dory hung up then. Sylvie held the phone against her breast for a long time. Carline had mentioned seeing Joel talking and laughing with Melody Pritchard outside the post office the other day. What hurt worse than his betrayal was knowing it might already be too late to offer forgiveness. Maybe he'd written her out of his life. Rianne rarely asked Sylvie over to the house anymore. At first it'd been almost a daily occurrence.

Panic began to set in as she considered the task she'd taken on. The dress needed more faux diamonds hand-stitched on one entire half of the underskirt, so they'd wink through the feather-weight tulle in the glow of candlelight. She had three Halloween costumes to construct for kids who'd be devastated if she didn't produce them on time. In addition, someone needed to twist people's arms to give up a Saturday afternoon and stand around for what could be a boring photo shoot. That sounded like a job for her charming, persuasive mother.

It took more effort to convince Nan Shea to help than Sylvie would've thought. But, maybe it was understandable. Her mother had stood by twice and listened to her cry her eyes out over hopes and dreams gone awry. What if she believed Sylvie would fall on her face again? That possibility only served to strengthen Sylvie's resolve to satisfy her obligations and see this last-ditch effort succeed. The proof—whether she had what it took to be a wedding-gown designer—would be in the pudding, as Grandmother Mary Shea used to say.

Sylvie threw herself into sewing every night. She barely broke for anything, and left most of the details of the photo shoot up to her mom and sisters. So much so, she gave Julie Kerr her mom's phone number as the prime coordinator for the project.

Sylvie did decorate her house for Halloween. All the kids in town counted on her to have her porch fixed up and looking spooky. She wore a witch's costume and served cold cider and hot doughnuts to anyone venturing this far out of town. She steeled her resolve to meet Joel face-to-face if he brought Rianne trick-or-treating, as he surely would.

She assumed they'd come in a group with Dory's two. Rianne had said Joel intended to walk with Grant and the kids.

The night was cold and crisp. Fall was upon them. Sylvie's trees had shed and a permanent smoky haze lingered in the air from burning fireplaces. The doorbell rang as Sylvie dipped out the first batch of doughnuts. She still had to toss them with cinnamon and sugar.

Racing to the door, she was totally unprepared to greet a ruddy-faced Joel peering back. His breath clouded in the cool night air. Rianne popped out from behind Sylvie's stack of pumpkins and shouted "Trick or treat!" Sylvie's throat worked convulsively. Time seemed to stretch and her voice failed her.

Joel laughed, the laugh Sylvie missed so much she ached at the memory. "Don't you look like the wicked witch of the east?" he said lightly. "I must admit I've seen you looking better."

That broke the spell that gripped her. Sylvie hugged Rianne and delivered her most practiced cackle. "Come, my pretty, I have food and libations in the kitchen."

Joel followed Rianne through a maze of hanging spiderwebs, dangling bats and leering skeletons to a room transformed into a witch's den. "This is so cool," he exclaimed. "I guess I've said it before but I'll say it again, Sylvie. You're a woman of many talents."

The Mercers stayed only long enough to partake of cider and melt-in-the-mouth doughnuts. After Joel's abrupt departure, Sylvie felt as though the joy had seeped out of the room. As though something fantastic had gone out of her life. She vowed right then to sit down with Joel after the wedding shoot. After she'd auctioned off the stupid dress. If there was the tiniest chance they could clear the air and start anew, Sylvie wanted the opportunity.

The days after Halloween turned blustery. It was good to be inside by a warm fire, sewing. She didn't surface for more than a week.

A day prior to Julie Kerr and crew arriving, Sylvie finished the gown. She'd also made matching long, green velvet dresses for Rianne and Kendra. She'd long since settled on a Christmas theme for the mock wedding and conveyed that to her helpers. Nan said once that Julie wanted real flowers. Her mom asked Sylvie's preference. "Carline said you used to talk about having a winter wedding yourself. If this was a real ceremony, what flowers would you want?"

"That's easy," Sylvie said, seeing the chapel in her mind. "Nothing but green pine boughs dotted with bright-green

Christmas balls tied with white satin ribbon. For flowers, I'd fill the dais with fifty or sixty ice-white poinsettias."

"Sounds simple enough," Nan said. "I'll send Jeff and Rob out to cut boughs. Poinsettias ought not to a problem this time of year."

"Mom, I've never asked. Who did you guys rope into standing in as groom? If you say Buddy Deaver, I may call Julie and renege on our deal, I swear."

"I'm not positive, honey. The groom is Carline's baili-wick. I know it's not Buddy. Last name I heard bandied about was Mason Walker. He's home on leave from the Air Force. The girls swear men in uniforms have universal appeal."

"Oh. I haven't seen Mason in a while. I guess he'll do," she said listlessly.

"You don't sound overjoyed, Sylvie. What's wrong?"

"No…noth…ing, Mother. It's all pretend. Mason's not very tall, is he? Maybe I'd better plan on wearing white ballet slippers."

"No. No. Heels I think, Sylvie. The boy's shot up. Must be what the Air Force feeds him. Six foot, they tell me. You don't want to look like Mutt and Jeff."

Sylvie had a hard time picturing the guy she remembered as a half-pint growing so tall after high school. "All right, Mom. Heels it is. I haven't heard back from Julie since you and she started communicating. I'm supposed to be at the church and dressed by three o'clock, right? Are you collecting Rianne, or is Dory coming by for her? She can ride with me."

"Sylvie, stop worrying. Nervous as you are, you'd think this was a real wedding."

"Don't you *dare* share this with anyone, but…it almost feels like it's real."

They signed off then. Sylvie was surprised her mom didn't have something snide to say in response to her confession. She must be slipping. Or else she accepted that the wedding vigilantes had finally had their first failure.

Saturday, Sylvie drove to the church alone. Parking, she carried her dress in a side door the pastor's wife had promised to leave unlocked. Sylvie couldn't resist peeking into the main sanctuary. The sight took her breath away and brought tears to her eyes, which she quickly wiped away. The place couldn't have looked more like the setting she'd envisioned so often. Drawing back, Sylvie closed the door tight and fanned a hand in front of eyes threatening tears again.

Her mother rushed through the door, followed by her sisters. Their opportune arrival drove away the last vestiges of melancholy gripping Sylvie. Their teasing laughter, and the children's excitement at the prospect of being part of a big production was infectious. "Are you sure Julie Kerr's plane landed on schedule?" Sylvie asked for the umpteenth time.

"Yes, honey," Nan said, setting a crown of entwined white rosebuds on Sylvie's smooth hair. "Haven't you heard all that bumping in the next room? That's the camera crew setting up. Smile, honey. This is going to be your finest hour."

Dory hugged her for luck, then Carline did. They each held Sylvie for a long moment. Their dresses were ones Sylvie didn't recognize, because she'd truly had no time to sew bridesmaids' gowns. However, they couldn't have been more fitting if she'd chosen them herself.

"We're going out now, Sylvie, so Julie can arrange us up front the way she wants us to appear in pictures. We'll take the girls and Roy." Dory handed her son a white pillow on which two glittering wedding bands were tied.

"Wait, guys. You're leaving me to walk out there *alone?*"

Nan stopped at the door. "Your father will be here in a minute to escort you. That was Julie's idea. She wants her photographer to capture your expression as you approach Reverend Paul. This is about giving an aura of reality."

"Oh, I didn't know. Sure, I guess. I don't know why I'm nervous. But I am." The next thing Sylvie knew, she stood by herself—but not for long. Her father walked in from out-

ide, bringing the sting of fresh, cold air. "Sweetheart, you're
beautiful."

"Stop, Daddy, you'll make me blush or cry."

"No tears. Brides are supposed to blush." Rob flung open
the door at the rear of the chapel and crooked an arm. "Ready,
princess?"

Grateful for his solid support, Sylvie slipped her arm through
his and donned a smile as they walked through the door. Her
feet abruptly stopped. The pews overflowed with people she
recognized. Friends from town. The chapel pews were full.

Her dad patted her hand. "You didn't suppose a secret like
having a big Chicago magazine come to our town wouldn't
leak, did you? As well, this gown has created a sensation. Everyone in town's been dying to have a look."

She shook her head as they turned the corner and stepped
onto the white runner. Somehow, she hadn't expected music,
either. But the wedding march brought everyone in the church
to their feet.

She and her dad were nearly down the aisle before Sylvie
glanced left, right or ahead. When she did, her knees almost
gave way. Mason Walker didn't occupy the groom's spot.
The very last man Sylvie expected to see—her neighbor, her
one-time lover and still the only man who owned her whole
heart—stood waiting. Love shone from Joel's eyes. At his
side, in the role of best man, stood Brett Lewis.

"Daddy?" Sylvie faltered. She much feared she sounded
like she had as a child, asking for her father's guarantee that
all was right with her world.

"Joel loves you, baby. He arranged this. Julie Kerr is his
friend. Her offer is legitimate, but so is Joel's. If you look honestly into your heart this minute and swear you can't marry
this man—a man your mother and I believe would lay his life
on the line to make you happy—I'm prepared to speak up
when Reverend Paul asks if anyone knows just cause why you
and Joel shouldn't be joined in holy matrimony."

Rob urged Sylvie forward to a point where Joel's love and that of his daughter's were reflected on their shining faces for her and all their friends to see.

Rising on tiptoe, Sylvie kissed her dad's leathery cheek. "So, this *is* real? I'm getting married today?"

Rob nodded, still gripping her damp, trembling hands. "So is a second chance at your career, Joel's gift to you."

She smiled, swept up the full skirt of a gown it'd taken her nearly six years to complete, and left her father. Sylvie ran the final steps down the slippery satin runner and launched herself into the waiting arms of her groom. "I do, I do, I do," she cried.

"So do I," Joel answered gruffly, tears flooding his eyes.

"Me, too," interjected Rianne from the side.

The confused pastor held up a hand. "Wait, everyone. We haven't reached that part of the ceremony." He said it twice before pandemonium ceased and the congregation stopped clapping and shouting. Tears appeared in the eyes of almost every person in the room, except for Julie Kerr's cameraman. He took in the scene through a wide-angle lens and captured the very real moments on film. It would be the shot mounted in the white leather wedding album. And the photo that would appear on the cover of *Bride's Delight* magazine. The same one would sit on Joel and Sylvie's mantel. A picture destined to catapult Sylvie Shea Mercer's wedding-gown design business into high gear.

At a meticulously planned reception later that evening, Grant Hopewell was overheard muttering to Jeff Manchester, "Gotta hand it to the city boy. He topped our romantic gestures by a mile or more."

Of course Joel acted smug. His eyes never left his wife, who talked animatedly with Lester Egan, his editor. Only Joel knew that his bride and his old boss were discussing a possible joint cartoon strip featuring newlyweds tackling dual careers at home.

"True, he topped us," Jeff lamented, tipping his glass to the newlywed. "I knew Joel was a force to be reckoned with when he brought in a pro ball player for our festival ball game. With a devious mind like his on our side, I'll bet we can finally surprise those three Shea women next Valentine's Day."

Rob Shea walked up, entering their tight huddle. Clinking his glass around the circle, he sipped before remarking, "Ahem. Make that four Shea women—and the fact that you need to gang up on them will remain our little secret. May I remind you young guys that just because there's snow on top of the volcano doesn't mean the fire's burned out."

Joel, who'd just joined the group, wasn't about to argue with his father-in-law, who'd first planted the idea that had made him the happiest, as well as the luckiest man in the whole world. He imagined the joy he'd have matching wits with Sylvie and her family for the next fifty or more years.

Welcome to the world of American Romance!
Turn the page for excerpts from our November 2005 titles.
CINDERELLA CHRISTMAS by Shelley Galloway
BREAKFAST WITH SANTA by Pamela Browning
HOLIDAY HOMECOMING by Mary Anne Wilson
Also, watch for a new anthology,
CHRISTMAS, TEXAS STYLE, which features
three fun and warmhearted holiday stories by
three of your favorite American Romance authors,
Tina Leonard, Leah Vale and Linda Warren.
Let these stories show you what it's like to celebrate
Christmas down on the ranch.
We hope you'll enjoy every one of these books!

We're thrilled to introduce a brand-new author to American Romance! Prepare yourself to be pulled in by Shelley Galloway's characters, who you'll just like. Cinderella Christmas is a charming tale of a woman whose need for a particular pair of shoes starts a chain of events worthy not only of a Cinderella story, but of a fairy tale touched with the magic of Christmas.

Oh, the shoes were on sale now. The beautiful shoes with the three gold straps, the four-inch heel and not much else. The shoes that would show off a professional pedicure and the fine arch of her foot, and would set off an ivory lace gown to perfection.

Of course, to pull off an outfit like that, she would need to have the right kind of jewelry, Brooke Anne thought as she stared at the display through the high-class shop window. Nothing too bold…perhaps a simple diamond tennis bracelet and one-carat studs? Yes, that would lend an air of sophistication. Not too dramatic, but enough to let the outfit speak for itself. Elegance. Refinement. Money.

Hmm. And an elaborate updo for her hair. Something extravagant, to set off her gray eyes and high cheekbones. Something to give herself the illusion of height she so desperately needed. It was hard to look statuesque when you were five-foot-two.

But none of that would matter when she stepped out on the dance floor. Her date would hold her tightly and twirl her around and around. She would balance on the pad of her foot as they maneuvered carefully around the floor. She would put all those dancing lessons to good use, and her date would be impressed that she could waltz with ease. They would glide through the motions, twirling, dipping, stepping together. Other dancers would stay out of their way.

No, no one would be in the way…they would have already

moved aside to watch the incredible display of footwork, the vision of two bodies in perfect harmony, moving in step, gliding in precise motion. They would stare at the striking woman, wearing the most beautiful, decadent shoes…shoes that would probably only last one evening, they were so fragile.

She would look like a modern-day Mona Lisa—with blond hair and gray eyes, though. And short. She would be a short Mona Lisa. But, still graceful.

But that wouldn't matter, because she would have on the most spectacular shoes that she'd ever seen. She'd feel like…*magic.*

"May I help you?"

Brooke Anne simply stared at the slim, elegant salesman who appeared beside her. "Pardon?"

He pursed his lips, then spoke again. "Miss, do you need any help? I noticed that you've been looking in the window for a few minutes."

"No…thanks."

With a twinge of humor, Brooke Anne glanced in the window again, this time to catch the reflection staring back at her. Here she was, devoid of makeup, her hair pulled back in a hurried ponytail, dressed in old jeans and a sweatshirt that was emblazoned with Jovial Janitor Service. And her shoes…she was wearing old tennis shoes.

*Pamela Browning has eaten breakfast with Santa.
It was a pancake breakfast fund-raiser for charity,
exactly like the one in her book, and she attended
dressed as Big Bird. She thought she'd be able
to relax with a big plate of pancakes after leading
the kids in songs from "Sesame Street,"
but some of the more thoughtful children had
prepared her a plate of—you guessed it—birdseed.
When she's not dressing as an eight-foot-tall bird,
Pam spends her time canoeing, taking
Latin-dance lessons and, lately,
rebuilding her hurricane-damaged house.*

Bah, humbug!

The Santa suit was too short.

Tom Collyer stared in dismay at his wrists, protruding from the fur-trimmed red plush sleeves. He'd get Leanne for this someday. There was a limit to how much a big brother should do for a sister.

The pancake breakfast was the Bigbee County, Texas, event of the year for little kids, and when Leanne had asked him to participate in this year's fund-raiser for the Homemakers' Club, he hadn't taken her seriously. He was newly home from his stint in the Marine Corps, and he hadn't yet adjusted his thinking back to Texas Hill Country standards. But his brother-in-law, Leanne's husband, had come down with an untimely case of the flu, and Tom had been roped into the Santa gig.

He peered out of the closet at the one hundred kids running around the Farish Township volunteer fire department headquarters, which was where they held these blamed breakfasts every year. One of the boys was hammering another boy's head against the floor, and his mother was trying to pry them apart. A little girl with long auburn curls stood wailing in a corner.

Leanne jumped onto a low bench and clapped her hands. "Children, guess what? It's time to tell Santa Claus what you want for Christmas! Have you all been good this year?"

"Yes!" the kids shouted, except for one boy in a blue velvet suit, who screamed, "No!" A nearby Santa's helper tried to shush him, but he merely screamed "No!" again. Tom did a double take. The helper, who resembled the boy so closely that she must be his mother, had long gleaming wheat-blond hair. It swung over her cheeks when she bent to talk to the child. Tom let his gaze travel downward, and took in the high firm breasts under a clinging white sweater, the narrow waist and gently rounded hips. He was craning his neck for a better assessment of those attributes when a loudspeaker began playing "Jingle Bells." That was his cue.

After pulling his pants down to cover his ankles and plumping his pillow-enhanced stomach to better hide his rangy frame, he drew a deep breath and strode from the closet.

"Ho-ho-ho!" he said, making his deep voice even deeper. "Merry Christmas!" As directed, he headed for the elaborate throne on the platform at one end of the room.

"Santa, Santa," cried several kids.

"Okay, boys and girls, remember that you're supposed to sit at the tables and eat your breakfast," Leanne instructed. "Santa's helper elves will come to each table in turn to take you to Santa Claus. Remember to smile! An elf will take your picture when you're sitting on Santa's knee."

Tom brushed away a strand of fluffy white wig hair that was tickling his face. "Ho-ho-ho!" he boomed again in his deep faux-Santa Claus voice as he eased his unaccustomed bulk down on the throne and ceremoniously drew the first kid onto his lap. "What do you want for Christmas, little girl?"

"A brand-new candy-red PT Cruiser with a convertible top and a turbo-charged engine," she said demurely.

"A car! Isn't that wonderful! Ho-ho-ho!" he said, sliding the kid off his lap as soon as the male helper elf behind the tripod snapped a picture. Was he supposed to promise delivery of such extravagant requests? Tom had no idea.

For the next fifteen minutes or so, Tom listened as kids

asked for Yu-Gi-Oh! cards, Bratz dolls, even a Learjet. He was wondering what on earth a Crash Team Bandicoot was when he started counting the minutes; only an hour or so, and he'd be out of there. "Ho-ho-ho!" he said again and again. "Merry Christmas!"

Out of the corners of his eyes, Tom spotted the kid in the blue velvet suit approaching. He scanned the crowd for the boy's gorgeous mother, who was temporarily distracted by a bottle of spilled syrup at one of the tables.

"Ho-ho-ho!" Tom chortled as a helper elf nudged the kid in the blue suit toward him. And when the kid hurled a heretofore concealed cup of orange juice into his lap, Tom's chortle became "Ho-ho-ho—oh, no!" The kid stood there, frowning. Tom shot him a dirty look and, using the handkerchief that he'd had the presence of mind to stuff into his pocket, swiped hastily at the orange rivulets gathering in his crotch. With great effort, he managed to bite back a four-letter word that drill sergeants liked to say when things weren't going well.

He jammed the handkerchief back in his pocket and hoisted the boy onto his knee. "Careful now," Tom said. "Mustn't get orange juice on that nice blue suit, ho-ho-ho!"

"Do you always laugh like that?" asked the kid, who seemed about five years old. He had a voice like a foghorn and a scowl that would do justice to Scrooge himself.

"Laugh like what?" Tom asked, realizing too late that he'd used his own voice, not Santa's.

"'Ho-ho-ho.' Nobody laughs like that." The boy was regarding him with wide blue eyes.

"Ho-ho-ho," Tom said, lapsing back into his Santa voice. "You're a funny guy, right?"

"No, I'm not. You aren't, either."

"Ahem," Santa said. "Maybe you should just tell me what you want for Christmas."

The kid glowered at him. "Guess," he said.

Tom was unprepared for this. "An Etch-a-Sketch?" he ventured. Those had been popular when he was a child.

"Nope."

"Yu-Gi-Oh! cards? A Crash Team Billy Goat…uh, I mean Bandicoot?"

"Nope."

Beads of sweat broke out on Tom's forehead. The helpers were unaware of his plight. They were busy lining up the other kids who wanted to talk to Santa.

"Yu-Gi-Oh! cards?"

"You already guessed that one." The boy's voice was full of scorn.

"A bike? Play-Doh?"

The kid jumped off his lap, disconcerting the elf with the camera. "I want a real daddy for Christmas," the boy said, and stared defiantly up at Tom….

This is Mary Anne Wilson's third book in her
four-book miniseries entitled
RETURN TO SILVER CREEK,
the dramatic stories of four men who became
fast friends as youths in a small Nevada town—and
the unexpected turns each of their lives has taken.
Cane Stone's tale is no exception!

A month ago, Las Vegas, Nevada

"I'm not going back to Silver Creek," Cane Stone said. "I don't have the time, or the inclination to make the time. Besides, it's not home for me."

The man he was talking to, Jack Prescott, shook his head, then motioned with both hands at Cane's penthouse. It was done in black and white—black marble floors, white stone fireplace, white leather furniture. The only splash of color came from the sofa pillows, in various shades of red. "This is home?"

The Dream Catcher Hotel and Casino on The Strip in Las Vegas was a place to be. The place Cane worked. The part of the world that he owned. But a home? No. He'd never had one. "It's my place," he said honestly.

An angular man, dressed as usual in faded jeans, an old open-necked shirt and well-worn leather boots—despite the millions he was worth—Jack leaned back against the semicircular couch, positioned to face the bank of windows that looked down on the sprawling city twenty stories below. "Cane, come on. You haven't been back for years, and it's the holidays."

"Bah, humbug," Cane said with a slight smile, wishing that the feeble joke would ease the growing tension in him. A tension that had started when Jack had asked him to go back to

Silver Creek. "You know that for people like us there are no holidays. They're the heavy times in the year. I look forward to Christmas the way Ebenezer Scrooge did. You get through it and make as much money as you can."

Jack didn't respond with any semblance of a smile. Instead, he muttered, "God, you're cynical."

"Realistic," Cane amended with a shrug. "What I want to know, though, is why it's so important to you that I go to Silver Creek?"

"I said, it's the holidays, and that means friends. Josh is there know, and Gordie, who's in his clinic twenty-four hours a day. We can get drunk, ski down Main Street, take on Killer Run again. Whatever you want."

Jack, Josh and Gordie were as close to a family as Cane had come as a child. The orphanage hadn't been anything out of Dickens, but it hadn't been family. The three friends were. The four of them had done everything together, including getting into trouble and wiping out on Killer Run. "Tempting," Cane said, a pure lie at that moment. "But no deal."

"I won't stop asking," Jack said.

Cane stood and crossed to the built-in bar by the bank of windows. He ignored the alcohol and glasses and picked up one of several packs of unopened cards, catching a glimpse of himself in the mirrors behind the bar before he turned to Jack. He was tall, about Jack's height at six-foot-one or so, with dark hair worn a bit long like Jack's, and brushed by gray—like Jack's. His eyes, though, were deep blue, in contrast to Jack's, which were almost black.

He was sure he could match Jack dollar for dollar if he had to. And where just as Jack didn't look like the richest man in Silver Creek, Cane didn't look like a wealthy hotel/casino owner in Las Vegas. Few owners dressed in Levi's and T-shirts; even fewer went without any jewelry, including a watch. He had a closetful of expensive suits and silk shirts, but he hardly ever wore them. Still, he fit right in at the Dream

Catcher Hotel and Casino. It was about the only place he'd ever felt he fit in. He didn't fit in Silver Creek. He never had.

He went back to Jack with the cards, broke the seal on the deck and said as he slipped the cards out of the package, "Let's settle this once and for all."

"I'm not going to play poker with you," Jack told him. "I don't stand a chance."

Cane eyed his friend as he sat down by him on the couch. "We'll keep it simple," he murmured. He took the cards out of the box, tossed the empty box on the onyx coffee table in front of them and shuffled the deck.

"What's at stake?" Jack asked.

"If you win, I'll head north to Silver Creek for a few days around the holidays...."

AMERICAN *Romance*

Presenting...

CHRISTMAS, TEXAS STYLE

A holiday gift for readers of Harlequin American Romance

Novellas from three of
your favorite authors

Four Texas Babies
TINA LEONARD

A Texan Under the Mistletoe
LEAH VALE

Merry Texmas
LINDA WARREN

*Available November 2005 wherever
Harlequin books are sold.*

www.eHarlequin.com   HARCTS1105

HARLEQUIN®

AMERICAN *Romance*®

This season, enjoy a holiday fairy tale by a
brand-new author…

CINDERELLA CHRISTMAS

by Shelley Galloway

(November 2005)

When she's wearing her mop-emblazoned
Jovial Janitor uniform, most people look
right through Brooke Anne Kessler. But
Royal Hotels executive Morgan Carmichael
has just been jilted by his date for the
company Christmas ball, and suddenly
he's seeing the petite blonde who dusts his
office in a whole different light.…

Available wherever Harlequin books are sold.

HARLEQUIN®

AMERICAN *Romance*®

COMING NEXT MONTH

#1089 CHRISTMAS, TEXAS STYLE by Tina Leonard, Leah Vale and Linda Warren
What makes a Christmas spent in Texas so special? Find out in three heartwarming stories about family, romance and the true meaning of the holidays, by three of your favorite Harlequin American Romance authors.

#1090 CINDERELLA CHRISTMAS by Shelley Galloway
When she's wearing her mop-emblazoned Jovial Janitor uniform, Brooke Anne Kessler finds that most people look right through her. But Royal Hotels executive Morgan Carmichael has just been jilted by his date for the company Christmas ball, and suddenly he's seeing the petite blonde who dusts his office in a whole different light....

#1091 BREAKFAST WITH SANTA by Pamela Browning
Fatherhood
When Tom Collyer unwillingly subs as Santa Claus for the annual Farish, Texas, Breakfast with Santa pancake fest, the last thing he expects is the request he gets from one five-year-old boy. Or how he and the little boy's breathtakingly beautiful mother will end up satisfying it!

#1092 HOLIDAY HOMECOMING by Mary Anne Wilson
Return to Silver Creek
Cane Stone is back in a town he couldn't wait to get away from—but only because he took a chance on a bet and lost. Holly Winston isn't too happy he's back, either. She can never forgive him for the breakup of her marriage. The odds are against these two having a relationship. But sometimes you *can* beat the odds.

www.eHarlequin.com